QUEEN OF GORGOS

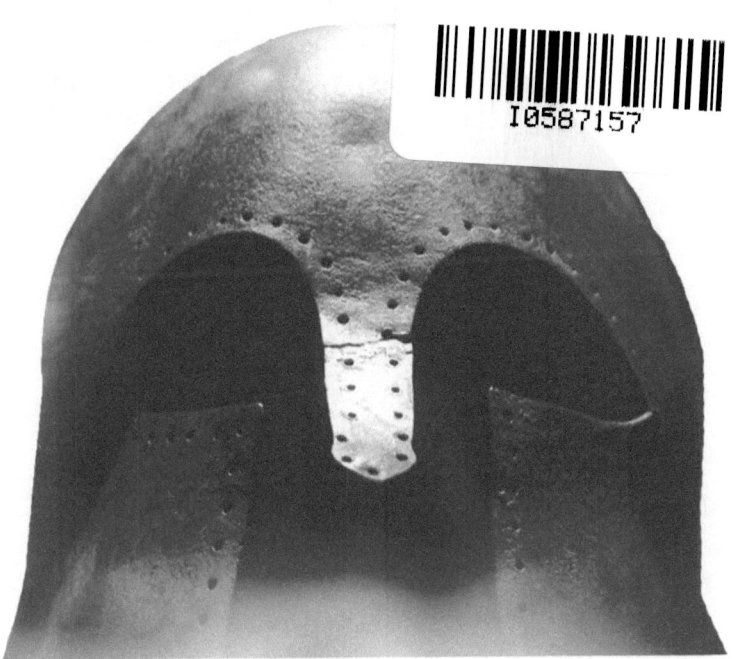

M. L. HOLLINGER

The Javik series Book Three

TotalRecall Publications, Inc.
1103 Middlecreek
Friendswood, Texas 77546
281-992-3131   281-482-5390 Fax
www.totalrecallpress.com

ISBN: 978-1-59095-290-0
UPC: 6-43977-82901-6

Library of Congress Control Number: 2014955309

Printed in the United States of America with simultaneous printings in Australia, Canada, and United Kingdom.

FIRST EDITION
1   2   3   4   5   6   7   8   9   10

To my daughters—

Queens in their own right

AUTHOR M. L. HOLLINGER

received an Aeronautical Engineering degree from Purdue University in 1957 and went into the Air Force right after college. He worked on several space program projects including; Titan III Space Booster, Space Shuttle, Star Wars and several other special studies for the Air Force. He attended the Air Command and Staff College and the Air War College. He served in Viet Nam from 1971-1972. His decorations include The Bronze Star Medal, Meritorious Service Medal, Air Force Commendation Medal, The Vietnamese Honor Medal First Class, The Vietnamese Gallantry Cross and five unit excellence awards. He retired from the Air Force in 1980 with the rank of Lieutenant Colonel and came back to Indiana where he joined the Indiana Corporation for Science and Technology. He is now fully retired.

I owe much of what I am today to two organizations; the Boy Scouts of America and Pi Kappa Alpha fraternity. The Boy Scouts transformed me from a shy, wimpy kid to a fit, capable, self-confident young man. The fraternity smoothed off the rough edges and matured a school boy into a man. Of the two, I feel I owe the most to the Boy Scouts. Scouting combined with my faith to provide the foundation for my life. I wrote this book to provide a role model for today's adolescent boys.

ACKNOWLEDGEMENT

I gratefully acknowledge the support of my wife and family in this project. They provided many helpful suggestions and a good deal of editing support.

PREFACE

Javik, the hero of my story, faces all of the problems boys face today and overcomes them through hard work and a determination to succeed. He has some help along the way, but all boys need someone to show them the right path. For most of us it's our fathers, but when there is no father, someone else must step in to provide the guidance so desperately needed. When that guidance is absent, sinister forces take over. Gangs often provide a warped set of values that lead to either prison or death. I sincerely hope Javik will provide a role model for those boys lacking a man's beneficial influence.

I also hope that the men who aid Javik along the way will inspire modern men to work with boys who lack the firm hand of a mature male in their lives. There are many fine programs available for that purpose; Scouting and the Big Brother program are only two. If you want to change the world for the better, get involved in the process of guiding our youth toward the path of success in life.

To the young men who read this story I say, "Javik is not a superhero. Any boy can do what he does, but it takes education, hard work and someone to guide you along the way. The men in Javik's life give him good advice. If there's no man to do that for you, learn from Goldar, Tao Shan, Browdat and Javik.

List of Characters

Javik: A boy learning to be a warrior in a cruel, medieval world.

Dana: Javik's mother.

Browdat: wealthy war leader in Javik's village who adopts him.

Goldar: A 'war leader' in Javik's village who marries Dana and becomes Javik's foster father.

Tao Shan: The best mentor in the kingdom. Javik has agreed to further training with him after Mauhad.

Sigurd: A fellow student at Tao Shan's school and now a close friend of Javik.

Noka: Javik's old roommate at Tao Shan's school.

Grazhda: A witch living near Javik's village and feared by all.

Allana: An escaped slave girl Javik encounters in the forest and falls in love with.

Bogard the Red: Another of Javik's former schoolmates.

Margan the Minstrel: A traveling troubadour who provides Javik with information about Allana.

Polla: A village girl who traps Javik into marriage.

Gilda: Javik's mother-in-law.

Garen: Javik's son.

Mordah: Javik's war dog.

Barinosh: Once an admiral in the now defunct Gogon fleet

Varuda: Once madam of a high class bordello who helps Allana gain wealth and power.

Vargon: King of the Turrek bandits.

Tumak: Vargon's second in command who becomes king of the bandits when Vargon is killed in battle.

Artun: A Ruzz warrior who helps Allana but proves to be a traitor for money.

Avra: An Argani healer who joins Allana's group as alchemist and healer.

Introduction

This is the third book in the Javik series. Allana has begun her quest to regain the throne of Gorgos by establishing a high class brothel in another land with the help of a former madam who has been disfigured by a rejected lover. Allana gains a great deal of wealth and some allies, but she must cross the territory of a ferocious bandit king, Vargon, to reach Gorgos. She bribes Vargon with her body in order to secure his promise of safe passage, but he captures her in spite of his promise and forces her to marry him.

A civil war in a kingdom bordering Vargon's lands lures the bandit king into an alliance with the rebel forces. He hopes to gain wealth and the island of Gorgos for Allana, but Vargon is betrayed. The rebel leader want's the bandits destroyed as much as anyone else and arranges a ruse to achieve that end. Vargon is killed in the battle, but his successor as bandit king forces Allana to promise to marry him as soon as the leadership of the bandits is settled in a bloody duel.

Javik wants to find Allana but has no idea where she is. Margan the Minstrel tells Javik about Allana's plight, and Javik assembles his friends to rescue her. They encounter Allana's friend, Barinosh, at Allana's old brothel, and he tells them about Allana's predicament.

The bandit's stronghold is impregnable, but Grazhda and Tao Shan have provided Javik with knowledge of a way around the fortress. Javik and his friends use their hand cannon to rescue Allana after she convinces the new bandit king to let her ride outside the fortress.

Gorgos is now part of the province of Ollon in the kingdom

of Tulla, and the group travels to Harrish, capital of Ollon, the seek some way to gain control of the island. Allana convinces Count Charlan, ruler of Ollon, to appoint her governor of Gorgos.

Once on Gorgos, the group begin to plan for Independence with Allana as queen. They develop cannon for use on ships, and Gorgos becomes ruler of the sea. War develops between Tulla and its bordering countries, and Allana and Javik take advantage of the conflict to force recognition of Gorgos as an independent state allied with Tullal.

Allana is crowned Queen of Gorgos and marries Javik.

The story continues in the next book, *The Wallan Prince*.

Chapter 1

Javik sat on a rock with Mordah panting lazily beside him, watching the river run gaily below and thinking about his life. Polla's death ended his unhappy marriage but left him with an infant son he wasn't prepared to cope with. He was now a recognized warrior with combat experience under his belt and his own hearth, but who would care for his son? Perhaps either his mother or Polla's would agree to care for the baby until he could find another wife?

Another wife—the thought evoked memories of Allana. Her deep black eyes and raven hair haunted his dreams, but she was gone—on a fool's errand as far as he was concerned. The escaped slave girl he found hiding in the deep forest had come a long way since he'd ended her ordeal by slaying her Sentii master. Things were going well until she discovered she was heir to a far-away kingdom. Now she was running a bordello in a far land and dreaming of becoming a queen.

A queen, bah. Queen of an island in ruins. I don't know why she'd want to leave the safety and security of Holliga and my love to chase such a foolish idea. Without powerful allies, how could she hope to gain a throne? Forget her, Javik. There's no hope of convincing her to come back. She's as stubborn as a mule once she makes up her mind. Maybe I'm better off with a more docile mate.

Mordah's growl caused him to turn with his hand on his dagger, but the familiar face of Margan the minstrel greeted him with a warm smile.

"Call off your monster, Javik," Margan called from a safe distance.

"Margan!" Javik calmed his war dog and ran to embrace the man who'd once saved his life.

"Where did you come from?" Javik asked as he held his friend at arm's length and studied him carefully.

"I've been far to the South in Zargaia, but when I heard of the plague in Berglaundia I had to come back to see if you were still alive." He thumped Javik on the chest and smiled. "It looks like I need not have worried."

"I was away at the fortress in the high pass when the plague struck. I was lucky to be there."

"And your mother?" Margan asked.

"She's well also, but the plague took my wife, though it spared our son."

"Your wife and your son?" Margan was truly surprised.

"Yes, after Allana left I was trapped into marrying Polla."

Margan knew of Polla by reputation, and he could imagine what kind of trap she'd laid for Javik. "I see, you had to do 'the honorable thing' I suppose?"

Javik smiled at Margn's delicate way of phrasing the obvious conclusion. "Yes, that's what happened. It's too bad I'd promised Tao Shan another year of training. I'd have left to find Allana right away but for that obligation. Now I'll never see her again. "

"You're probably right. I stopped by her bordello before setting off for Berglaundia, and a lady in a quaint mask has the house now. Her name is Varuda, and she told me Allana left to find her kingdom several weeks before I arrived. She also told me Allana was captured by the Turreks as she crossed Magda on her way to Gorgos. Varuda heard this bandit King, one Vargon, intends to force her into a marriage with him."

"The Turreks? Who are they?"

"A fierce tribe of bandits who live by pillaging the caravans crossing their territory in Magda. I thought Tao Shan would have told you about them."

Javik shook his head and frowned. "No. He didn't spend much time on Magda. He only said it was a primitive country that must be crossed cautiously." He sighed heavily. "It's just as well. I'm sure she's forgotten all about me by now."

"She's not forgotten you, Javik. She loves you as much as she ever did, but she wants to be Queen of Gorgos before she sends for you."

"Humpf! 'Sends for me', eh? I don't intend to be a queen's lap dog."

"She's not like that, Javik. Yes, she's matured far beyond the girl you knew, but her love for you has never changed. Even if she does have to marry this Vargon, you will always be the man she really wants."

Javik sat down again, and Margan sat beside him. Mordah settled down beside Javik and rested his head on his front paws.

"I still dream of her, but the woman in my dreams is not the woman you describe now. I've decided to find a new wife here in Holliga where I'm a respected warrior. I could never live the life of a courtier. I only have my dreams of Allana now."

It was Margan's turn to sigh. "Javik, Javik, you will never understand women."

"What do you know of women?" Javik laughed and punched the minstrel's shoulder.

"Ah, Javik. You have so much more to learn. Do you think my humped back glows in the dark? You'd be surprised what women overlook when they're romanced properly. A song about love is a potent narcotic for the feminine soul."

The men talked until the sun was overhead, and then walked back to the village for lunch.

Javik found his mother busy baking bread. Her face was wet with perspiration, and her hair was tied back with a scarf, but Javik felt she was still a lovely woman. He was glad Goldar asked to court her, and happy that she seemed to welcome his attentions. She noticed Javik and Margan at once.

"Margan, how good to see you again." She embraced the minstrel, leaving flour hand prints on his tunic. "Sit down. I'll get some food for you two after I get these loaves in the oven."

"We're in no hurry, Mother." They sat down at a table and watched her work as Javik brushed the white powder off Margan's clothes.

"How are your hands, Margan?" Dana asked as she turned back to her baking.

"They've healed well, Lady, thanks to your attentions. I play as well as ever."

"I suppose Javik's filled you in on everything that's happened since you were last here?"

"Yes, and I told him about Allana's adventures in Zargaia."

"How is she?" Dana asked.

"As I told Javik, she's a rich and powerful woman now. She went off to restore her kingdom, but the Turrek bandits captured her and their King intends to marry her."

Dana paused in her chores. "Oh Javik, I'm so sorry," she said.

"It's all right, Mother. I've decided forget her."

Dana looked at her son and smiled knowingly. "Forget her? And, how will you do that?"

"By finding a new wife here in our village and raising my son to be a man. At least my new wife will not be a whore and the wife of a bandit king."

"Javik, you don't mean that," Margan said.

"No, son, no matter what she's become you two are still in love with each other, I know that much," Dana said. "You won't have true peace of mind until you hold her in your arms again. Any wife you take now would only be a substitute for Allana, and that wouldn't be fair to her. She'd always know your heart was not really hers. She'd never have you completely."

"Listen to your mother," Margan said. "She's telling you the truth. She knows how a woman feels about love, and she knows you will never forget Allana."

"And, Allana will never forget you," Dana added. "Do you think I'm blind? I saw how you two felt about each other, and I know true love when I see it. You are so like your father in many ways, and I saw the same man who loved me so dearly every time I saw you with Allana. Don't delude yourself into thinking you could ever be happy without her."

"You and I both know even the most beautiful woman in this village is only a poor second choice compared to Allana," Margan added.

"Even if what you say is true, how would I be able to wrest her from this bandit king? I'd need an army to do that, and what man would follow me on such a fool's quest?"

"I would," Margan said.

Javik smiled at the minstrel and placed an arm around his shoulder. "You are a good friend, but your hands are more suited to the lute than the sword."

"Don't underestimate the power of song, Javik. Music has a way of grasping a man's soul as well as a woman's."

"I know that's true, but going after her now is just as foolish as her quest for a throne. I must be practical about this."

Dana shook her head as she placed the last loaf inside the glowing cavern. She wiped her brow with her apron. "I've given you a woman's opinion, but speak to Tao Shan before you give up on Allana. He's always given you good advice. Then speak to your father if you decide to pursue her. You're a ma, and you don't need his blessing, but as your father, he should be consulted."

Margan broke the serious mood by demanding food. "Could we talk more over some food? I haven't eaten since last night."

Dana laughed and began ladling some broth into bowls. She sat them in front of the men and added a freshly baked loaf of dark brown bread. She sat down herself and turned to Margan. "Did you only come here to give us such sad news about Allana?"

"That and to see how the plague treated you. I'm glad to see both of you alive. They said the plague was quite devastating."

"We lost many fine people, but it's past us now," Dana said.

Dana broke off a chunk of the bread. She dipped it into the broth and ate before continuing.

"Thank Zhou it spared your son, Javik. Have you thought

about what to do with him?"

"I will speak to the Lady Gilda to see if she will keep him until he is weaned. Would you be willing to keep him after that, Mother?"

Dana smiled at Javik and took another piece of bread. "You know Goldar will ask me to marry him?"

"I thought as much. I would welcome him as a step-father."

"A match blessed by Zhou," Margan added.

"Goldar must wait a suitable time after Ruda's death before we marry, but with a new wife, I don't know if Goldar would like small children around. His sons are grown and off on their own, and he knows I'm too old to bear any more."

"I think he would do anything you asked, Mother." Javik smiled slyly as he ate another soggy morsel of bread.

Dana laughed and wiped her hands on her apron. "I think he would, Son. Yes, I'll keep little Garen for you, if Goldar agrees to it. I don't think I've forgotten how to be a mother yet."

"Do you want me to speak to Goldar about Garen?" Javik asked.

"No, I'll handle that part." She turned to Margan. "Will you stay in our village long?"

"Now that I see you're all well, I should be moving on, but I'll stay until this oaf makes up his mind about Allana. If he decided to go, I'll go with him, and if he decides not to go, he'll need someone to console him with song." He nudged Javik with his shoulder. "Am I welcome at your hearth, Javik?'

"Always, stay as long as you like. My mother will see to your arrangements. I think I'll talk to Tao Shan about Allana before I see Browdat." He turned to Dana. "I'll be back before the evening meal."

Dana leaned across the table and kissed her son on the cheek. "I'll see to Margan while you're gone."

* * * * *

Javik waited patiently while Tao Shan finished his training session with the new candidates for Mauhad then approached his old mentor.

"Javik, it's good to see you," Tao Shan said. "What can I do for you?"

"I need some advice, sir. Do you have a moment?"

"I always have time for my old pupils. Let's go inside." He led Javik to his private quarters and told a servant to bring wine. After their cups were filled, Javik spoke. "Margan is here, and..."

"Ah, I'd like to see him. Where is he staying?" Tao Shan interrupted.

"He's at my hearth. He brought me news of Allana, and..."

Once more Tao Shan couldn't wait. "How does she fare?"

"Not good. She's been captured by bandits in Magda, and the bandit king is forcing her to marry him."

"Which bandits?" Tao Shan asked.

"Margan said it was the Turreks."

The old mentor's face took on a serious expression, and he rubbed his chin for a moment. "That's very bad news. The Turrek are known for their brutality and their bloody rituals. This bandit king has undoubtedly given her a choice of marriage or death."

"That's what I'm afraid of, but I see no way I could help her. I've almost decided to leave her to her fate. What would you advise?"

Once more Tao Shan went into a deep thought mode. Javik sipped his wine as he waited. He knew it was not wise to interrupt the old fox while he was thinking. Finally, Tao Shan shook his head and frowned. "I see no way either. The Turrek headquarters is in an almost impregnable mountain stronghold. The kings of Zargaia and Tulla have often lost entire armies trying to storm it. The fortress's only vulnerability is from the North, but there are no passes through the mountains from that direction suitable for moving large armies. The only pass is narrow and treacherous. It could be traversed by men on horseback moving in single file, but only in the summer. All other times snow and ice make movement impossible."

"Can you show it to me on the map, sir?"

Tao Shan moved to his map cabinet and rolled out a map of Magda. He moved his finger to a large lake. "Here is the Turrek stronghold."

Javik moved to the mentor's side and studied the area on the map. A large lake filled the space between two mountain ranges. A wide river flowed into the lake from the North. A black dam blocked the river at a waterfall where it spilled into the lake.

"There's no indication of a castle here," Javik said as he moved his finger around the dam area.

"The dam itself is a fortress. The rest of the headquarters is inside the mountain in a series of caves. The battlements are 100 meters above the lake's surface. There is no way for an army to bring in siege engines or towers. They must scale the mountains to approach the defenders, and as a result, they are easily picked off one-by-one by bandits using arrow slots in the West cliff faces. The mountain is honeycombed with interconnecting caves and tunnels. Only an army approaching from the North could hope to defeat the Turrek, but as I said, there are no passes suitable for that tactic." He pointed to a spot that appeared to be all mountains. "Here is the single pass from Tulla to the Turrek lands leading to a point behind the fortress. As you can see, it's too narrow for any army. It's entrance is also difficult to detect from either side of the mountains."

Javik sank back into his chair and sipped his wine. "Then she is truly lost to me."

"She may still find a way to escape her captors, but she would have to reach Tulla to be safe, and that's quite a ride. The Turrek are excellent horsemen, and they would probably be able to recapture her before she could reach the Tullan fortress guarding the southern border at Othis. Your only hope is that she can do that and send word to you later."

"No, I'll not waste my life hoping and dreaming. I must forget Allana and find a new wife. Eventually, I'll forget her entirely."

Tao Shan remembered the boy so eager to liberate the wild forest girl and the expression on his face every time he was near her. "I wish you luck in that quest." He raised his wine cup to his former pupil.

"I will need luck, but thank you for your usual good advice." Javic raised his cup and the pair drank the last of their wine. Javik bid his mentor good day and left the longhouse to walk in the forest while he tried to erase all trace of Allana from his mind. He hadn't gone far when the growl of a bear caused him to turn and draw his dagger. He was relieved to see the bear beside the witch Grazhda.

"Hail, Prince Javik," the old witch said.

"Oh, it's you. I thought I was a dead man when I heard that growl," Javik said as he re-sheathed his dagger. "Why the bear?"

"The forest is a dangerous place. An old woman needs protection when she travels alone. I sense a disturbance in your aura. What's troubling you?" The bear laid down and rested its massive head on its front paws.

"I've had word of Allana, and it's not good. She's a captive of the Turrek and will be forced to marry their King."

The old woman spat on the ground. "I could have told you that weeks ago, but you never bother to seek my advice."

Javik hung his head and mumbled his reply. "What advice could you give anyone about love?"

"Ha-ha-ha-ha. Brash warrior, do you think I was always this old? I've loved and lost more times than any six other women. Even today I have the power to transform this shriveled body into a form rivaling Allana's. I stay in this wrinkled prison because it commands more respect from the ignorant masses. I tell you now that Allana is well, and you will rescue her from her plight if you have the courage to try."

Javik bristled at the suggestion he was a coward. "I'd fight any man for her, but I just sought Tao Shan's advice, and he tells me it's impossible. Several Kings have tried to defeat the Turrek and died before the walls of their fortress. Even if I could command such might, I'd fare no better."

"That old fox only convinced you that might is wasted on this quest. The Turrek are too well fortified to be taken by force. You must use guile and cunning to rescue Allana—that and your superior weapons. I saw your little demonstration for Browdat."

"Even so, I know nothing of that country except what Tao Shan told me just now. I can't just blunder into danger and hope to survive."

"You will find the help you need at the House of Orgama in Ullum if you decide to go."

Javik frowned at the mention of the bordello. "What help could I find among a collection of whores?"

"Not the whores, but one who serves Allana—one of her countrymen named Barinosh."

"I would not set foot in such a place." Javik folded his arms across his chest and assumed an arrogant pose.

"Then you will not rescue Allana. You might as well stay in Holliga and marry some simple, delicate thing who will grow fat bearing your children. Do you find hunting and farming preferable to adventure?"

Javik decided to change the subject. "You called me Prince just now. Why?"

"If you rescue Allana that's what you will be after you marry her, but I see you have no stomach for that quest. Farewell, farmer." Grazhda turned to leave, and the bear rose to follow behind her.

The witch may be right. It will only take a journey to Ullum to see if she is, Javik thought.

"Wait!" Javik called, and Grazhda turned back to him with a wry smile on her face.

"What is it?" she asked.

"You've always given me good advice in the past. I believe you now, but I can't undertake this quest alone. How many fighting men will I need?"

"That's more like it," she said. "You have friends who

fought beside you against the Sentii. If you ask them, they will go."

"Then I'll go. My mother was right. I'll never forget Allana as long as there's any possibility we could be together. Thank you for telling me what I must do."

"My thanks will come with your son's visit. Farewell, Prince."

A stag ran across the path between Javik and Grazhda, and when he'd passed, the witch and her bear were gone.

Javik strode off to see to the care of his son and seek his father's blessing for the quest.

* * * * *

Javik found Gilda busy cleaning up from the noon meal. She was ordering servants around while she did as much work as any of them. All hearths had lost slaves to the plague, and the women who were once creatures of leisure now found themselves back to work. She stopped working when she noticed Javik.

"Javik, welcome. Have you come to see your son?"

"Yes, and to speak with you for a moment, if you have time."

Gilda issued a few more orders and led Javik into the baby's room. Little Garen was awake and gurgling happily as he watched a contraption made from sticks, string and bits of cloth swirl above his crib. Javik leaned over his son and spoke.

"Good day, Garen."

The baby's eyes changed focus to his father's face, and a look of consternation overtook the previous smile.

"He knows his name," Javik beamed.

"Since you gave him his name, we've been trying to use it as much as possible," Gilda explained.

Little Garen began to frown at Javik and looked like he was about to cry. Gilda noticed his consternation and picked him up.

"He's not used to you yet, Javik. You need to spend more time with him."

"That's what I've come to talk about. I'm afraid I must be off on another adventure soon."

Gilda sighed as she patted Garen on the back and walked back and forth with him.

"Is it that wild thing you found in the forest?"

"Yes, Allana. I must find her."

"Polla is not yet cold in her grave and you must go off to find a stranger rather than take a new wife from your own village."

The tone of Gilda's voice cut into Javik's soul. Had Polla been able to keep her wanton ways a secret from her own family when the entire village knew of her? He doubted that, yet he fully understood that one's own children were seen in a different light.

"I'm sorry, but I still love Allana, and I must find out if there is any future for us. I would have a mother for my son, and if it can't be Allana, I will return and take a wife here in Holliga."

Gilda laid Garen back in his crib and sat down on a chair. She looked away from Javik and pulled a kerchief from her bosom. She blew her nose quietly before speaking.

"I'm sorry, Javik. I know what Polla was, and you did an honorable thing marrying her. I should be grateful to you."

Javik knelt beside her and placed a hand on her arm.

"I understand, Mother. Who else would I trust with my son

but someone so wise and compassionate as you?"

"We have a wet nurse and must care for him at least until he's weaned. Do you want us to keep him longer?"

"No, I've asked my mother to care for him after that."

"Rumor has it she will soon marry Goldar. Will they want a baby?"

"She will speak to Goldar, but I'm sure he'll agree," Javik said.

Gilda sighed heavily, "To tell the truth, it will be hard for me to give him to Dana. We've come to love him so. Our children are all grown, and even Challa, my husband, has come to enjoy a child again, though he often told me he was glad to be rid of his own."

"I know how you feel, but my mother and Goldar may want some time together before taking on my son. May I ask you to keep him until they are ready? I promise to return before his sixth winter so I can be a proper father to him and help him grow into manhood."

"Yes, Javik. You may count on us."

Javik noticed the tears in Gilda's eyes for the first time. He knew she was thinking of a small child with no father. Not a father away on a trip, but one who was lost forever in a foreign land.

"I will come back, Gilda."

"All you men say that, Javik. We women have no choice but to believe you and hope the gods agree."

* * * * *

Browdat was supervising some plowing when Javik found him. The big war leader looked quite strange in only a cotton shirt and knee britches. For the first time, Javik noticed his legs were on the spindly side compared to the bulk of his torso. Several purplish scars told of the battles he'd experienced. He hailed Javik as his adopted son approached.

"Javik, come here. Maybe you can help me beat these stupid farmhands into obedience." He beckoned to Javik then turned to a man following a plow and two large horses.

"No, no, no! That furrow is too close. Move left, move left!"

Javik smelled the fresh aroma of newly exposed earth, and he loved the way it made him feel full of life, but he was also glad he was not a farmer. The backbreaking work associated with that life made war look easy.

"Father, I've come to ask your blessing for an adventure."

Browdat stopped in mid harangue and turned to face his son.

"Certainly, as soon as the plowing's done. Stay here with me and learn how to do this. Someday you will own land, and you must know how to manage it."

"I could have no better teacher than you, Sir, but I must leave immediately to rescue Allana."

"Allana?" Browdat growled. "That woman is gone forever, Javik. Forget her."

"I wish I could. All the long winter, I thought of nothing but her. Now Margan has returned with dire news about her. She's been forced into a marriage with a bandit King, and I have to set her free again."

Browdat placed an arm around his adopted son and turned him away from the field. They walked for a while before the war leader spoke again.

"I knew you'd want to do this, and I can't forbid you to go. Zhou knows that woman has enchanted you, and you won't be able to break that enchantment until you see her again. Do you know where to look?"

"Margan saw her in Ullum last year, but she's gone from there to Magda. I'll start in Ullum and gain what intelligence I can there. I know we can't face the Turrek with a few warriors, but perhaps there may be some way to free her without the need for an army. I spoke to Tao Shan, and he said there was a pass into Magda from Tulla allowing a small force to enter the bandit's territory secretly."

"Who will go with you besides the crippled minstrel?"

"I think Berda and Karl will go, and I'll also ask Noka and Sigurd, they were fellow students at Tao Shan's house."

"That's a small group. Take some of my servants, and maybe Mikka would join you. He'd at least bring some maturity to the effort. You will face some perilous moments, Javik."

"Mikka would certainly be welcome, but would he take orders from me?" Javik could not imagine a warrior of Mikka's caliber serving under one so young as himself.

"He will if I tell him to," Browdat blustered.

"Father, if Mikka comes along, it must be of his own free will. I don't want him to serve me under duress."

"Well, just let me speak with him before you approach him."

Javik gave Browdat a wary look.

"I promise not to threaten him. What can you pay him?"

"Only whatever booty we can garner along the way and whatever lies at the end of our quest. We will all share equally in everything."

"Except Allana!" Browdat slapped Javik on the back and laughed heartily.

* * * * *

Karl agreed readily to join Javik's quest, Berda had to seek his new wife's approval. Mikka even offered his services, and assured Javik he was under no pressure from Browdat. Preparations took nearly a week with the bulk of that time waiting for Berda to obtain Clara's blessing, but the group assembled early one bright morning to depart with half the village assembled to see them off.

Dana knelt before her son. "Be safe, my son, and return with honor or not at all." It was the traditional speech for a woman sending her husband or son off to battle

Javik pulled her to her feet and embraced her. "I will return soon, Mother."

Goldar took Javik's hand in a firm grip. "I wish I were going with you, Javik. Don't worry about your mother while you're gone. I'll take good care of her."

"Thank you, Sir. I'll count on that."

Gilda held little Garen up to his father. "Say goodbye to your son, Javik."

Javik took the boy and held him high above his head. "I'll be back to make you into a man, little Garen, I promise."

Javik embraced Gilda and handed the baby back before shaking hands with Challa. Next in line was Frieda.

"Javik, my boy. Be very careful." She smothered Javik in a great hug and turned away crying.

Tao Shan stepped forward and took Javik's hand.

"Remember all of my lessons, Javik. I know you will learn many things on this adventure. You must return and tell me all about it."

"I will, Mas..., I mean, Sir."

Browdat came out of the longhouse carrying a sword. He presented it to Javik.

"Take the sword of Aelin the Red with you, Javik. You won it in battle, and it will protect you well."

Javik stared at the sword in its ornate sheath.

"Father, I sold you this sword. It is yours to keep."

"And mine to give. Take it."

Javik took his sword from his belt and handed it to Browdat in exchange for the sword of Aelin.

"I will bring greater honor to this sword than it has ever known, I promise you, Father."

The men embraced, and Javik mounted his horse. The group rode away to the cheers of the villagers and a boisterous song from Margan. Javik did not turn back to see the tear trailing down Browdat's black beard.

Chapter 2

Javik's band reached Timann, Noka's village, just before sunset. They camped outside the stockade wall while Javik went to find his friend. The report of a hand cannon told Javik where to look, and he found Noka demonstrating the device for a group of awed war leaders.

"Have you found more powder?" Javik shouted, and Noka turned to the voice. His face lit up with the unexpected surprise of seeing his friend so soon after their defense of the fortress in the pass.

"Come here, Javik. I want you to meet these men."

Noka made the introductions while informing the men it was Javik who learned the secret of the magic powder from Tao Shan. Javik was bombarded with questions, and answered them as best he could without revealing the secret of the mixture. After each man took a turn with the hand cannon, the session broke up, and Noka led Javik to his hearth.

"Mother, Father, come and meet Javik," Noka called as he entered the building.

A slightly graying woman looked up from her cook pots and smiled warmly at the stranger, and a portly man with hair every bit as red as his son's came forward to extend his hand.

"Welcome to our hearth, Javik. I am Ranjel, Noka's father and chief of the village. This is my wife, Leila. Noka has told us much about you. Sit down and have some qush."

Javik took a chair, and Noka sat next to him while Ranjel took a seat opposite.

"What brings you to Timann, Javik?" Ranjel asked.

"I've come to ask your son to accompany me on a quest, Sir."

"You're finally off to find Allana!" Noka beamed.

"Yes, Karl and Berda from my village are with me along with one of our great warriors, Mikka, and some of my father's servants. Margan the minstrel is with us to help the time pass with his songs. We have plenty of brawn, what I need are brains, and your brains in particular."

"Well, you have them," Noka stopped short and looked at this father. "If my father will approve."

Ranjel smiled broadly at his son and slapped him on the back. "You have no need to ask my permission, young warrior. Besides, I'm sure your mother would be glad to have you out of our longhouse for a while."

"Nonsense, husband," Leila scolded, but smiled as she did so. "But, he is a man now and able to make up his own mind about these things."

"Then, I must go with Javik," Noka said. "I want to do something besides inventory the stores at least once in my life." He turned to Javik. "I can be ready in two days. What should I bring?"

"Your weapons, your baggage, your horse and the loan of a cart, if you have one," Javik replied.

"As long as I don't drive the cart," Noka said.

* * * * *

Two days later the group was larger by one warrior and one

cart. One of Browdat's servants was assigned to drive the cart while Noka rode beside Javik and Mikka. The next destination was Odum, Sigurd's village.

Somehow, Sigurd had learned of their journey and was ready when they arrived. He was camped outside his village stockade wall with several horses, three servants and a Wagon full of supplies.

"By Zhou, I'm pleased to hear you've decided to go after Allana. What happened to that wife you had back home? I hope you gave her the boot as soon as you got back," Sigurd asked as the band rode up to his tent.

"She's gone Sigurd, but not that way. There was a plague in our village, and she died of it."

Sigurd's manner changed from bold humor to somber seriousness.

"I'm truly sorry, Javik. I would not have jested had I known."

"It's no problem, Sigurd, but what is all this?" Javik waved a hand to indicate the camp.

"Javik! These are the bare necessities for a person of my stature. Besides, I figured you poor wretches would need some provisions. The wagon is my donation to our cause. When do we ride for Allana?"

"Well, if you don't mind us setting up our common tents alongside your canvas palace, here, we'll camp the night and start in the morning," Javik said.

"Be my guest," Sigurd said with a flourish of his hand. "I'll have two barrels of qush brought out so we may properly inaugurate our quest. I'll even throw in a slab of venison for your hound." He snapped his fingers at a servant who nodded and moved off toward the village gate.

That night, the qush flowed freely as the old friends relived their youthful adventures and spoke of the journey to come. Margan serenaded them with songs of war, bravery and tender maidens.

* * * * *

The camp was quiet the following morning as the warriors slept off their celebrations. The sun was two hands high above the trees when a horn sounded and awakened the revelers. Javik stepped from his tent and rubbed sleepy eyes into focus on a sight he hadn't seen since Tao Shan's longhouse.

"By Zhou, this is the laziest bunch of adventurers I've ever seen." The speaker slid from his saddle and embraced Javik.

"Bogard? Is it really you?" Javik asked.

Bogard fluffed his red beard in Javik's face and said, "Who else do you know with this flaming accoutrement? Of course it's me. Sigurd sent me a messenger telling me of your quest to find Allana. I decided you two would constantly be at each other's throats without someone to stand between you and beat some sense into your thick heads, so here I am."

Karl and Berda ran up to Javik in their night clothes. "Who's this?" Karl said.

"Bogard, these are two warriors from my village, Karl and Berda." He turned to his friends. "Bogard was a student with me at Tao Shan's."

The men exchanged greetings as Sigurd appeared fully dressed for the day. "I thought I heard that obnoxious horn of yours, Bogard." He embraced his fellow alumnus of Tao Shan's school. "You made good time. Did you travel alone?"

"No, my men are camped a short ride away. We couldn't

quite make it all the way in last night. From the looks of these drunks, it's probably a good thing we didn't join you. We'd be in no shape to ride today."

"How many are with you?" Javik asked.

"Two of my father's servants, but both are good archers. Shall I have them come in?"

"By all means. We still have a barrel of qush left to celebrate your arrival," Sigurd said.

At the mention of more qush, Karl and Berda turned a bit green. "I think I'll go back to bed for a while," Karl said.

"Me too," Berda said, and he followed his friend to their tent.

"Get dressed, Javik. My servants are preparing a fine breakfast, and it should be ready soon. You can fill Bogard in on your story over some venison stew," Sigurd said.

"As long as there's some bark tea to drive the devils from my head," Javik said, as he returned to his tent.

* * * * *

Over breakfast Javik filled Bogard in on his life since they parted two years ago and told him of Allana finding she was a princess.

"I can't believe it. That wild girl from the forest is a princess?" Bogard said.

"It's true, Tao Shan verified it," Javik said. "She was running a brothel in Zargaia until a few months ago. Now she's been forced to marry some Turrek bandit king."

Bogard sputtered out his bark tea at that news. "A brothel? By Zhou I'll be one of her customers. Where is this place?"

Margan broke in, "In Ullum, the capital city of Zargaia. It's called 'the house of Orgama'. She doesn't serve as a whore there, she owns the place. Besides, she's not there anymore, as Javik told you."

Bogard wiped the tea from his beard and sat back with a disappointed expression. "Orgama, the love goddess. What an appropriate name for a brothel being run by a woman who is a love goddess herself. What do you think of this, Javik?"

"What can I think? Margan says she still loves me, and no matter what she's done, I love her. I must rescue her from this bandit so we can be married," Javik said.

"Well, that makes this quest even more interesting," Bogard said. "Even if the treasure to be gained is small, we will help Javik marry the love of his life.

After breakfast the group moved off toward Zargaia.

Chapter 3

Allana slammed her wine goblet down on the table and glared at the wall.

"Damn, Barinosh! Is there no way we can escape this place?"

"I've been all over the fortress, Lady. Vargon's men have every possible exit covered. Even if we did manage to get outside the walls, it's many Leagues to the Tullan border. They'd surely overtake us before we could reach safety."

"I have no choice, then. I must agree to marry Vargon."

"Lady, I see no other way out." Barinosh was well acquainted with the barbarity of the Turrek. They had captured him and his partner in the pearling business two years ago when they attempted to cross Magda without the protection of a caravan. The old man was forced to watch while the bandits crucified his partner, and the same fate awaited him until the bandit King noticed the Gorgon tattoo on his arm. Vargon was familiar with Allana's tattoo and questioned Barinosh about its meaning. After he learned the royal significance of Allana's mark he sent the old sailor to her. Clearly, the bandit King had ambitions to become ruler of Gorgos with Allana as his Queen.

"There are poisons we could employ," Allana mused.

"Yes, but these bandits have strange ways concerning the wives of their Kings. Vargon covets Gorgos, and marrying you would legitimatize his claim to that throne. However; once outside of Magda, he would be separated from his main power. The people of Gorgos would rally to you once they knew who you were. Even if he took a sizeable force with him to the island, the people would not rest until you were free to rule them as their Queen. Marry Vargon, but wait until the time is ripe to eliminate him."

"You are very wise. We must play along with this bandit until we have the strength to resist him. Besides, we need to be on the right side of any civil war in Tulla. What do you hear on that score?"

"Many say Oliga almost has enough power to overthrow the King now. If Vargon joins him, he will have all he needs. He only waits for the proper time to challenge Queen Nonia."

Allana sat silent for a while before asking her next question.

"What do you hear of Nonia?"

"She is the true power in Tulla. The King does as she commands, and the people fear her magic. She is high priestess of their sea god, Godon, and she is said to have performed many miracles in his temple. Vargon even fears her, though he claims he fears no magician."

"I want to be sure I'm on the correct side in this war. Could you gain an audience in the court of Tulla?"

"I think so, lady, but Vargon will not let me leave."

"I'll tell him I agree to his proposal, then, I'll ask him to let you go on to Harrish to work our pearl business. He'll relent once I tell him how much gold you'll bring back to him."

"But your highness, we'll need that gold to rebuild Gorgos," Barinosh protested.

"And, we'll keep most of it out of his reach. I'll tell him you will bring 1000 gold crowns. That's a fortune to these brigands. Bring that to Vargon but deposit the rest with one of the Argani in Agam."

"A good plan, Lady. Let me know when I may leave."

"I will speak with Vargon tonight. Tomorrow you should be able to leave. I'll sign over my letters of credit to you. I won't need much money here. Once you've purchased a new ship and restarted our pearl business, go to the royal court and find out all you can about this coming fight. Report back to me when you know something."

"I hate to see you chained to this bandit, Lady."

"Don't worry about me. Vargon worships me, and I've endured worse than him. Our plan is settled, then. We will take the first step tonight."

Vargon's dinners were little more than brawls. The bandits did as much drinking as eating, and the entertainment was often watching one of their victims being tortured or raped. Allana took most of her meals in her cave, but she decided her acceptance of Vargon's marriage offer needed a full audience.

This night, the entertainment was a simple duel between two men who claimed the same woman captive. Allana stayed in the background until one of the combatants lay dying, and then she made her entrance. The room fell silent except for the groans of the dying man. Vargon spoke first.

"Allana! I'm glad you could join us tonight. Come to me." Vargon patted the pillows on his right after shooing away a concubine. "Get him out of here," he commanded, and servants raced to remove the nearly dead loser from the floor of the large cave that served as a combination dining room, throne room and exhibition chamber. Other servants moved in to clean up the blood while the winner unchained the captive woman and led her off. Her pleas for mercy fell on deaf ears.

Allana walked toward the bandit chief inhaling the aroma of the food as it mingled with the perfumes of the women and the sweat of the men. Several men were smoking water pipes, and the aroma told her the smokers were in another world even before she noticed the blank look in their eyes. She sat down next to Vargon.

"I see you are scraping the bottom of the barrel for entertainment lately," she said.

"It's winter. The caravans don't come as often, and some of the passes are closed. We make do with what's available. I haven't even had a good flogging to put on for weeks. All the men seem to be behaving themselves. Maybe you're a good influence on them?"

"I hardly see them, and I'm not interested in becoming acquainted with any bandits."

"I'm still waiting on your answer to my proposal. Perhaps a bandit chief is more to your liking?"

A group of musicians moved to a small stage and began to play. Allana knew the music, and she knew Vargon was a sucker for a provocative dance. She hadn't planned on dancing that night, but her clothes were very amenable to the routine demanded by the music.

"I'll give you my answer with a dance, if you like."

Vargon's smile broadened as his eyes moved over her body. He licked his lips in anticipation. "I anxiously await your decision," he said as he pushed her toward the floor. "Play that again," he commanded the musicians. "Allana will dance for us."

The bandits cheered loudly as Allana moved to the center of the floor. She nodded to the musicians, and the crowd fell silent.

The notes flowed like a river wandering through a long valley. Allana closed her eyes and let her body sway in time to the rhythm of the drum. Her arms entwined above her head like two serpents as her hips undulated sensually. As the beat picked up tempo, she moved in a circle around the floor hesitating on alternate steps to shake her upper body. Her raven hair swung around her head like a black cloud tossed by a gale. The tune sank back into a melancholy strain, and she collapsed on the floor writhing in imagined passion. Like a cobra rising in anger, she slowly rose to her feet and implored the audience as she moved in a slow circle. She pulled off her sash revealing a bare midriff. Falling to her knees, she undulated her stomach and moaned like a woman in labor. The music swelled to a new high as she sprang back to her feet and danced like a dervish around the room. Suddenly she turned to Vargon and ran directly at him as the drum pounded out a crescendo. On the last beat, she leaped into his arms. The bandits went wild.

"I take it this is yes?" Vargon said.

"On one condition."

"Name it."

"You allow Barinosh to travel to Harrish to restart our pearling business. You will need the extra money if a war comes, and my share is 500 gold crowns." Allana expected to have to bargain with Vargon, but the bandit King's ambitions were lower than she anticipated.

"Done!" the bandit chief roared. He dumped Allana on the

cushions and rose to address his men.

"My brothers! Allana has agreed to marry me."

A rousing cheer greeted his announcement.

Vargon signaled for quiet.

"The wedding will be in two weeks. I expect each of you to provide a suitable gift for my bride. Now, bring out the best wine. We will toast my newfound happiness."

Allana watched the proceedings with amusement. Vargon gave them two weeks to steal something appropriate.

Barinosh left the next day with a company of the bandits as guard and carrying the letters of credit.

Chapter 4

Barinosh arrived in Harrish three days after leaving Vargon's men behind at the Tullan border. After a good night's rest, he pressed on to Harrish. Once there, his first order of business was to settle his partner's debts. He wasn't looking forward to this business. He hated dealing with the Argani, but he had to admit that it was much easier carrying around letters of credit than a chest full of gold. His first stop was the house of Imram.

"Barinosh, you've been gone a long time. Welcome home," the Argani greeted his debtor's partner.

Barinosh looked at the swarthy little man with disgust. The curly black beard and the peculiar hat some of them wore complemented his dark face and even darker eyes. He stood only 14 hands high, and wore a garish dress of purple velvet with a large gold chain around his shoulders. His house was quite a contrast to the one he'd seen in Ulum. There was no pretense of poverty here.

"I have a letter for you from the Argani Gallam in Ulum." He handed the moneylender a scroll, and the man unrolled it carefully.

"Ah, I see your partner did well with the pearls. I'll get you a note for the remaining balance." The Argani called for a clerk and spoke to him in their guttural language. The clerk bowed and left the room.

"My partner is dead, the Turrek made short work of him, but they enjoyed every minute of his agony."

Imram's face took on a serious expression, and he clacked his tongue. "Tsk, tsk. I'm glad we live far from that border. They are a barbarous people. Will you have some wine?"

Barinosh couldn't remember Imram being this polite on previous visits when they were here to beg for more repayment time.

"Yes, some wine would be good."

Imram poured two goblets of rich, red liquid and passed one to Barinosh.

"To a prosperous future." Imram raised his goblet, and Barinosh did the same before taking a short sip.

The wine was very dry, and went down smoothly. They drank and talked of happenings while Barinosh was away until the clerk returned with the new letter of credit. Barinosh finished his wine and moved on to the next creditor.

The last stop was an Argani named Jehu. The sum owed him was the lowest, but Barinosh trusted him more than any of the others. He decided Jehu might be the best one to use in cashing out the final letter of credit.

The ritual at Jehu's house was like the others. As they shared a cup of hot tea, Barinosh presented the final letter of credit and a personal letter from Allana allowing Barinosh access to her funds. Jehu studied them all carefully before responding.

"Your paperwork seems to be in order. The Lady Allana has used all the proper code words in her documents. I'm not acquainted with her, but I do know Gallam's signature and code words, and I trust Gallam. How much gold do you need?"

"I'll need to buy a new boat and pay my crew and divers, if I can find them all. I'd say 2,000 crowns should do it."

"You have it. The best boats are built on the island of Gorgos, but I assume you know that being a Gorgon yourself."

"I know the island well. There's one particular builder I'm interested in."

"And, who is that?"

"Nimosh, he's an old friend of mine from my days in the Grogon navy. I know he'll give me a fair price."

"Hmm," Jehu thought for a moment. "Nimosh owes me some money, a minor sum, but the interest could build, in time. I think I can help you out. The funds you've deposited with me plus the interest I earned on your partner's debt are very useful to me right now. Tell Nimosh I will cancel his debt if he subtracts the amount from the price of your boat."

Barinosh was taken aback. He'd never known an Argani to be so generous with his gold before.

"That's very good of you, no matter how little he owes."

"A trifling matter of 300 gold crowns, but the Lady Allana's funds will help me realize an investment that should make us both rich." Jehu leaned closer to Barinosh and whispered, "You know there's to be a civil war?"

"I've heard rumors."

"Well, certain noble houses are prepared to support the winning side, but they need gold to be successful, and they're willing to pay handsomely for it."

"You speak as if the winner were a foregone conclusion."

"Agh, no. War is always a chancy thing, but these houses will wait until the outcome is clear before helping the pendulum swing fully to their side. They will take no chances."

"Bah, how can you trust a house that won't side with the right?"

"The right doesn't always win wars, and some houses believe the right side is the side that wins."

"A nasty business, but if it helps me get a boat, I'm grateful."

"Why should we care who rules Tulla, as long as there's a profit in it for us?"

The clerk returned with the receipt and a chest of gold. Barinosh opened the chest to find 1,000 crowns and a letter of credit for 2,000 crowns.

"But I only need 2,000," he protested.

"You should not be undercapitalized, Barinosh. Use the letter to buy the boat. Nimosh will give you the excess gold. Use the coin to help crew your ship."

Barinosh looked at the Argani with a stern face radiating an aura of distrust.

"Don't worry, it's not a debt. Your lady's account is good for more than I need, and you might as well make use of it. By the way, when do you expect her?"

"Not for several weeks. She's marrying Vargon of the Turrek next week, and they'll want a honeymoon, if I know Vargon."

Jehu gasped in astonishment. "Marrying that barbarian? Surely, he won't want to come here with her? I believe there's a price on his head in Tulla."

"He hopes to be on the right side of the coming war also. I thank you for your generous dealings, Jehu. Let's hope we all gain from the coming turmoil." Barinosh drained his cup and left with one of Jehu's servants carrying his chest of gold.

Within a month, a boat newly christened "Allana" was on its way to the pearl islands, and Barinosh was off to Agam, capital of Tulla with a letter of introduction from Jehu to Charlan, Count of Ollon. Ollon was a rich province along the seacoast surrounding its capital, Harrish. The Count had grown rich on the trade between Tulla and the other maritime countries. He also commanded a large naval force protecting those trade routes. Barinosh was pleased to be his guest at court.

The apartments of Count Charlan were not impressive. While at the Tullan court, he lived simply in a fashionable section of the city with only a few servants. He received Barinosh in a small room just off the hallway.

"Welcome to my house. Any friend of Jehu's is a friend of mine. What brings you to the capital?"

"Sir, I've heard rumors of a coming conflict between the Queen and Oliga, the Chamberlain, and I was hoping to see which way the winds of fate were blowing."

"Sit down, and have some wine." The Count indicated a chair and signaled a servant to pour another cup.

"Thank you. The journey from Harrish was cold and miserable."

"Hopefully, spring will come soon, but I fear it will bring war as well as good weather."

"How do you see the situation?" Barinosh asked.

Charlan turned his cup as it sat on the table and studied the motion of the wine as he contemplated Barinosh. This man was not known to possess any great wealth or power, and his connection with Jehu was one of a paid-up debtor. The Count's intelligence pegged him as a simple pearl merchant. Before answering this question Charlan needed more information.

"I'm curious as to why an honest pearl merchant should care about the politics of the royal house."

Barinosh smiled and took a sip of the wine. It was a good vintage. He would try honesty and see how long he stayed alive for his trouble.

"My partner is a lady who bears the royal mark of Gorgos. She is the one most interested in the happenings in Tulla. I, as you have learned, am simply a pearl merchant who once served the royal house of Gorgos."

Charlan seemed to jump a bit at this news, but quickly regained his composure.

"I was not aware that any of that house survived."

"It's true. I have not seen the mark myself, but I have it on good authority she bears it."

"Gorgos could be one of the bones tossed to the dogs of the winning house in this struggle. Does she command any forces or control any magic?"

"She has neither of her own, but she will soon wed the chief of the Turreks."

"Phew," Charlan gave a soft whistle. "A formidable force, indeed. They could swing the balance if they laid their swords on the scales. Do you know which side they favor?"

"My lady tells me Oliga has promised Gorgos to their lord, Vargon, in return for his aid."

Charlan smiled as he contemplated his options. He was sitting on the fence now. Both factions wooed him because of his naval power and control of the sea trade, but he could also field a sizeable army if the need arose. His navy also possessed knowledge of the sticking fire weapon for sea battles. The catapults on his ships could throw the blazing balls half a league. He'd been leaning toward Nonia, but perhaps Oliga was now a better choice. He didn't think anyone else at court knew of this arrangement yet, and he would try to keep the secret.

"Oliga is very free with my territory. Gorgos is now part of Ollon. If I joined Nonia, she would once more command the mightiest force. I need to speak with Oliga about this."

"As a legitimate heir to the throne of Gorgos, my Lady would bring great progress to Gorgos, and her loyalty to you would be sincere—with or without Vargon."

Charlan laughed and drained his wine cup. "I see your Lady's true motive in all this, but you must tell no one else of any possible alliance between Vargon and Oliga or your Lady and me. You must play the role of the simple merchant if you wish to save your hide. It will also give you a reason to come to court on a regular basis."

"I will seek an exclusive royal franchise for supplying the king and queen with pearls."

"Good, I'll support your request, but make sure you keep me informed about the Turreks. We are allies now, you and I, but we must hide our true loyalty until the outcome is clear. If Nonia gains an advantage, I'll try to find some way to warn your Lady so she may also be on the winning side. I'll introduce you at court tomorrow. Will you dine with us tonight?"

"Gladly, sir."

"Good! The food is excellent in this city."

Chapter 5

Vargon delayed the wedding two weeks to allow time for the bandit chiefs to gather. The other tribes of Magda would need time to make suitable arrangements for hostages in order to insure the safety of each clan's leader.

Magda consisted of four major bands beside the Turrek. The largest was the Lugga, almost twice the size of the Turrek, but only one fourth as fierce. Next came the Pinosh, about the same size as the Turrek, but located deep in the interior of the mountains. They lived more by animal husbandry than banditry. The Qualla and the Zagra were smaller tribes who constantly juggled alliances to remain independent. There was no degree of trust between the tribes on any issue, and peace was maintained through the exchange of hostages from time to time. The wedding was such a time. None of the other chiefs would willingly walk into Vargon's fortress unless they held very important Turrek captives.

At last, the big day arrived. Vargon's cave palace was never so gay. Allana was amazed at the way the bleak caverns were transformed into bright, festive rooms. Even the food was cranked up several notches in quality and quantity, and the best wines were looted from a rich caravan to satiate the palates of the bandit kings. Allana put on her best gown and as much jewelry as she trusted the thieves with. Rugina, the Turrek servant Vargon gave her, was awed by the result.

"Lady, you are truly the most beautiful woman in Magda. My Lord is very fortunate to have you," Rugina said as she wove a string of pearls through Allana's black hair.

"Fortune had no part in this arrangement. Vargon gave me no choice in the matter, but if I can return to Gorgos, marrying even that brigand will be a small price to pay."

"I'm sorry you do not love him, Lady. He's a very good man in many ways."

"I don't know of any yet."

Rugina giggled before speaking. "You may find some of those ways tonight, Lady."

"Oh please, I've already lain with your king, and I only hope he remembers some of what I taught him."

Rugina stifled an outright laugh. "I've heard he is very powerful in the bedchamber."

"I guess he'd come in handy if you had to throw a large bear out the bridal bed."

The women laughed together at the thought of Vargon battling a bear on his wedding night.

The main chamber of the huge cave complex was aglow with torchlight, and the large fireplace was ablaze with a larger fire than usual. The guests assembled at their tables around the central floor as servants ran to and fro pouring wine, beer and whatever other beverages were available. A group of musicians played gay tunes as the crowd waited for the big event of the evening, the arrival of the bride, but they were not prepared for Allana's grand entrance.

A large gong sounded, and the musicians fell silent. Two

women dressed in filmy pantaloons and velvet tops strode onto the floor strumming harps. Four nearly nude women dancing erotically and beating tambourines followed the harpists. Behind these, four of Vargon's strongest men carried a closed litter. They moved to the center of the floor and set down the litter as the women made a pathway between the curtains and Vargon. The gong sounded again, and the side curtains of the litter dropped to reveal Allana seated comfortably on a divan. She smiled at Vargon and extended her left hand in an invitation to the bandit chief.

Vargon smiled broadly as he left his chair and moved to his bride to be. He lifted her to her feet and led her to the chair beside his. He turned to face his guests.

"My friends, this is my bride, Allana, Princess of Gorgos."

A wave of excitement ran through the crowd as Allana glared at her soon to be husband.

"Yes, you heard me correctly. This woman is the last of the royal house of Gorgos, and I will soon restore her to her people and reign as King."

A cheer arose spontaneously, or as spontaneously as the Turrek guards around the room could prod out of the quests.

"Let the ceremonies begin!" Vargon shouted, and the musicians broke into a serious opus as the litter was carried from the floor and the dancers and harpists marched out. As they left, four bandits in polished armor and a somber looking man in a black, hooded robe marched in from the other side of the floor. A terrified man, naked and bound in chains, marched in the midst of the bandits. The procession stopped in the middle of the floor, and the man in the black robe pulled back his hood to reveal a silver skull where his head should have been. The crowd gasped in horror. Though they all knew the ritual, the unveiling of the skull mask was always a shock. Allana thought the mask was very cleverly constructed since it was realistic in every aspect. The man in the robe and skull mask began to speak, and the jaw of the skull moved convincingly as he did.

"Men of the Turrek and guests, we assemble this night to solemnize the joining of Vargon, King of the Turrek, and Allana, Princess of Gorgos. Anyone objecting to this union may speak now without fear of death." He turned around as if soliciting a response, but none came.

"A union of this magnitude demands the most solemn of ceremonies. Prepare the altar!"

Allana watched in horror as the naked captive was chained to a table brought to the center of the floor by four other bandits. He appeared to be pleading for help, but only groans and gasps came out of his mouth. She fought back her repulsion as she realized the man had no tongue.

"Let the bridal pair approach the altar," the skull priest intoned.

Vargon rose and took Allana's hand. He pulled her to her feet and led her toward the poor wretch now serving as a human altar. A low drumbeat began behind them.

They stopped with the skull priest between them and the silently pleading man chained to the table. Two acolytes dressed in black robes approached from the other side of table. One carried a golden goblet, and the other held an ornate knife. Allana could only guess what might happen next, but she knew it would take all of her courage to keep from fainting. She would have to put up the best front of her life now, and she wondered if she was up to it.

"Now the two become one," the priest chanted. "Allana, you die as a maid with this thrust." He took the knife and drove it into the victim's chest just below his ribcage. He drew the blade to one side making an arcing cut just under the last rib. There was surprisingly little blood, and the victim's eyes grew wide with the stroke, but he was still alive.

"Vargon you die as a single man with this thrust." The priest repeated the cut but on the other side of the victim's chest. A bright red, shallow "v" now marked the knife's path as the priest handed it back to the acolyte who cleaned it with a white cloth before placing it beneath his cloak.

The priest held up his hands throwing his sleeves back to his elbows.

"Now the living heart will provide the consecrating wine for the union of this royal couple."

Allana nearly fainted as the priest drove his hands into the victim's chest through the v-shaped cut. Amazingly, he was still alive, though his face contorted into a mask of pain and disbelief. The priest removed his bloody hands holding the still beating heart of the victim, as the crowd roared their approval.

The dizzying nausea nearly overcame her, but she fought back bravely as the second acolyte held the golden goblet under the dying heart. The priest turned it over and let the still warm blood lurch into the cup with the last beats of the grisly trophy. He squeezed it gently to extract the last few drops before placing it on the victim's stomach. Allana saw the man's eyes glaze over and roll back in his head as she struggled to hold back the hot, burning gorge in her throat.

The priest turned to Vargon and Allana.

"With this cup you become one in a new life from the soul of the sacrifice."   He handed the goblet to Vargon who took a hearty swig and passed it to Allana.

She took the cup and felt the warmth of the poor man's life ebbing away into the soulless gold. She dared not smell the dark liquid and held her breath as she lifted the cup to her lips. She had tasted blood many times, but never from a human being. Amazingly, it was much the same taste as any other kind. She swallowed with great difficulty and handed the cup to the priest. The crowd cheered again, and the musicians broke into a gay song.

The skull priest bowed to Allana and Vargon. "May you have every happiness, my Lady and my King." He spoke as if he had just given them an expensive gift instead of a grizzly toast to each other.

Allana was recovering quickly now as the victim was cleared away and the floor cleaned of any stray stains. The priest backed away from them still bowing low. His bloody hands were now hidden in his sleeves, and the event quickly passed into a horrid memory.

"Bring gifts to my bride!" Vargon commanded as he led her back to their chairs.

Allana was glad to be seated, and she took a long draught from her wine cup to wash away the metallic taste of the ceremonial cup.

A procession of men lined up in front of Vargon and his new bride, as Tumak announced each one. Allana had recently learned Tumak was second only to Vargon among the bandits. Rugina said most of the men preferred him to Vargon, but he was fiercely loyal to his chief.

One by one, the bandit chieftains placed rich treasures at Allana's feet. She thanked each one as Vargon inspected the gifts making a mental note of whose gift seemed too cheap for his tastes. The next order of business was a lavish banquet followed by entertainment and large quantities of wine. It was well past midnight when Vargon rose and declared it was time to retire with his new bride. Jeers and catcalls greeted the announcement, but Vargon ignored it all as he dragged Allana toward the bridal chamber.

Several burly guards stood outside the doors of Vargon's section of the caves, and he gave them strict orders he was not to be disturbed for any reason. For the first time, Allana saw the bandit chief's private rooms. They were a mess.

The walls were bare except for some peculiar looking stains Allana could not identify. She suspected they were the results of fits of rage taken out on some part of a past dinner. Several large tables groaned under the weight of various treasure items, bowls of fruit, nuts and some moldy loaves of bread. A cabinet on one wall hung open to reveal a few scrolls and some writing equipment. The chairs were scratched and gouged from random encounters with armor and weapons. One corner held an assortment of weapons in a stand next to an armature with a helmet, chain mail and breastplate. A large shield rested against the wall behind the chain mail. Guttering candles flickered eerily giving the room a sinister aura.

Vargon led Allana past this confusion into a more brightly lit bedroom. A huge bed occupied the center of the room covered in silken sheets and an array of pillows. A pile of furs rested near the head of the bed, and the hide of a brown horse served as a rug. Allana noticed that some of her clothes had been moved from her apartments to this room. She could hear water running somewhere and guessed Vargon had his own toilet.

"Your boudoir, wife," Vargon slurred. "Make yourself at home."

Allana walked around the room while Vargon undressed. She found the toilet. A spring gushed out of one wall of the small room and dropped into a shallow pool before flowing out through a hole in the opposite wall. A wooden stool spanned the small stream just before it vanished into the rocks. Here was both bath and toilet. She tested the water with her hand and found it ice cold. It would take a lot of hot water to make the bath useable.

Vargon came up behind her and threw his arms around her waist.

"I've waited too long for this, but I won't make you shave for me."

"I've already done that, husband. I knew you'd want me smooth for our wedding night."

"This I have to see." Vargon picked her up and carried her to the bed. He laid her on the soft sheets, and Allana wondered that so vulgar a man could tolerate such luxurious bedclothes. He undressed her with more gentleness than she thought him capable of, then he stepped back and admired his conquest.

"You'll never be sorry you married me, for tonight, I have everything a man could desire."

Allana fought back her revulsion as they made love.

* * * * *

It was several weeks before Barinosh returned to Vargon's fortress. Allana received him in her private apartments. It seemed Vargon didn't want her to sleep in his quarters on a regular basis. He only sent for her every few days now, and she was glad of the respites.

"What news from the court of Tulla?" she asked.

"Lady, there will soon be civil war. Oliga and Nonia have gathered their allies, and the sides are evenly matched. The Queen commands the royal army of 2,000 men, but most of them are on border and garrison duty outside the capital. The real power lies in the hands of her aristocracy. The counts of three provinces have promised her 3,000 men each, but two powerful counts are holding back to see which way the winds of chance will blow; Charlan, Count of Ollon, and Rollum, Count of Tourno. Ollon controls the sea trade, and a large segment of the Tullan economy. Their military might is great on the sea, but not large on the land. The Count of Tourno could muster over 4,000 men on short notice."

"And what of Oliga?" Allana asked.

"He is allied with the two most powerful men in Tulla. The Count Drago and the Count of Modin both control armies of 4,000 men each. He has sought allies among the bandits of Magda, but only Vargon has promised him any aid."

"And what is Vargon's promise?"

"2,000 men, all battle hardened bandits. Oliga is confident he can win with Vargon as an ally. The forces are gathering, and open conflict will come soon. Both Oliga and Nonia have been putting on shows of their magic powers in the temples, Nonia in the temple of the sea god Godon, and Oliga in the temple of the fertility goddess. I witnessed their performances several times."

"What do you think of their magic?"

"Ptah," Barinosh spat on the floor. "They're charlatans, like all magicians, but the people believe in them. Many follow only because they fear magical reprisals if they don't."

Allana thought for a moment before speaking again.

"Then, Vargon is the key to Oliga's victory. Take him out of the mix, and Nonia wins easily," Allana mused.

"True, Lady, but if one of the other neutral counts decides to side with Oliga, the scales are balanced again. Neither will attack unless they feel they have superiority. Take Vargon away now, and Oliga will delay his move until he has another ally."

"Then Vargon will be Oliga's ally. With Oliga comes Gorgos, and I will deal with Vargon once the island is mine again."

Chapter 6

Oliga smiled broadly as he moved the tiny pieces across the map table.

"I think we have her where we want her, Bergin."

The old general was a veteran of many battles, but never against his own people. This was a new experience for him, and he was not comfortable with being a rebel. Queen Nonia was responsible for his new situation. She was the one who insisted he retire. She was the one who replaced him with her own lover so he could be close to her all the time. Now she would pay for her folly, even though it ran against his grain to oppose his sovereign.

"Bringing in the Turreks was a master stroke, Oliga, but they must pass the fortress at Othis to reach Nonia's rear echelons. It has enough heavy cavalry and infantry to block the largest force the Turrek can muster. If he's hung up there, how will that help us?"

"If she leaves the Othis garrison in place, her front lines will be too weak, and she can't afford that. My guess is she'll post them to protect the baggage train then plan on using them as reinforcements for her front once the Turrek are defeated," Oliga said.

"But, won't Vargon sack the city instead of attacking

Nonia?" Birgen asked.

Bergin laughed softly. "Nonia knows Vargon will not be able to resist looting her baggage train. Besides, the local militia there can defend the walls against the bandits. Vargon has no siege machines, and he won't risk the losses he'd incur in scaling the walls. No, he'll bypass the city once he knows they won't have a large force at his rear."

"Aha, but if he knows a large force will be defending the baggage train, he may not attack," Bergin said.

"Nonia is no fool. She'll convince Vargon's spies that the entire garrison is bound for her front, then, she'll set an ambush at the baggage train and surprise him completely."

"I won't rely on Nonia's actions. I'll also make sure their spies understand the entire Othis garrison has been sent to the front lines against us. The Turrek scum will be decimated by the heavy cavalry and crossbowmen from the fortress," Bergin said.

"We kill two birds with one arrow. Nonia is defeated, and we eliminate a bandit problem. That fool Vargon will blunt the edge of our enemy's sword with his bones. They're bound to inflict some casualties on the Othis garrison, leaving a weaker force to face us." Oliga took a long draught from his wine goblet and sat back smiling contentedly.

"Timing will be the main issue there," Bergin said. "We must attack while Vargon is engaging the rear guard."

"Precisely. We will delay our attack until Vargon is dealt with, but move on Nonia before she can move the Othis garrison to her front," Oliga said.

"Even if the Turrek are successful, they'll just loot the baggage train and limp back home after suffering too many casualties?" Bergin said.

"Perhaps, but our success is not dependent upon them doing any more than delaying the movement of the Othis garrison. Once Tourno sees the Turrek have engaged and the garrison from Othis will not be in the front lines, he will join with us. Together we will overwhelm her," Oliga said.

"So, we wait to be sure the Turrek attack before we move. Is that it?" Bergin asked.

"Yes, if Nonia must send reinforcements to her rear, so much the better. We must hit before what's left of the Othis garrison can join the main force. All we have to do is convince Nonia we are not planning to attack immediately."

"I think that will be no problem. We will give her spies every indication we're delaying our move," Bergin said.

Oliga raised his goblet in a toast. "To liberty."

"To liberty," Bergin responded.

* * * * *

Inside Vargon's fortress, Allana was busy studying the bandit chief's lieutenants. They were a scruffy lot with the exception of Tumak.

Tumak was rather fair skinned for a Turrek, and had good features. Tall and muscular, he carried himself with an air of authority, which demanded respect from the bandit rabble above and beyond that fostered by his skill with weapons. No one dared challenge him, and Vargon relied on him completely to control the routine aspects of his banditry operations.

On this particular day, Allana was to dine with him in private, having set up the meeting on the pretext of selecting a bodyguard, but first, she was eager to hear Barinosh's report on the intrigues surrounding the Tullan throne. The old man had a cheerful expression as he entered her private chambers.

"I take it you have good news from Tulla," Allana said as she offered him a goblet of wine.

"Aye, Lady. Oliga grows stronger by the day, and Nonia's allies are wavering."

"What is the cause?"

"They fear the entry of Vargon and the Turreks has tipped the balance. Ollon or Tourno may swing to Oliga's side, and if one of those two should join him, he will win easily."

"What holds Charlan back? He knows Vargon is Oliga's ally."

"He only suspects that is true. He awaits my confirmation, and in any case, he will not decide which side to join until he sees the Turrek attack is successful."

"A wise position. Have you learned anything of Oliga's plans?"

Barinosh drained his goblet and declined another cup before answering.

"Only by hearsay. A source Charlan considers reliable says Oliga plans to march on the capital through the Idlum River valley before the spring floods make the river impassible. Come, I'll show you."

Barinosh led Allana to another table where he spread out a map of Tulla. He pointed to a narrow spot between two sets of low mountains.

"Here is the Idlum River, and here is the point where Nonia plans to meet Oliga. Oliga could not use the Turrek in his front. They'd have to pass through her entire army, but he could use them as a mobile harassing force in the Queen's rear areas. This means they'd have to enter the Idlum valley through this pass."

Barinosh pointed to a low pass through the mountains north of the river.

"The Queen will have to use part of the Othis garrison to guard her rear, leaving the city without fighting men, but she believes Vargon will not attack the city because of its formidable walls. She cannot afford to position any of her main force to stop the Turrek, and she needs the Othis garrison at her front if she hopes to defeat Oliga. It's her only hope. She feels the royal infantry and heavy cavalry will make short work of the bandits in a set battle, then she would move that force to the front against Oliga after the Turrek retreated. Even though her force would suffer heavy casualties against the Turrek, she still needs them against Oliga. Oliga would face a weaker royal force, and the Turrek would be decimated. He has the best of both worlds."

Allana smiled at the duplicity of Oliga, but one did not become royal chamberlain by being completely honest. It was a plan worthy of her old master Grucheaux – let the Turrek bleed to weaken the Queen.

"I agree with your analysis. Oliga plans to sacrifice the Turrek in his conquest of Tulla. This may work to our benefit. If Vargon is killed in battle, I will go to Oliga and claim Gorgos as Vargon's heir. If he survives, I'll deal with him at Gorgos, as we'd planned. I win either way."

"But Lady, if Vargon dies the bandits will expect you to either throw yourself on his funeral pyre or marry his successor," Barinosh said.

"That's why I'm playing up to Tumak. I'm sure he will claim leadership once Vargon is no more. We can pursue the same plan with him we had in mind for Vargon, but I don't think Tumak will want any part of Gorgos. I'll convince him that I should have the island as a wedding present. We will wait and see how this battle turns out, and then we will act accordingly. Go back to our pearl business, but keep your eyes and ears open."

"I am your servant, Lady," Barinosh said as he bowed before Allana and kissed her hand.

Barinosh left Allana just as Tumak entered her apartments. Vargon's chief lieutenant strode into the room dressed in his best tunic and pantaloons. His high boots shone with the effort of many slave's work, and his hair and beard were neatly trimmed and combed to perfection. His blue eyes were a rare thing among the Turrek, and they riveted you with a purposeful glint.

"Mistress, I am honored to dine with you," Tumak said as he bowed low before Allana.

"You are welcome, Tumak. Please sit, and my servants will bring our meal." Allana indicated a chair at one side of a small table. Tumak sat down and Allana sat opposite him. She called for the meal and poured two cups of wine.

"I have several names for you to consider for a bodyguard, Lady. I think you will be pleased with each one, and I can have them called in for inspection if you desire. The first one is..."

Allana cut him off with a motion of her hand. "First we must toast the success of the Turrek in the coming war in Tulla." She raised her cup toward him.

"Why, yes, Lady, but..."

Once more she silenced him with a fingertip to her lips and nodded toward the cup. They both drank, and Tumak leaned forward before speaking.

"What do you know of the coming war, Lady?" His tone was hushed, and he was clearly uncomfortable.

"I have my own spies, Tumak. I'm not sure Vargon is acting wisely. I've recently had word that treachery is afoot in the camp of Oliga."

"Bah! Vargon ignores my counsel by dealing with Oliga. The Tullans hate us Turreks, and they'd like to see us eliminated. I also fear treachery."

"I don't know if it involves the Turrek at all. I only know that Oliga intends to sacrifice one of his allies to make his own job easier. Perhaps it is Drago or Modin?"

"Not likely. They can contribute far more might than we can. They have heavy infantry and armored cavalry, and if it comes to a siege of Agam, they have siege machines. We are only lightly armed horsemen."

Allana tried to contain her jubilance. Tumak was not happy with the arrangement. He would be easily turned to her purpose should Vargon return from the war alive.

"I will speak to my husband. He should not ignore your wise words. I've heard the men speak very highly of you, and many would prefer you as leader of the Turrek."

"I am flattered, but I serve Vargon as long as he lives. I would appreciate it, though, if you could make a few hints about your spy's information."

"He rarely listens to me. He says I'm only a woman, and not fit to share the councils of men." Allana put on her best pouting face.

"He makes a great mistake, Lady. You are a paragon among women, not only in your beauty, but also in your wisdom and cunning. I've seen the way you manipulate him."

"But, it's true. I'm only a woman. If I manipulate my husband, it's because he can deny me nothing out of his love for me. I only have my female wiles as weapons."

"They are more formidable than any sword, Lady."

Allana leaned closer to Tumak. "I must tell you, though. I don't think I will be able to manage him much longer. I think he's growing tired of me. He hardly ever invites me to his bedchamber anymore."

Tumak began to sweat profusely, and he stammered a bit as he responded.

"I, I, I can't b-believe he could ever grow tired of one so lovely as you."

"It is a sad thing, but true. To be honest with you, I requested a bodyguard because it would be a good excuse to have a virile man nearby in case the need became too much for me to bear. I'm only a woman, after all."

Tumak licked his lips and sat back in his chair. He was rescued by the arrival of dinner.

Allana changed the subject to bodyguards after the meal, and requested three of Tumak's candidates for inspection the next day.

Chapter 7

Allana stood on the wall of the bandit fortress and watched the rushing torrent swirl by below. The once clear water was now a dull brown and carried dirty black tree trunks and limbs along with it as it plunged over the cliff. The melting snow swelled the river, and it nearly filled the opening in the fortress wall. It would not be long now before Vargon would be off to war. Her next move depended upon the outcome of that war, and she hoped she could avoid killing him. He loved her more than his own life, she knew that, and that knowledge helped her endure his attentions.

She switched her gaze to the valley beyond the lake. The snow was almost gone now, and the ice on the lake was beginning to break up into large chunks. She could see the road winding through the valley and wondered if Javik was somewhere along that distant path. It had been over a year now, and no word from him. He would be a real man now. Perhaps he'd forgotten her and married some girl from his village? No, she couldn't believe that. If Vargon loved her madly, Javik loved her even more. She had to believe he'd be there one day. One day she'd be standing on the wall and see his blonde hair shining in the sun. She'd know him from a distance of several leagues. Yes, he'd come. He had to come.

The sound of a trumpet stirred her from her dreaming, and she turned to see a rider galloping to the mountain entrance of the bandit castle. His horse was well lathered, and she knew this meant the war was beginning.

* * * * *

Vargon strode into his great hall with Tumak close behind. The messenger knelt as he approached.

"Well, what news?" Vargon thundered.

"Oliga sends his greetings, sir. He is ready to begin his attack and asks if your strength is gathered and ready to move as agreed."

Vargon studied the man. He was one of Oliga's guards, and he'd seen him before in the Chamberlain's palace. He could trust this man with his answer.

"Tell Oliga that I will move from here in three days and attack Nonia on the fourth day. I will wait for his messenger at the appointed place to be sure Othis is not defended and to receive confirmation of his attack before I move. Take that message back to your master."

The messenger saluted and rose to leave.

"You'll need a fresh horse," Tumak said. "I'll see that one is provided."

"Thank you, sir," the messenger said as he backed out of the room.

Tumak instructed one of the guards to see to the man's horse and turned to Vargon.

"I will send riders to each of our captains telling them to assemble here in two days."

"And, contact our spies in both camps. I want to know this is not a trap before we go too far," Vargon ordered.

"Yes, sir," Tumak said as he saluted and left the room.

Allana entered from the other side of the room. "Is it to be war, husband?"

"Yes, as you probably know too well by now. What do your spies say?"

"I haven't heard from them, but I'll let you know anything I find out."

"I wish I could believe that," Vargon said as he pulled her into his arms.

* * * * *

Two days later, the soggy valley behind the fortress was filled with bandits. Vargon called all the chiefs to a council of war to be followed by a lavish banquet. The Turreks traditionally prepared for war by drinking themselves into oblivion.

Vargon was in a gay mood that night. As servants cleared the remains of dinner from the tables, he rose and lifted his wine cup to his assembled captains and their ladies.

"Men of the Turrek! I have news from Oliga of Tulla. In two days we move to strike down Queen Nonia and her tyranny. The moment you've all been preparing for is here. Drink to our victory!"

"Hail Vargon!" the men cheered as they stood and lifted their cups in response.

After the toast, Vargon continued. "Tonight we celebrate, but tomorrow you must gather your men and load your wagons. We will camp at the low pass until word comes of Oliga's attack. He's assured me the garrison at Othis will be in Nonia's front, and he will move through the Idlum valley to meet her forces head-on while we will attack swiftly from the rear. You all know what lies at the rear of Nonia's army, her baggage train."

A mixed chorus of shouts and whistles met this announcement. None of the Turrek were very keen on a pitched battle with regular soldiers, but they could all appreciate looting a baggage train while the enemy was engaged elsewhere. Once more, Vargon signaled for silence.

"Nonia needs all of her strength to face Oliga. It will be easy to take the treasure, but Oliga has promised us even more if we continue to attack Nonia's rear. I intend to force her to divert enough units to insure Oliga's victory."

Tumak stood for recognition.

"What is it, Tumak?" Vargon asked.

"This plan depends upon a weakened garrison at Othis and Oliga attacking Nonia's front so that she may not send troops to counter our intrusion. What if Othis resists us or if he doesn't attack?"

"He's given me his word on both matters," Vargon responded.

"And you trust him?" Tumak said as he looked to the other lieutenants for signs of their reaction to the plan. A few negative remarks came forth, but most of the men only looked on impassively.

"No, I don't trust him. We will wait on word from our own spies before we move."

"You are wise, as usual Vargon," Tumak said as he sat down.

The rest of the evening was spent in pure debauchery. Allana tired of the spectacle early and excused herself from the orgy.

* * * * *

Bergin walked into Oliga's tent with a broad smile on his face. "Good news Oliga."

"You look cheerful enough tonight. What's the news?" Oliga poured a cup of wine and held it out to his General.

"Ah, thank you. Treachery is thirsty work." Bergin took a long swig from the silver chalice before continuing. "Vargon has gathered his forces and plans to attack in two days."

"Good, good! Now the difficult part begins. We must convince the devil's spies that we're on the attack while convincing Nonia we are doing just the opposite. What plans have you made?"

Bergin sat down opposite his master and took another drink. "It will take Vargon a full day to reach the low pass. He plans to wait there for confirmation of our attack. Of course, we will send our messenger, but he will not believe him. He will wait on word from his own spies. The guards on the camp have orders to let any rider leave until we begin our march, but to let none enter or leave afterwards. Vargon's spies will ride out once they see our forces leaving camp. We will march to a point just short of Nonia's lines and halt. Nonia's spies have been told of Vargon's attack, so she'll have to wait until Vargon is defeated before moving any forces to face us. That is, as long as she knows we won't attack at the same time. I will instruct our men to light cooking fires once we've stopped. That will convince Nonia we do not intend to attack until the next morning."

"An excellent plan Bergin," Oliga smiled broadly as he poured himself another goblet of wine. "To our success," he said as he held out his goblet toward his general.

* * * * *

In Nonia's camp preparations were well underway to block Oliga's advance. The Queen watched as markers representing her forces were placed on the large map table. Satisfied that all units were in place, she let her gaze wander to the large mirror just inside the entrance to her private quarters. She sighed at the toll this civil war was taking on her beauty. She was still a fine-looking woman in spite of being on the downhill side of forty. Her figure was as good as ever, and her blond hair was not yet showing any trace of gray, but her face betrayed the stress of her position with fine lines around her eyes and at the corners of her mouth. Her steel gray eyes could still flash like lightning, but even they revealed the doubt plaguing her thoughts about the outcome of this battle. The entrance of General Darga with one of her spies caused her to re-focus on the situation at hand.

"My Queen! This man has vital news," Darga said as he knelt before his mistress.

"I hope it's good news. Our cause could use a little of that right now," Nonia said as she turned to the dirty horseman kneeling beside her general. "Rise and give your report."

"I fear my news is not good, Madam. Vargon is on the march toward the low pass with over 2,000 horsemen. He plans to attack your rear when Oliga attacks your front. Oliga hopes you will divert forces from your front to counter Vargon's attack."

"How do you know this?" Nonia asked.

"I was in Vargon's fortress when he spoke to his captains. The Turrek accepted me as a fugitive from your justice. I moved freely among them."

"You did well," Nonia said as she tossed a bag of coins to the spy. "Leave us now and refresh yourself."

Darga turned to leave also, but Nonia stopped him.

"Stay, Darga. We must review our plan for this dual attack."

"Lady, Vargon has only light horsemen. The Othis garrison we assigned to the rear guard will crush the Turrek easily. Then we can move them to our front to deal with Oliga's attack."

"I'm concerned about Vargon, but I worry more about Tourno. When Rollum sees Vargon attacking with Oliga, he will join him against me. They can block our retreat to Agam or strike our left."

"Oliga hates the Turrek as much as we do. I believe he will sacrifice them before his attack. Tourno will see the Turrek ploy for what it is and will not move until he thinks Oliga has gained the upper hand on your front. If we can defeat Vargon quickly, which I think is a certainty, we can reinforce our front to stop Oliga and keep Tourno out of the fight or, possibly, win him to our side."

Nonia stared at the map table as she pushed her hair back from her face.

"You're probably right. Vargon will run back to Magda once his force is decimated. We must only pray that Oliga does not attack at the same time. How can we be sure of that?" The Queen rubbed her chin as she contemplated a solution.

Darga spoke. "I have an idea, we will move the infantry and cavalry into the forest here and here." The General indicated positions on the map table. "Then we remove the baggage from the wagons and replace it with crossbowmen. They will stay under tarpaulins until the last moment, then rise to shower death on the Turrek from the front while our heavy troops attack from the forest on each side.   The Turrek will be decimated."

"Won't Vargon's scouts discover the ambush?" Nonia asked.

"We will let their spies know we're moving the garrison to the front lines.   When they see the troops leaving the baggage area, they will be convinced.   Our troops will act like they're moving to the front, but they'll double back and set the ambush. Vargon's scouts will see weak force guarding the baggage and attack immediately," Darga said.

The Queen's frown turned into a smile.   "A clever plan.   The troops will already be packed and ready to move after defeating the Turrek.   We could then use the garrison to aid us against Oliga.   If we are fortunate, we will hold the main attack long enough to convince Tourno to stay neutral or join with us.   All we need is a little luck, Darga, a little luck."

* * * * *

Vargon halted his column within sight of the fortress at Othis and called for Tumak.

"Send scouts ahead to determine if the garrison will oppose our entry into Tulla.   Oliga says the garrison's gone to oppose him, but I don't trust him.   We'll camp here until we receive word of Oliga's attack."

"It will be done," Tumak saluted and rode off to relay his leader's orders.

Vargon dismounted and stretched his saddle weary back. Two slaves rushed forward with a chair and a pitcher of wine. One made his master comfortable while the other poured a large flagon of wine.

Tumak soon returned and dismounted next to Vargon.   "We

should know about the garrison in a short while. I told the men they could have cooking fires."

Vargon nodded agreement. "Good, good. They can get a hot meal before the battle tomorrow. Oliga plans to attack just after dawn. Make sure the men are ready to ride before first light. Come, have some wine." Vargon snapped his fingers, and a slave appeared with another chair and cup. Tumak sank into the rough camp chair eagerly and savored the wine.

"Tomorrow we will know if Oliga keeps his word," Tumak said.

"I'm not worried about that. We will loot the baggage train even if he doesn't attack as planned. Nonia needs all of her strength against Oliga. She'll have none to spare for us. If Oliga holds back, we'll grab the gold and run. We're much too fast for any units she could send to pursue us."

"But, he's promised you Gorgos. If he reneges on that, what will Queen Allana say?"

"She's my wife now, and she'll obey like any other wife or face the consequences."

The slaves set up a camp table, and soon a supper of roast game and bread appeared. They had barely finished when a breathless rider fell to one knee in front of Vargon.

"Well, what of the garrison?" Vargon asked.

"They are not there, Master. The fortress is undefended except for some townspeople on the walls with bows."

"You see, Tumak. It's as I said. Nonia has every man she can muster facing Oliga. The baggage train is ours for the taking."

* * * * *

Rollus, Duke of Tourno, liked what he heard. Vargon was

poised at Nonia's rear while the might of Oliga was, poised to engage her front. Tomorrow would prove whose side was strongest, and he would join that side as soon as the matter was settled. His main force was aligned to go to Nonia's aid, but he could easily shift their mission from aid to attack. It was all working out nicely.

* * * * *

The morning dawned bright and fair. There was no frost, and the air held a hint of summer to come. Vargon's spies reported Oliga breaking camp and marching to the attack. The bandit king gave the order to move out, and his army rode past Othis toward the waiting baggage train.

* * * * *

Oliga ordered the attack and watched Vargon's spies slip away to report the fact. Once they were well on their way, he halted the advance within view of Nonia's forces.

* * * * *

Nonia smiled as she saw Oliga halt his men and allowed them to light cooking fires. The riders standing by to call up the ambush forces were told to relay her order to slay the Turrek instead. As she expected, the Chamberlain felt his forces were sufficient to defeat her even if the Turrek were defeated. Her trap was set, and once the Turrek were no longer a threat, she was confident Rollus would swing his forces to her cause. She was sure Oliga had blundered greatly.

* * * * *

The Turrek spread out to attack a baggage train their scouts said was only sparsely guarded, but rich in wagons stacked high with booty under the drab, brown tarpaulins. Each bandit licked his lips in anticipation of rich plunder as the command for attack was sounded. They thundered toward the wagons shouting fiercely and waving their swords high above their heads.

Vargon was the first to fall as the crossbowmen threw back the tarps and fired their volley. The Turrek charge was not daunted, however, and the bandits began to cut up the bowmen in revenge. They hardly noticed the heavy cavalry and infantry descending upon them from the forest on their flanks. Soon a melee was in progress with whirling horses wreaking chaos and the clash of arms and armor almost drowning out the shouts of the men. Tumak and four men surrounded Vargon's body as two of the bandit captains rode up brandishing bloody swords.

"Tumak! We are betrayed. What shall be do?" one shouted.

"We must retreat. You and Burtus gather as many as you can. We will fight our way out of this trap back toward the fortress. I don't think they'll pursue us past that point. I'll take care of Vargon's body. I don't want these Tullans to make a spectacle of it."

The two captains saluted and rode off into the melee once more.

Tumak tied Vargon's remains to his king's horse and mounted his own. The fight was pressing closely around them, but the bandit warriors were holding back the Tullan army so far. More and more bandits joined his group as the captains spread the word to assemble on Tumak. Soon he found himself sitting like an island in a stormy sea.

"This is all we could muster, Tumak," Burtus shouted as he rode up. His left arm was hanging limply at his side and a deep slash across his right cheek was bleeding heavily. Behind him, a trumpeter sat shaking in his saddle.

"See if that trumpeter has enough balls left to sound retreat," Tumak commanded.

Burtus turned to the terrified youth and gave the order. The first call was weak and unsure, but a slap across his back with the flat of Burtus's sword produced a much stronger call on the second attempt.

"Keep him at it," Tumak shouted as he turned his horse and began to cut his way back toward the pass.

Bandits fell in on either side creating a wedge forcing its way through the Tullan lines. The ambush force was not that large, and the bandits soon found themselves fighting a rear guard action as they retreated. Tumak looked back at the battlefield as he topped a hill and saw the carnage. About half of his force was dead, dying or still engaged with no hope of retreat, but Tullan bodies lay stacked two and three deep on the bloody ground. The bandits had sold their lives dearly. Vargon would have been proud of them.

* * * * *

Oliga sat his horse with Bergin beside him surveying his army. All was ready. Vargon had attacked as planned, and his scouts told him the Tullan and Turrek had both paid a heavy price in the action. Nonia's front was no match for his strength, and there would be little help from the forces engaged with the bandits. He gave the order for attack.

* * * * *

Nonia heard the bad news. The bandits had caused heavier casualties than expected even though they left over half their force lying on the field. The Turrek were taken care of, but the fight with Oliga would be less certain unless the remains of the Othis garrison could move quickly to her front. Her army braced for the assault as they watched the rebels advance through the river valley toward their breastworks. The beat of the war drums was matched by the noise of weapons striking shields and the guttural chants of the warriors.

Nonia's archers let fly a volley when the army came within range, but Oliga's forces formed turtles and kept advancing. An answering volley rained death on the defenders, but crossbowmen took up positions on Nonia's front lines and began to pick off individual warriors. The advancing tide of men stopped at the abatises only briefly as woodsmen stepped forward to hew a path through the sharpened branches. Oliga's crossbowmen fired from behind shields in an effort to cover the axe men, but nearly all of them fell before a surge of infantry plunged into the gap cut at the expense of their lives.

Now the infantry on both sides joined the battle, and it raged through the trenches as more gaps were cut in the defense works. Oliga's forces cut their way to the second line of breastworks where the fighting was even fiercer than at the first line. There seemed to be no end to the river of warriors pouring into the trenches, and Nonia stood looking on in horror as the sounds of death came closer to her tent. Darga approached with a worried look.

"Can we hold, Darga?" Nonia asked.

"My Queen, I fear the rebels are too many for us. We need the help of the Othis garrison immediately or we are lost."

"They should have been here by now. Should I give the order to retreat?"

"No, Lady. The dice of war may roll our number yet."

At that moment, a trumpet sounded, and the first ranks of the Othis garrison appeared from the forest behind Nonia's defenses.

"Thank the gods, they're here," Darga shouted as the commanders led their men into the melee.

His joy was short lived. The new supply of men soon petered out with little effect on the advancing rebels.

"They are not enough, Darga," Nonia called. "Sound the retreat."

Darga found a trumpeter and gave the order. As the notes sounded, horses and a wagon appeared before Nonia's tent. The Queen lost no time in making her escape while Darga stayed to supervise a somewhat disorderly retreat.

* * * * *

The messenger knelt before Rollus, dirty and tired from a long, hot ride.

"My Lord, Nonia's forces are beaten. They retreat before Oliga's might. The Turreks are routed and make their way back home through the low pass. The day belongs to Oliga."

"Then our path is now clear," Rollus said as he turned to his generals. "Advance to prevent Nonia from reaching Agam. Torrou, fly to Oliga's camp and offer him our support. Tell him we will block Nonia's retreat. If he asks what I want in return, tell him that I simply wish to be treated fairly under his rule. He will understand."

"Yes, Lord." Torrou saluted and left the room.

"Come, gentlemen. We ride to victory on the side the gods favor," Rollus shouted.

* * * * *

The bleeding column was a sad sight as it approached the bandit's mountain fortress. The news of the defeat preceded their arrival, and many women were waiting to see if their loved ones had fallen. Allana watched from the walls as the lead horsemen emerged from the mountainside. She knew Vargon had fallen, and she had to put on her best mourning widow act in spite of the joy leaping up inside her. Behind Tumak, a cart carried Vargon's body while his horse, led by one of the bandit Captains, walked behind. Soon, the wails of the women reached the top of the walls. It was over, and Allana had won.

Chapter 8

Six bandits carried Vargon's body into the center of the great courtyard. He was dressed in his finest armor and his hands were clasped around the grip of his long sword. Allana stood with her servant next to Tumak, as he had instructed her. The mournful dirge of the peculiar bag-like instruments favored by the Turrek added a mysterious note to the slow cadence of the drums. Nearly all of the men gathered around the funeral pyre were wounded in some way. One or two rested on litters, but the rest stood with red, weary eyes as they watched the procession circle the pyre once before placing the body on top. It was growing dark, and the light from the many torches around the courtyard flickered in the breeze casting dancing shadows on the stone walls. Allana thought they were the shadows of demons attending the last rite for one soon to join their band.

The skull priest appeared accompanied by four acolytes swinging censures of incense. He stopped on the side of the pyre opposite Tumak and Allana, and raised his arms in the air. The music and drums stopped, and the silence enveloped the courtyard like a dense fog. Allana could not even hear a bird sing or a dog bark, and she began to tremble a bit.

The priest intoned a chant in a language she hadn't heard before, but the men present responded in unison in the same tongue. The light from the torches made the skull mask even more sinister as the priest moved around the pyre to face Tumak and Allana. He raised his arms again and spoke, this time in the Turrek language.

"The Lord Vargon has fallen bravely in battle. He now sits with the gods on the high mountain and enjoys a hundred virgins. He led the Turrek well, and he is deserving of all honor and praise. Join me in our final tribute to this great leader." He paused a moment before continuing. As he spoke the rest of the men joined in with him. "Hail Vargon, hail king of the Turrek, hail son of the gods, rest in peace with the immortals in the vast gardens of Virinias. We who remain salute you."

An acolyte passed the priest a torch, and he jammed it into the pyre. The other captains followed suit on all sides. Tumak was the last to cast his torch on the now blazing bier. He turned to Allana.

"It is traditional for the king's wife to die with her husband by throwing herself on the pyre."

"You have to be joking. I will not sacrifice myself for that pig. You'll have to kill me first."

"That will be done unless you accept the alternative." Tumak smiled as he fixed Allan in a sinister gaze.

"I know. I must agree to marry the next king of the Turrek. Do you think you will be the next king?"

"I know I will. No man here will dare challenge me for that title, and the only way to gain it is by combat to the death between claimants. What is your decision?" Tumak drew his sword and positioned the point at Allana's throat.

"What choice do I have? It's death or you, and as distasteful as it is, I choose you."

Tumak sheathed his sword to a great cheer from the other captains and raised Allana's hand in his.

"Hear me, men of the Turrek! I claim the title of King, and by that title the hand of the Lady Allana. Let any who dispute me step forward now."

The blazing pyre now filled the courtyard with light, and the heat was barely tolerable even at the ten-meter distance between the crowd and the flames. The captains muttered among themselves but diverted their eyes from Tumak's scan of their faces. Allana was beginning to think Tumak was correct about them when one warrior stepped forward. It was her bodyguard, Dallak.

"I challenge you, Tumak. I challenge you for the throne and the lady."

Allana thought she saw Tumak's smile fade a bit at this challenge, but he quickly resumed his arrogant manor.

"The challenge is accepted. We will settle the matter in ten days as the law requires. Now we must tend to our wounded and mourn our dead. Until then the Lady Allana will be confined to her apartments and see no man of the Turrek. What say you, priest?"

The skull priest stepped back into the firelight. "It shall be as our laws demand. Prepare yourselves. Ten days from now the gods will decide."

The crowd dispersed, and Vargon was left to burn into his spirit self and join the gods.

The next morning, Allana was surprised to see Barinosh enter her apartments.

"Barinosh! It's good to see you. I didn't think they'd let you in."

"They counseled on the matter and decided I was too old to do any damage to your virtue. I've come to tell you that the King of Tulla is dead by his own hand, and the Queen is a prisoner of the rebels. Oliga will be crowned king next week."

"Have you heard anything about his promise of Gorgos to Vargon?"

"Nothing, Lady. I've asked Count Charlan to press your claim as Vargon's heir and a legitimate claimant to the old throne of Gorgos, but he needs to tread softly until his position is sure. His forces took no part in the rebellion on either side, and he's not sure of Oliga's favor yet."

"I pray he will act quickly. I was forced to agree to marry the next king of the Turrek, and that matter will be decided nine days from today. I fear Tumak may be my next husband unless I can escape from here and be sure of Oliga's protection on Gorgos."

"I fear you will hear no good news before then, Lady, but perhaps I can find some way to get you away from the Turrek. Charlan is willing to aid you, but I know he has designs on you himself. He's heard stories from spies and travelers about your beauty. You may leave one bad situation for another. Charlan has a wife, and she would not tolerate a rival."

"Do what you can. How is the pearl business going?"

"It goes very well. Between that and the payments from the House of Orgama, you are becoming a wealthy lady again."

"The Turrek still have all of the treasure I left Zargaia with, but I doubt I'll be able to take any of that out with me, even if I should be able to escape."

"There's no way we could get you out of this fortress. If you could manage to let them allow you to ride outside the walls, we might be able to set an ambush and get you back to Othis before the Turrek could catch up with us."

"That's impossible until after the succession ceremony, whatever that entails. I assume it's some bloody battle to the death with very intimate weapons. That seems to be the way these barbarians do things."

They were interrupted by one of the guards. "Your time is up, old man."

"I must leave now, but I will return in nine days with a plan to free you, one way or another. I go now to the House of Orgama to collect your payment, but I will come again after I see Charlan. Farewell, Lady." He bent and kissed her hand.

"Farewell, Barinosh. I hope your next visit brings good news."

Chapter 9

As war raged in Tulla, Javik and his band camped outside the walls of Ullum, capital of Zargaia. Javik was impressed with the city. He stared at the walls for a long time before Sigurd nudged him.

"It's only a big city, Javik. Don't act like the country boy you are."

"Can you imagine trying to storm those walls? I'd be dizzy before I got half way up," Javik said.

Sigurd lifted Javik's jaw back to its normal position. "You don't storm walls like that. You either starve the place into submission or knock the walls down. Weren't you listening in any of Bandor's classes?"

"Yes, yes, but I never imagined walls like these. King Kullan must be a very wealthy king."

Margan joined Sigurd and Javik and offered his more extensive knowledge of Zargaian history. "Kullan? He didn't build these walls, his grandfather finished them, and they were begun several generations before that."

"Still, there's nothing like this in Berglaundia," Javik said.

"We don't need walls. The mountains are our walls," Bogard added.

"Come, Javik. We'll go to the House of Orgama to ask about Allana." Margan tugged on Javik's arm to draw him away from the splendid sight of the city walls.

"Oh, yes. I'm coming." Javik fell in behind Margan and Bogard as Sigurd stifled a laugh.

If Javik was in awe of the walls, the House of Orgama floored him. He almost stumbled into the fish pool at the entrance because his eyes were fixed upon the waving draperies and the marble statues of naked women. Varuda welcomed Margan.

"Margan, it's good to see you again. We've missed your songs." She embraced the minstrel and turned to Javik.

"Have you brought us customers?" she asked.

"No, Varuda, this is Javik." Margan stood back and snapped his fingers to break Javik's trance. "Javik, Javik, this is Varuda."

Javik had not seen a woman so beautiful since Allana. At least her figure was as lovely. He could tell nothing of her face as it was hidden by a mask painted a pale white with ruby lips and pink spots for cheeks. Her skin was fair but darker than Allana's, and her hair was a riot of red curls. Eyes like fine emeralds shone from the openings in her mask. A filmy, light green gown barely hid her ample assets, and her jewelry was richly loaded with precious stones. Was this what Allana looked like now? He could only hope.

"So this is Javik. Allana said you were a country boy, but she gave me the impression you were not so easily awed by women. She certainly didn't lie about your looks." Varuda moved close to Javik and felt his muscular arms. "Yes, she didn't exaggerate a bit about that."

"I, I , I'm pleased to meet you, Varuda," was all Javik could muster.

"We've come to find news of Allana," Margan broke in to save Javik from being raped by Varuda.

"Ah, Margan. Must you spoil this moment with business? I really want to know Javik better."

"What would Allana say about that?" Margan cautioned.

"We could have a few secrets between us, couldn't we Javik?"

Javik could feel the perspiration beading on his chest as Varuda brushed her breasts against his arm.

"I'm sorry, Varuda. I'd love to know you better, but Allana is my quest now. I must pry her away from this bandit king."

"Javik, you don't know what you're saying," Varuda said. "The Turrek are barbarians. They'll cut you up just to hear you scream."

"I don't care. I'll challenge this Vargon for Allana."

"I've seen Vargon, Javik. As tall and muscular as you are, you're no match for him," Varuda offered.

"Then I'll die trying. I've not come this far to be turned away now for fear of some bandit."

Javik started to leave, but Varuda stopped him.

"Wait, Javik. A friend of Allana's, a man named Barinosh, comes here once each month to collect my payment for this house. I know he sees Allana from time to time. He's due here tomorrow. Why don't you wait to speak to him before you attempt anything rash?"

Javik thought for a moment. What Varuda said made sense.

"Very well, we're camped outside the south wall. Send word to me when this Barinosh arrives, and I will come to him here. Come, Margan, we must let the others know of my plans."

Margan hesitated. "Javik, I will stay here for a while, if you don't mind. The ladies love my music, and I wouldn't want to disappoint them." He gave his friend a sly wink.

"Fine, you can stay as long as you like, but I'll be going back." Javik turned to leave. "Are you coming Bogard?"

"I think I'll stick around for while myself, if you don't mind," he said.

"Javik, are you sure you won't stay a while also?" Varuda cooed.

"You're a fine woman, Varuda, but I must say no. Remember, send me word when Barinosh arrives." Javik left the House of Orgama and returned to the camp.

* * * * *

"What did you find out?" Berda said as he rushed to greet his old friend.

"I'll tell everyone at once. Gather our group together, Berda."

Berda thought for a moment. "Let's see, Sigurd is not here. He decided to go into the city to see the sights. He said he'd be back by morning. Mikka went to see the blacksmith about two of our horses, but he should be back by supper. Karl and Noka heard there was a library in the city, and they've gone to see what scrolls are there. They said they might not be back for supper. The servants are here, but they really want to go into the market to buy fresh supplies. I told them to wait for your orders. Sigurd's men are complaining that they can't go into town, and they want you to overrule Sigurd."

Javik heaved a sigh and rolled his eyes skyward. Tao Shan trained him to be a leader, but he had no idea how difficult the job would be in real life.

"Very well, then I'll tell everyone at breakfast tomorrow before they can vanish again. Right now I need some qush."

* * * * *

The next morning, Javik explained the situation to his band. Bogard was the first to speak.

"I've heard of the Magda bandits. Let's see there's you, me, Sigurd, your two friends, you say you have a strong warrior from your village, I have two archers and Sigurd has two warriors. The rest are slaves or servants." He counted up on his fingers. "That's ten able bodied men. I figure we're about ten-thousand men short if you plan to face them head-on."

"Surely, you count the three of us as the equal of any nine bandits," Sigurd said as his face broke into a broad smile.

"More than that," Javik said. "Our hand cannon double that number."

"I heard you had them," Bogard said. "Will you show me how they work?"

"As soon as I finish this breakfast," Javik said.

Chapter 10

Sigurd, Bogard and Margan accompanied Javik as Varuda's messenger guided them to the House of Orgama. She led them to the lavish gardens of the bawdy house where Varuda and Barinosh greeted them.

Javik was surprised by Barinosh's age. He had expected a much younger man, and the vitality of this obviously ancient mariner belied his white hair and beard. Even the firmness of his handshake was astonishing, but it matched the sparkle in his soft, brown eyes.

"I am so pleased to meet you, Javik," the old man said. "My Queen has told me much about you."

"How is Allana?" Javik tried to restrain his excitement, but the thought of speaking to a man who had actually seen her was making his heart pound so loudly, he was afraid Barinosh could hear it clearly.

"She is well, but in a difficult situation. She must marry the king of the bandits."

"But, I thought she was married to him already," Javik seemed confused.

"Vargon was her husband, but he was killed in the recent war. Tumak now claims the throne of the Turrek, and he also claims Allana as his bride. It's all part of their peculiar laws. I don't understand it, but I promised my Lady I would find some way to rescue her if at all possible. The duel for the throne will take place in only six days, and I must return to Tulla as quickly as possible."

"Why Tulla?" Javik asked.

Varuda interrupted to explain. "Charlan seeks Allana's hand also. He is her only hope of rescue from the Turrek. He could send an army to storm the bandit fortress."

Margan broke in. "Not very likely, from what I've heard of that place. It would take a mighty army indeed to storm those walls."

"I fear that is our only hope," Barinosh said.

"Treachery may work where strength would fail," Javik said, remembering Grazhda's words. "We have a band of good warriors here with us, and a weapon the bandits have not seen before. If we could catch Allana outside the fortress with a small escort, we might be able to rescue her with our own resources. Would that be possible?"

Barinosh stroked his white beard for a moment before answering. "It might be possible. They keep her confined to her apartments now, but they may allow her to ride for exercise. The problem is, they would only allow her to ride north of the fortress, and the only way to that area is through the fortress itself."

Javik leaned closer to Barinosh and spoke softly. "I know a pass north of the fortress suitable to our purposes."

"What?" Barinosh almost shouted.

"Softly," Javik cautioned. "The news is not for unfriendly ears."

"How many are you?" Barinosh asked in a near whisper.

Javik counted up the warriors in his band. "There's ten of

us. How many Turrek are with you?"

I travel with two bodyguards. You'd have to deal with them before we could try anything," Barinosh said.

"That's an easy matter, and our hand cannon make us the equal of twice our number," Sigurd added.

"Count me as one of your warriors also," Barinosh said.

Sigurd laughed. "You'd better stay with the baggage, old man."

Barinosh bristled and reached for his sword. "Step outside, and you'll find I'm not too old to teach you a few tricks, young whelp."

Bogard stepped in. "I'm sure Sigurd was only thinking of your safety as a valuable servant to Allana. He was not insulting your prowess as a warrior, were you, Sigurd?"

Sigurd took the hint. "Certainly not, please accept my apology, Barinosh."

"Granted freely, but never doubt my ability in battle."

"Can you help us set up an ambush?" Javik asked Barinosh.

"I think I could. Take your group to the city of Othis in Tulla and wait for me there. I must return to Harrish with my Lady's funds then I will join you at Othis. We will make further plans there after I speak with Queen Allana again."

"How do we get to Othis?" Javik asked.

"The caravans leave here every day, and they always need escort troops. Offer your group's services to one of the caravan masters, he'll be glad for the extra men. I will take you to them before I leave."

"Won't you travel with us?" Margan asked.

"No, I move freely among the Turrek because they know I serve Queen Allana. I have no need to travel with a caravan."

"How long will it take to reach Othis?" Sigurd asked.

"The trip through the Turrek country is two days. I will meet you there in four days. I will, then, go to the bandit fortress to meet with Queen Allana and plan her escape. We will make our move as soon as my Lady is free to leave the fortress."

"Take us to the caravan masters, then," Javik said.

"If you don't mind, Javik, I think I'd like to stay here with Varuda a while," Sigurd said.

"And, I should stay and see he doesn't get into any trouble," Bogard added.

"And, I must serenade the ladies while they work," Margan strummed a chord on his lute.

Javik smiled at his friends. "Very well. Meet me back at our camp before supper. Come, Barinosh."

Javik and Barinosh left for the caravans while Varuda led the other men inside the House of Orgama.

* * * * *

The caravan section of the city was not a very pleasant place. The odor from the horse and mule corrals overpowered even the pungent smell of the fermented cabbage favored by the Dubbans, the dark foreigners who made up the caravans and drove them across the mountains of Magda into Tulla. Two inns served as quarters for the Dubbans and the men who rode with them. One was rough and served the drivers and escort troops, while the other was only a bit more refined and reserved for the caravan masters. Barinosh led Javik into the masters' inn.

The common room was dark and smelled of stale beer. All of the tables were taken up by Dubbans in their deep blue cloaks and black turbans. They were men of a land beyond the great sea who seemed to appear any place commerce needed their talents. Anyone dealing with them faced expert negotiators. Their customers were always fleeced, but they walked away from the deal believing they had cheated the Dubbans terribly.

Not even the protection of these fierce people was a guarantee of reaching Tulla safely. The Turrek only attacked them when they had superior numbers, but one in every five caravans suffered some degree of loss from the bandits.

Barinosh found the table he sought in a more brightly lit section of the great room. A large, dark man greeted him like an old friend.

"Ah, welcome, Barinosh. It's been a while since I've seen you. Sit down and have some wine."

"I will Jamuda, I want you to meet Javik, a friend of mine."

Javik extended his hand, but Jamuda ignored it and placed his hands together in front of his face while he bowed from the waist.

"The Dubban don't shake hands, Javik. This is their form of greeting." Barinosh bowed to Jamuda, and Javik followed suit.

"Sit down, sit down." Jamuda motioned two of his men away from the table and indicated the chairs to Javik and Barinosh. "This is a fine looking warrior you've brought me. What is his price?"

"Javik is the leader of a group of warriors wishing to travel to Tulla. He would offer you his services in return for traveling with your next caravan."

Javik had remained silent, but now he felt Barinosh was missing an opportunity. Jamuda seemed to be interested in him, and perhaps, it might be a way to make some money.

"Barinosh is very generous with our services, Jamuda. All of my warriors are battle-hardened veterans. Should you be attacked by the Turrek, we would make the difference between defeat and victory."

Javik felt a short kick from Barinosh under the table, but ignored it.

"Ah, but to which side would you swing the pendulum, young warrior? Toward defeat or victory?" Jamuda smiled and revealed a row of yellowish teeth that seemed to fit in well with his dark skin and black beard. His deep black eyes were absent of emotion, but Javik knew they masked a diabolical brain.

"We have a weapon I don't think any man here has ever seen, and I have a war dog of fierce aspect. We would work for your usual fee."

"My usual fee, as you put it, is one percent of the fee for the total caravan, provided we make it safely to Tulla, but that is for seasoned veterans of many trips across the mountains. For green youths like yourself, I only pay half that."

Javik had no idea what one half of one percent of the fee would amount to, but he was sure he and his men were worth as much as any man in Jamuda's employ. "If you had seen us in battle, you would gratefully pay twice your usual fee for our swords."

Jamuda smiled, and Javik felt a second sharp kick under the table from Barinosh.

"I've seen my men in battle against the Turrek. Who have you fought, young warrior?"

"The Wallans and the Sentii, most recently." Javik added the last part to give the impression these were but two of many previous opponents.

Jamuda rubbed his beard, and his look grew more serious. "I will make you an offer. Ride with my caravan for one half of one percent. If we are attacked by the Turrek, and you acquit yourselves well, I will pay you a full one percent."

Javik felt another kick, and he noticed Barinosh frowning.

"A handsome offer, Jamuda, but I will make you a counter offer." Javik was pleased he remembered Tao Shan's guidance on bargaining. Always praise an offer, but counter above your settling price. "We will travel with your caravan, and if you are attacked, we will drive off the Turrek by ourselves. If you have to come to our aid, we get nothing, but if we succeed, you pay two percent."

Javik now felt two kicks and noticed Barinosh beginning to sweat. Jamuda only smiled broadly.

"Javik, my friend, you are too hard on me, but since you are a friend of Barinosh, I will accept your offer, but only if you agree to one percent."

"Done," Javik almost shouted and reached a hand across the table to Jamuda.

"You forget the custom of my people, Javik. We do not touch hands as your people do. We seal our bargains with wine." Jamuda snapped his fingers, and one of his captains appeared at his side. "Bring the cup of agreement and two other men to witness our bargain," he commanded.

In a few moments the man reappeared with an ornate silver cup and two brawny Dubbans bearing heavy curved swords. The captain produced a white dove from under his cloak and held it over the cup as he slit its throat. The bird's blood flowed into the cup, and when it was drained, the captain threw the dead bird to a servant.

"I call on you men to witness the bargain between myself and my friend, Javik." Jamuda repeated the bargain, and the men nodded understanding. Jamuda lifted the cup and offered it to Javik. "Drink to seal our bargain, Javik."

Javik took the cup and sipped the still warm blood before passing the cup back to Jamuda. The Dubban drank the remainder of the blood and slammed the cup brim-down on the table to show it was empty. The Dubban warriors grunted their approval and left.

"We leave at dawn tomorrow, Javik. Be ready." Jamuda stood and bowed to Javik.

"We will be there." Javik and Barinosh bowed to Jamuda and left the inn.

Outside, Barinosh breathed a sigh of relief. "Javik, I thought you were in over your head, but you did well. You got nearly one half of what your services are worth."

Javik stopped and stared at the old man. "What do you mean? You offered our services for no fee at all."

"I know, if you hadn't butted in, Jamuda would have offered me two percent to start with. Once you opened your mouth, I had no choice but to remain silent. Still, you did better than I thought you would."

The next morning Barinosh left for Tulla alone while Javik and his friends joined Jamuda's caravan.

Javik had never seen so many animals in one place since his first war. A large field outside the walls of Ullum seemed to be alive with horses, mules, wagons and carts. In one corner, a herd of cattle milled around under the watchful eyes of mounted Zargaians. The cries of the animals mixed with the shouts of the men and the wail of babies in a symphony of chaos. The smells of the animal dung mixed with the smoke from the cooking fires and assaulted the nostrils of anyone unlucky enough to be downwind of the marshalling area. Even Mordah sneezed to rid his nose of the putrid scent. Jamuda stood on the steps of his house on wheels surveying the scene, and Javik made his way to that point.

"Good morning, Jamuda. We are here as we bargained."

"Good morning, Javik. This is Mohama, my troop commander; he will show you how to position your men. We will leave as soon as the sun is above the trees."

Mohama stepped forward and bowed to Javik who reciprocated as he learned to do the day before.

"How many are you?" Mohama asked.

"We are ten warriors, all experienced," Javik answered.

"And your monster?" Mohama pointed to Mordah.

"He has more experience than all of us. In a fight, he'd be worth two men."

"We may test his skills on this trip. He will come in handy when we camp. Bring your men to me at that wagon in a few moments. I will assign their positions in the caravan. Each of your men will be partnered with one of mine since this is their first trip. The Turrek are very bold, but they are also very good at ambush. If they don't know what to look for or where to look, this could be their last trip."

"I'll bring them at once," Javik said as he saluted Mohama in the manner of his people.

Javik's group joined fifty Dubban troops in front of Jamuda's wagon. The escort commander stood on the steps of the rolling house in a shining breastplate with a curved Dubban blade at his side and a wicked looking dagger in his belt. Jamuda stood beside him to reinforce his authority. Mohama spoke.

"Assignments are as usual except that each squad will be augmented with two of these Berglauni warriors. Javik, here, will ride with me in the middle of the caravan. Squad leaders step to this side. Javik, assign your men as you wish. We leave when the sun clears the trees. Achma, you will ride point."

The Dubban captain bowed his acknowledgement.

Javik assigned his warriors to Mohama's squad leaders. Only Sigurd protested about being subservient to someone of lower rank, but Javik's frown was enough to quiet his arguments.

A bugle sounded just as the sun cleared the trees, and the caravan rose as one from the soft, cool earth of the field. Achma led the first section out, and the other groups moved off in line behind it. Mohama's men took up their positions on either side of the column as it snaked off into the distance. Javik joined Mohama next to Jamuda's wagon, and moved off at the midway point of the long line. He wondered if sixty men would be enough if they were attacked.

"Mohama, how large are the bandit groups that attack the caravans?" Javik asked.

"Usually only thirty or so, but sometimes as many as fifty."

Javik was taken aback by the answer. "That doesn't give us much of an edge spread out the way we are. Do you think you have enough men?"

Mohama laughed. "No, Javik, not if the bandits are determined to have the entire caravan. In that case they will bring three hundred men, and we'll have no choice but to flee. They usually know what they want and where their target is in the caravan. They have spies everywhere. We try to keep them from taking anything, but many times we must sacrifice a part of the caravan to save the rest."

"Why don't you just bring more men?"

"Men cost money. The more men, the lower each man's share. We've learned how to survive with a minimum number of troops. Your men are extra protection this time. Perhaps the bandits will not attack when they see our increased strength."

Javik rode on in silence for a while contemplating what he would do in the event of an attack. Tao Shan always stressed that planning was the best way to avoid failure.

"When do the bandits usually attack?"

"You never know, but usually late in the day when the caravan has spread out and the animals are tired. They only attack that part of the train they're interested in. We're spread out all along the caravan line, and it takes us a while to react in force. Sometimes, their initial attack is a feint, and when we react to that, they strike at another place in the line. You see how the line is spread out already."

Javik looked back. He could barely see the last unit, and the front of the caravan was already out of sight. "How can you hope to defend this line with only sixty men?" he asked.

"As I told you, we can't. We react to the bandit's strike as best we can, but sometimes, they take what they want and vanish before we can engage them."

"Then what good are we?"

"We keep the Turrek from looting the entire caravan and from attacking at night while we camp. When the caravan is drawn up for the night, we have plenty of men to protect it."

"You must know what you're doing, but it seems like foolishness to me. I'd have twice this many men, at least."

"Jamuda spoke of a new weapon you Berglauni possess. Is that it in the case tied to your saddle?" Mohama indicated the leather case for Javik's hand cannon.

"Yes, it's a hand cannon. If the bandits strike, they'll have a nasty surprise coming."

"May I see it?"

Javik pulled the hand cannon from its case and handed it to Mohama.

"This looks formidable enough as a club. Does it do anything else?"

"It fires balls from this end." Javik indicated the barrel.

"Hmph!" Mohama hefted the weapon and looked into the barrel. "I suppose you know what you're doing, but I'll take a good strong bow any day." He patted the quiver and bow attached to the left side of his saddle.

The day passed without an attack, and camp that night was routine. Half the men stood watch on an early schedule and the remainder took a late shift. The caravan was on the move again at dawn. They had not gone far when a rider approached Mohama.

"Sir, the bandits are waiting in ambush at the next pass. I can't tell how many, but I could see only a dozen, or so. What are your orders?"

"I think they're after our shipment of carpets. Put the defense wagons with the carpet wagon. Second squad in the front wagon, and third squad in the rear one. They'll let the carpet wagon through before they block the pass. Perhaps the second defense wagon can make it also. Alert the first squad to watch for another attack. If none comes, they can come back to help defend the carpet wagon."

Javik interrupted. "What are the defense wagons?"

"They're wagons that look like regular cargo wagons, but the sides drop down. Archers inside can fire volleys at the attackers."

"Two of my men also have hand cannons. Put us in the front wagon along with whatever archers will also fit. I think we can guarantee a warm reception for the Turrek."

"Very well, gather your men. Abbah, here, will show you the wagon."

The wagons were loaded with defenders and positioned on either end of the wagon Mohama suspected of being the Turrek's target. Inside the front wagon, Javik, Sigurd and Noka loaded their hand cannons with four small balls in each gun and lit their matches. The four archers in the wagon with them watched in amused silence as they positioned their quivers for easy access. It was not long before the shouts of the bandits could be heard as they hurled stones down blocking the pass. Mohama had guessed correctly, the bandits charged toward the carpet wagon. Fortunately, the second defense wagon managed to also clear the pass before it closed.

One of the archers dropped the side of Javik's wagon, and the Berglauni warriors raised their weapons.

"Sigurd, take the right. Noka, take the middle. I'll take the left. Fire!"

The roar of the hand cannons was amplified by the confined space of the wagon, and Javik's ears were ringing as the smoke cleared. Six bandits lay dead before the carpet wagon, and two more swayed in their saddles. The archers took over pouring murderous fire upon the bandits while Javik and his friends reloaded. The next volley from the hand cannon sent the

Turrek into panicked flight. The archers in Javik's wagon stood open mouthed, gaping at the fearsome, death dealing tubes. Each one wanted to inspect them, and they murmured among themselves until the pass was cleared behind them. They didn't even bother to loot the dead, but Sigurd and Noka took care of that chore bringing what booty they could find to Javik.

"We'll place all booty in the defense wagon. Jamuda will tell us how he wants to divide it at the end of the trail," Javik said.

At that moment, Jamuda rode up on a well-lathered horse.

"I heard thunder. What happened?" Jamuda said.

One of the archers ran to him and jabbered something in Dubban while pointing to Javik, Sigurd and Berda.

"Show me this weapon which has made cowards of my best men," Jamuda commanded as he dismounted.

Javik walked to Jamuda and handed him the weapon. Jamuda was surprised by its weight and almost dropped it. He touched the barrel and drew back his hand quickly.

"It's hot! Did you shoot fire at them?"

"No, only balls of lead, like this." Javik took several balls from his pouch and held them out for Jamuda's examination.

"Show me," Jamuda commanded.

Javik loaded his gun and had one of the archers prop up a dead bandit against a tree. He stepped back several paces and fired nearly blowing the head off the cadaver.

"By all the gods, what a marvelous weapon. Do all the Berglauni have these?"

"No, only we three, and a few others, but I suspect the blacksmith who built these is swamped with orders for more."

"How much do they cost, and where can I find this blacksmith?" Jamuda asked.

"The cost is probably well over a hundred gold crowns by now, and the smith lives at the fortress in the low pass on the other side of Berglaundia. The weapon does you no good without the knowledge of how to make the powder it uses, and only we three possess that."

"You must let me set you up in business to make the weapons and the powder. I will finance the whole enterprise and share the profits equally with the three of you."

Javik remembered his bargaining session with Jamuda before they began traveling and declined the offer. "No, Jamuda. We are on a mission to find someone, and we may not stop to make money now. Once our quest is completed, I may take you up on your offer."

"Please, Javik. Don't let anyone else in on this until you speak with me," Jamuda pleaded.

Javik felt the Dubban was completely in his power. He seemed to be honest in his pleading, and Javik decided he would give the man a chance when the proper time came.

"Jamuda, I will give you the first opportunity to bid on whatever business I begin."

Mohama rode up and stared at the dead Turrek bandits. "What killed these men? There are no arrows in them."

Jamuda spoke up as he raised Javik's hand cannon to the rider. "These weapons of fire and thunder. Didn't you hear them?"

"I heard a loud noise, but we had to clear the pass before I could investigate. I guess it's all you said it was, Javik." Mohama passed the hand cannon back to Javik and turned to Jamuda. "The pass is clear now. We can go on."

"I suppose we'd better move on before those Turrek return

with reinforcements," Jamuda said. "Give the order."

There were no more attacks, and the caravan arrived at the Tullan fortress guarding the border just before noon. Jamuda paid Javik and his men one and one half percent, much to Javik's surprise.

"You are too generous," Javik said. "Our agreement was only for one percent."

Jamuda laughed heartily and slapped Javik on the back. "You are very young, Javik. If you'd have let Barinosh bargain for you, you'd be paid two percent for such a performance as you rendered against the Turrek. Farewell, young warrior. May the Barakha be with you."

Javik bid Jamuda farewell, and his group took the road to Othis.

Chapter 11

The Turrek assembled in the great hall to witness the duel for the throne. Allana was escorted in by four guards and seated on a divan next to the vacant throne. Neither Dallak nor Tumak were to be seen. The crowd fell silent as a gong sounded and the skull priest strode to the center of the floor.

"Who claims the throne of the Turrek and the Lady Allana?" the priest intoned.

Tumak entered from Allana's left. He was completely naked and carried no weapons at all. "I, Tumak, claim the throne."

Dallak entered from her right. He was also naked and unarmed. "I, Dallak, say that Tumak's claim is false, and I am the rightful king."

"The claimants will advance," the priest chanted, and the two men marched to face each other. Two acolytes appeared and handed vicious looking daggers to each man.

"By the ancient laws of the Turrek, Tumak and Dallak will do battle with the sacred knives, and the gods will decide which will be king. There is no quarter to be asked or given here. Only the death of one of you will satisfy the gods. Do you both understand?" He turned to Tumak.

"I do," Tumak almost shouted.

The priest turned to Dallak. "I do," Dallak responded even

louder.

"Then move to your positions. On my signal you may begin the combat. May the gods have mercy on both of you." The priest backed away from the combatants and shouted, "Begin!"

The two men circled each other warily. The crowd was deadly silent.

Dallak lunged first. He was quick as a cat, but Tumak sidestepped him easily and slashed downward barely missing the bodyguard's back. Dallak recovered and began circling in the other direction.

Tumak's face now held a look of supreme confidence. He smiled, and his eyes were like daggers themselves. Allana could feel the intensity of Tumak's concentration. She looked at Dallak and saw a hint of fear in his eyes.

Tumak lunged, and Dallak moved to block the knife arm, but Tumak quickly circled his blade around the heavy forearm and upward past Dallak's chest leaving a scarlet line across the bare skin. Dallak winced, but resumed circling.

"First blood is enough for me, Dallak. Give up now, and I'll let you stay with me," Tumak said.

"This is to the death, as our laws demand," Dallak answered.

"Then your blood is not on my hands," Tumak said as he lunged again. Dallak caught his hand at the wrist and drove his own dagger toward the captain's stomach, but Tumak countered by gripping Dallak's dagger arm. Allana noticed a small drip of blood from Tumak's arm where Dallak's knife must have grazed it during the parry. The two men struggled against each other for a few seconds before Dallak whipped a leg behind Tumak's knees and sent them both sprawling on the floor with Dallak on top.

Neither man seemed to be able to gain any advantage as they struggled. Dallak's position allowed him to use his weight to keep Tumak's dagger hand pinned to the stone floor, but his attempt to position his own dagger for a strike was thwarted by Tumak's strength. Dallak could only manage to move his dagger to a position over Tumak's chest. The bandit captain stiffened his arm into a solid beam supporting his attacker's dagger arm and the weight of his upper body. Allana knew if this situation went on much longer Tumak's strength would begin to fade, and Dallak's dagger would descend to its intended target. Tumak knew this too, and waited for the inevitable last thrust from Dallak. He would attempt to drive his dagger home with a sudden surge of energy, hoping to surprise Tumak. When it came, Tumak was ready. He deflected the power of Dallak's thrust to his right, and the dagger crashed harmlessly against the floor.

The movement was enough to throw Dallak off balance, and Tumak used the bandit's momentum to roll him off toward his own dagger hand. As the big man fell, Tumak managed to turn his dagger upward to meet the bare back of his opponent. Dallak impaled himself.

The bandit's eyes opened wide, and a short gasp escaped his tightly closed lips. Tumak felt Dallak's grip relax on his dagger arm and released the now empty dagger hand of his rival. As swiftly as a cat, Tumak straddled the dying bandit and retrieved Dallak's dagger from the floor. Blood was beginning to flow from Dallak's mouth as Tumak raised the dagger and plunged it deeply into his challenger's chest. Again and again he struck at the limp form until the floor ran red. At last, his anger ebbed, and he slowly stood to acknowledge the cheers of the Turrek men. He held the bloody dagger over his head and turned around several times as the shouts of praise grew louder. He knelt next to Dallak's still body and cut off the dead man's penis. As the men roared their approval, he inserted the grizzly token in Dallak's mouth. Any virgins Dallak had earned by his valor would now be sorely disappointed. Tumak once more buried the dagger in Dallak's chest, and, leaving it there, he walked to Allana.

She recoiled from the blood-spattered figure before her, but he took her arm and led her to the center of the floor as servants were removing Dallak's body.

"I claim Allana as my wife now. Our wedding will be one week from today." The assembled bandit captains cheered even louder at this announcement as Tumak enfolded Allana in his bloodstained arms and kissed her.

* * * * *

The next morning Allana was glad to see Barinosh. The day of her wedding was fast approaching, and she was not thrilled about another gory ceremony requiring the sacrifice of a prisoner no matter what his crime.

"What news, Barinosh?" she asked as he knelt before her.

"Good news, my Queen." He looked to either side before kissing her hand. "Can we speak freely here?"

"Yes, these bandits don't have a high enough opinion of women to even spy on them."

"Javik is coming, Lady." The broad smile on his face told Allana the old man was well aware of her feelings for the young warrior. She relaxed as if a great load had just been taken from her shoulders.

"Where did you see him?"

"He was in Ullum at the House of Orgama."

Allana bristled a bit at this news. "As a customer?"

"No, Lady. The minstrel guided him there looking for you. Varuda told him about you and the Turreks. She bid him speak to me before he made any move to find you. He has several men with him, and I saw at once a chance for your escape."

"Oh, if there were only some way to be with him again, Barinosh. Have you thought of a plan?"

"I have, Lady. Will they allow you to ride outside the fortress?"

"I fear not, but I will plead with Tumak for the privilege. I may be able to get him to agree, but I'm sure he will insist on a heavy escort force. He is not as enthralled with me as Vargon was, but I think he is pliable. What would you do if I'm allowed outside?"

"Javik and his men could ambush your escort. If they manage to kill all of them, Tumak will have no news of the escape until time for your return. If we are lucky, we will be over the mountains and in Tulla by the time Tumak realizes you're gone."

"Over the mountains? How is that possible?" Allana asked.

"Javik said he knows of a pass suitable for men on horseback leading to the land north of the fortress. All he needs to know is the path you will take."

"If Tumak allows me to ride, I will take the trail closest to the Eastern Mountains," Allana said.

"That area is mostly forest. There should be several places suitable for an ambush. According to Javik's map, the pass is 10 kilometers from the fortress. Will he let you ride that far?"

Barinosh asked.

"I don't know, but that's only an hour or so out and the same back. He has to allow that much. Your plan also depends upon the number of men Tumak sends as my escort, but I doubt he would send more than four or five. First, I must see if I can get him to agree to my ride. I dine with him tonight. Come back tomorrow, and we will talk more."

* * * * *

Tumak seemed to be in an excellent mood that night. The dinner was very much to his liking, and he was definitely in the mood for Allana. Over dessert, she broached the sensitive subject of her riding.

"Tumak, I'm tired of being cooped up in these caves all day. Couldn't I ride outside the fortress for a while each day? You could provide an escort to see that I'm not molested."

"I'm not stupid, Allana. I know you'd make a break for freedom at the first opportunity."

"How could I escape you if I only ride north of the fortress? Besides, how am I to gain Gorgos without you?"

"Oliga played us false. He let Nonia bleed us as we bled her. He has no need to keep any promises to us in our weakened state. Forget about Gorgos."

"Gorgos is my homeland, Tumak. Vargon promised me I would rule as Queen."

"Vargon is dead, and his promises died with him." Tumak pulled Allana close to him and bent to kiss her. She pushed him away.

"I should have thrown myself on Vargons funeral pyre. He might keep his promises in the underworld better than his successor keeps them here." She stood up and moved to the window. A fresh summer breeze blew the curtains into gentle waves while they also lifted her raven hair off her shoulders. She turned to let the declining sun show the silhouette of her body through her filmy gown.

Tumak felt his heart pound at the sight of the woman he'd lusted for since he first laid eyes on her. She'd not allowed him to have her since Vargon's death, but tonight he would remedy that situation.   He moved to her and enfolded her in an embrace.

"If it will please you, I'll ask Oliga to keep his promise, but only if you love me tonight."

"No Tumak," Allana said as she pushed him away. "You don't trust me. How can I make love to a man who won't even allow me the privilege of riding in my own land? I'm to be your bride in only three days, you can wait until after the ceremony."

"I can't wait, Allana. My soul burns for you every minute of the day. I can't stand the agony of seeing you and not having you." He pulled her to him again, and again, she pushed him away.

"If you take me now you take a statue. I will not respond to being raped. You are strong enough to compel me, but is that what you want?"

Tumak pushed her away roughly. "Witch, I should have thrown you on Vargon's pyre."

The pair stood in silence for a long moment as Tumak stared out the window at the gathering darkness. He turned back to Allana with a look of resignation.

"Very well, you may ride, but with an escort of my choosing, and only for the span of two hand-widths of sun travel."

"And you will plead my cause with Oliga?"

Tumak frowned more deeply and turned away from Allana. "Yes, I'll ask Oliga for Gorgos."

Allana rushed to embrace the bandit king. "Oh, Tumak, you are truly a husband to be proud of." It took all of her resolve to utter the words in a convincing tone.

Tumak lifted her chin and kissed her gently before leading her to the bed.

* * * * *

After breakfast Allana entered the stables to find four of Tumak's best men waiting for her. Allana rode for the prescribed two hand widths and returned to the fortress to advise Barinosh of the route she'd follow. He left immediately to inform Javik.

Allana repeated her riding routine the next day, but Javik didn't come. There was only one day left before the wedding, and she prayed he would come before that day dawned. She doubted Tumak would consent to her riding on her wedding day.

The day before the wedding dawned dark and gray. As Allana approached the stables, a light mist began to fall. The men of the escort were waiting dismounted inside the stable building. One of them bowed to her as she entered.

"Lady, will you ride in such weather?" He indicated the sky with a sweep of his arm.

"I have my cloak. We will not stay out long. Are Turrek warriors afraid of a little rain?"

The men grumbled, but they mounted their horses as a groom helped Allana into her saddle. They rode off into the forest with Allana praying Javik would strike today. She didn't have long to wait.

106 M. L. Hollinger

A sound like three claps of thunder startled the horses as the two riders in front of her fell to the ground. Behind her, one of the escorts turned and began to gallop off toward the fortress while the other drew his sword and moved toward Allana. A brawny warrior she recognized from Javik's village rode to intercept the swordsman while a blur of gray fur sped off toward the fleeing rider. The clash of swords lasted only a moment before the Berglauni warrior dispatched the bandit bent on defending Allana. A scream from back on the trail sent another rider off to settle that matter. She was almost sure it was Javik, but in the swirl of the action she couldn't be sure. Soon, all was quiet again, and the first warrior dismounted to clean his sword on the bandit's cloak before relieving him of his purse and weapons. Two more warriors appeared out of the trees and began to pillage the other bodies as Barinosh rode up to her.

"We must fly, Lady. The sound of the guns will bring curious bandits from the fortress," Barinosh said.

"Where is Javik?" Allana pleaded.

"He is here," Javik said as he rode up behind her carrying the last bandit's goods. A huge, gray dog loped by his horse's side.

Allana dismounted and ran toward Javik as he left his horse and dropped his booty. They embraced in silence for a long moment before Sigurd broke the mood.

"Javik, you can kiss her later. We must be away from here."

"First we must kill the horses," Javik said. "They will return riderless and give warning of our attack. I took care of the one back down the path."

"Can't we just take them with us?" Noka asked.

"No, they'll hold us up, and if one bolts off we don't have time to round it up." Javik drew his sword and plunged it into the closest horse as Mikka did the same to another. Bogard killed the third horse.

Javik helped Allana mount and looked up at her. "I'm sorry we don't have more time for a proper greeting, but I will make it up to you at Othis."

Allana looked down at Javik with moist eyes that seemed to glow in the gray drizzle. "Until Othis, Javik."

The group was soon off down the trail toward the pass at a full gallop.

* * * * *

One of Tumak's captains burst into the bandit council meeting and knelt before his king. He had a sour look, and Tumak knew the news was not good.

"Sir, Lady Allana is gone, and her escort has been murdered."

"What? How can that be?"

"I don't know who helped her. There were tracks from six other horses nearby and seven horses proceeded to the North. I've sent twenty of our best men after them."

"Someone told the witch about the high pass. That pass is rough going. They can't have gone far. Bring them to me alive if you can, but I want the Lady Allana alive at all costs. If you need more men, take them."

"One thing, Sir. Two of the men with your lady were killed in a peculiar fashion."

"What do you mean?"

"There were no sword or arrow wounds only several small holes in each one. We found these in the holes." The captain laid six lead balls on the table in front of Tumak.

"What are these? Are they from a sling?"

"No sling could drive them so deeply into a man's chest. It must be some kind of magic."

"Nonsense! It's only some new weapon we haven't seen before. Tell your men to be careful approaching whoever rides with her. They may be more dangerous than normal. Go, and send me word as soon as possible."

The captain saluted and left the room. Tumak broke up the meeting and went to his rooms to think.

* * * * *

"We'll rest the horses for a while. Dismount and walk," Javik called.

Allana dismounted and moved to Javik's side. She noticed him limping.

"Javik, you're hurt," she said.

"It's nothing. That last bandit was a better swordsman than I estimated. He got in a good hit on that leg before I could kill him."

"You're bleeding," Allana said. She turned to Barinosh, "We have to stop for a while. Javik's hurt."

The old man moved to Allana's side and noticed Javik's leg.

"We must stop to see how badly you're hurt, Javik. Come, sit over here." Barinosh led Javik to a fallen tree and sat him down.

Allana moved toward Javik, but Mordah barred her path growling low from deep inside his chest.

"Javik, call off your monster," Allana said. "He's so huge, you can ride him if your horse fails you."

Javik called Mordah to his side and sat him down. "He's

safe now. He just had to get to know you as my friend."

Allana approached cautiously. She drew a small dagger from her belt and used it to slit Javik's bloody pants leg, revealing a wicked cut just beginning to clot over.

"This must be cleaned and dressed, Javik, or I fear an evil spirit will enter it."

"We don't have time for that, Allana. The bandits will be after us by now, and we're no match for more than a few of them. Our only hope is to reach Tulla and the safety of Othis. I can ride, and I can walk for a little while."

"He's right, Lady," Barinosh added. "You know better than anyone what fate awaits us at the hands of the Turreks. We must go on."

"This will only take a moment, and it may mean the difference between saving his leg and losing it. Find me some dark green moss from a rotting log and give me your canteen."

Barinosh knew it was useless to argue with Allana once her mind was made up. He went to do her bidding as Noka, Sigurd and Bogard came up to see what was wrong.

"That will make a magnificent scar," Sigurd said with an air of envy in his voice.

"Sigurd, you always were an ass," Allana snapped at the young warrior as she washed Javik's wound.

"Well, it's true. I don't think it's as serious as you make it out to be," Sigurd snorted.

"It does need attention," Bogard said. "We'll go back along the trail a bit to look for any pursuers."

"A good plan, Bogard. Take Sigurd with you before Allana kills him with her tongue. He can fire a shot to warn us if you see anything," Javik said.

Bogard and Sigurd departed, and Barinosh returned with the moss. "Is this what you wanted, Lady?"

Allana inspected the moss and nodded her approval. "Good, now wash the dirt off the back of the moss and find me something to use for a bandage."

Barinosh used Javik's canteen to rinse the tree bark from the moss, but he could find no suitable material for bandages. He returned to Allana.

"Lady, we have nothing to use for a bandage."

"Never mind, I'll use this." Allana used her dagger to cut a swath of cloth from the hem of her dress. She bound the moss in place and helped Javik to his feet.

"How does that feel?" she asked him.

"Like someone put tree moss on my wound," Javik said.

"Javik, you haven't changed a bit. Now get on your horse."

"I can walk," he protested.

"No, you can't. Barinosh will lead your horse and his." She turned to Noka. "You, ride back down the path and bring the others."

Noka looked at Javik for confirmation, and he nodded approval, making sure Allana didn't see him do it.

"I guess I need to introduce you to my friends," Javik said as he mounted.

"That can wait until we're safe. We'll walk the horses to rest them," Allana said.

"The horses will need water soon," Allana said. "Is there any nearby?"

"Yes, Lady. We forded a river coming to rescue you. It's not far," Barinosh said.

The other members of the party rode up before Allana had

gone too far. Bogard dismounted and walked up to Javik.

"We saw no pursuit, Javik. They may not be aware your lady's missing yet."

"We'll walk until the horses are less winded. There's a stream ahead. We'll water them there. Sigurd!"

"Yes, Javik," Sigurd said as he replaced Mikka by Javik's side on the narrow trail.

"As soon as your horse is rested, ride back and serve as rear watch. We need to be ready if the bandits come after us."

Sigurd acknowledged the order and dropped back leaving only Allana by Javik's side.

"You're even more beautiful than the last time I saw you," Javik said.

Allana looked up at the boy who was now an experienced warrior. He was much the same, yet, his face held a more sober look, and his eyes seemed to be more cold, but only when he wasn't looking at her. As she caught his eyes with hers, she saw them soften into the same boyish innocence she'd fallen in love with when she first saw him in the green uniform of Tao Shan's house.

"And, you're a man now, Javik. I can see it in your face and in the way you give orders to these companions of yours. Who are they?"

"You know Bogard and Sigurd, of course. The red headed one is Noka. I shared a room with him at Tao Shan's house. You saw Mikka at our village, even if you haven't met him formally yet. They all wanted to help me find you. Margan is back at our camp along with some other men from my village and some warriors from Sigurd's village. We're camped outside the walls of Othis. Barinosh tells me you are a widow now."

"It's a long story, and I'll tell you all about it later. Tell me about your life since we were last together."

"I was crushed when you weren't there to greet me after the war with the Wallans. I pined for days until I realized it was no good mourning you. I finished my year with Tao Shan just as war broke out with Sentius. Our village was tasked to provide men for the fortress at the pass, and I spent the winter there. That's where we made the hand cannons." Javik showed her the weapon. He deliberately left out his marriage to Polla and their son.

"Is that what made the awful noise when you killed those bandits?"

"Yes, I'm afraid Noka missed the one behind you. He was afraid of hitting you. Mikka was ready to block him, though."

"And your demon dog felled the fourth?"

"His name is Mordah, and he's quite friendly once he knows you're not an enemy. You can probably pet him now."

Allana reached out toward the massive animal walking between her and Javik's horse. She was ready to pull back quickly, but Mordah allowed her to ruffle his fur a bit before shaking it back into place.

"He's so coarse. I expected him to be softer."

Javik laughed. "He's a war dog. He isn't supposed to be soft."

"Why didn't you come after me when you were finished with Tao Shan?"

"I was trapped into a marriage, and had no choice but to stay with my wife. She was pregnant with our child."

"You're married and have a child?"

"I was married. While I was away at the fortress, a plague

hit our village. My wife was a victim, but our son lives."

"I'm both sorry and glad, Javik. Sorry for the loss of your wife, but glad you are free to be with me now. Was the boy healthy?"

"He's a fine boy. I named him Garen."

"A peculiar name. I don't think I've ever heard it before. How did you come up with that name?"

"Grazhda, the old witch, told me to name him Garen. It has something to do with the royal line of Wallandia, I think. Anyway, Grazhda has helped me in many ways, and I felt it best to humor her."

"Did she speak to you about giving him to her?" Allana asked.

"Yes, she did. My mother said she also spoke to you about him."

Allana smiled and shook her head as if finally jogging her memory into place. "She said I must give up something I would feel no pain in getting and no pain in letting go. She was right. Polla suffered the pain of his birth, and since he's not my son, I feel no pain in releasing him."

"That pain is mine. I don't feel right about letting the witch have him for a year, but she doesn't seem to want him for anything but training in the art of magic."

Sigurd rode up to break the mood. "Javik, there is a party of twenty, or so, men coming up at top speed. We'd best start running again."

"The horses aren't fully rested, but we can't stand against that many unless we find a suitable ambush site. Into your saddle, Allana. We must ride hard."

Allana and Barinosh mounted, and the group took off at the

gallop once more. They splashed into the stream, and Javik called a halt. As the horses drank, Javik consulted Barinosh and Sigurd.

"The path gets narrower from here on. The party pursuing us must ride single file just as we do. I remember one area where we could set an ambush a bit farther on. We'll stop there and thin out their ranks a bit. Perhaps there's some way to block the path also.

"Yes, that's a good idea," Sigurd said. "I remember the spot you're speaking of. It's just past the summit of this pass. We might make them think twice about following us if we can cut a few of them down."

"A good idea. Lead the way," Javik called.

Javik liked this tactic. If they succeeded in blocking the path, it would give Javik's party time to rest and water the horses while they evened the odds a bit.

Javik knew he was feverish from his wound, but he also knew he must go on. The ambush spot quickly came into view, and Javik signaled a halt.

The left side of the trail was a sheer drop of several hundred meters, and the right side rose steeply to a small plateau. A path up to the plateau was hidden from anyone coming up from below.

Javik took Sigurd and Bogard up to look for suitable positions for archers or marksmen.

"This is good," Sigurd said. "I see five good positions. We will use the three hand cannon and two archers. That's you, me, Noka, Bogard and Barinosh."

"No, Barinosh must go on with Allana. He can take the rest of the party on to the foot of the path in Tulla and wait there.

We'll keep Mikka here. He's a good archer. Barinosh can leave our five horses farther down the trail.

The party descended to the pathway, and Javik gave his orders.

Allana moved to embrace Javik. "Javik, I'll stay with you. If you don't escape, I'd rather die with you than live without you, even as a Queen."

Javik held her tightly for a moment. "No, you must go on. This is a perfect ambush site. We'll be fine, and I'll join you in Tulla." He pushed her away and took his party to the top of the plateau. The climb was difficult for Javik, but he pressed on in spite of the pain. Once on the top, they took up positions allowing for concentrated fire at the trail. They lit their matches and waited.

It was not long before the sound of the horses on the rocky path alerted them to the bandit's approach. Javik licked his lips and swallowed the last water from his canteen just before the riders came into view. The shot was only about twenty meters. Javik rose and signaled for Sigurd and Noka to take the first three riders along with him, then instructed Mikka and Gogard to use their bows to make sure none of those bandits continued. Javik was banking on the shock of the hand cannons forcing a retreat allowing them time to reload.

As the first riders appeared around the bend in the trail, Javik gave the order to fire. Three of the riders dropped instantly and a fourth slumped in his saddle with an arrow point protruding from his back. They were not wearing armor, and Javik was glad of that.

The rest of the bandits stopped and turned back toward the safety of the bend in the path.   Javik gave the signal to reload.

Once more the bandits dared to show themselves, and once more two fell to the hand cannons before they retreated again. Javik knew there would not be a third charge. The bandits would try to outflank them by climbing the rocks to a position above them in order to use their own bows.

As Javik reloaded, Bogard moved to his side. "I believe they might be able to get above us, Javik. See that ridge up there?" He pointed to the spot. "From that point we're easy targets. We'll have to move out of here."

"I see what you mean, but it will take them some time to reach that spot by climbing. We'll keep one man here to turn them back if they try the path again. They won't risk coming around that bend single file, but they'll stick their noses out enough to test our vigilance." Javik turned to the other men. "We must leave this position. Who will stay behind to keep the path clear?"

Noka spoke. "There's no need for that. I think we could use our magic powder to move that boulder." He pointed to a rock perched precariously at the edge of the plateau.

'Yes, that would start an avalanche to block the path," Sigurd said.

"Sigurd, take Mikka and Bogard down and get the horses ready. I think Noka may have a good idea," Javik said.

Sigurd replied, "No, you and Mikka go to the horses. A cripple can't run fast enough once we set the powder off. I'll stay and guard the trail. Bogard can help Noka. Give Noka your powder horn."

Javik handed Noka the powder, and Mikka started to help Javik back down to the trail.

Javik shook off his hand. "I expect to see all of you back at the horses," he said.

"We'll be there. Just be ready to ride," Sigurd said.

Once more Mikka steadied Javik as they left the plateau.

Noka turned to Bogard. "Dig a hole at the base of that rock. We'll use what powder we have left in our flasks. I hope it will be enough."

"Take mine also. I've loaded my hand cannon for one last shot," Sigurd said as he handed his powder horn to Noka.

"We'll have none left to defend ourselves if they reach us before we can light the fuse," Noka protested.

"We still have Bogard's bow," Sigurd said. "Get busy digging."

Noka soon had a hole big enough for their powder. They emptied their flasks, and Noka produced some fuse.

"It's not much, we'll have to get away quickly," Noka said.

The report of Sigurd's hand cannon stopped conversation. "That's the end of my powder, but they won't risk another man until they reach their position above us. Light that fuse, and let's get going."

Sigurd and Bogard moved down the path toward the horses. They hadn't gone too far when Noka joined them.

The concussion wave from the explosion was mild, and Noka hoped it was enough. He turned back to look at the rock, and his heart sank to see it still in place. They pushed on, but the pursuit did not overtake them. The blast must have been enough to make them hold back.

They were only a few meters from the horses when a rumbling sound caused the men to pause and look back again. The sight of the boulder bounding down toward the pathway, dragging a river of rocks and debris with it was a welcome sight. Sigurd and Bogard cheered when they saw the result. The three men reached the horses, and mounted quickly.

"What's the hurry now," Javik said. "It'll take them the rest of the day to clear that mess."

The rest of the party laughed as they walked their horses at a leisurely pace toward the summit of the pass.

Chapter 12

Tumak listened to the report of Allana's escape in silence, but his hands gripped the arms of the ornate throne so tightly his knuckles were turning white. One vein in the side of his neck was pulsing visibly, and his eyes betrayed the bonfire of anger burning behind them.

"We were forced to give up pursuit when they called down the thunder god to block the mountain pass trail. Your lady is now inside the walls of Othis."

The kneeling captain licked his lips and began to sweat as the bandit chief rose from his throne and walked down the four steps toward him. He watched as the leather boots came to a stop beneath his nose, but he dared not take his eyes off the floor. He cringed as he heard a dagger being drawn from its sheath.

"I should slit your throat here and now, but I will need every man we have to attack Othis and retrieve my bride." Tumak kicked the captain backwards, and the bandit slithered away quickly.

Gurzak stepped forward from the group of men watching the scene with morbid curiosity. They had expected an execution, and most of them seemed to be disappointed.

"Tumak, we cannot attack Othis. Our forces are decimated from the war, and the men are weary of battle. She was

Vargon's whore, and you're well rid of her."

Tumak sheathed his dagger and rubbed his beard in thought. Allana was the most beautiful woman he had ever seen and well worth every man it would cost storming the walls of Othis, but he knew Gurzak was right. An attack on the city was foolishness, even with the Turrek at full strength.

"You're right, Gurzak. Leave her to the brothels of Tulla." Tumak spat on the floor to emphasize his disgust with the woman and strode off to his rooms to weep over her loss.

* * * * *

By the time the group reached the camp outside Othis, Javik was not doing well. Allana noticed he was becoming weaker as they approached the walled city. She rode next to him and placed a hand on his forehead.

"Javik, you're burning up with fever," she said.

"I'm not feeling very good. How far to the camp?"

Allana turned to Sigurd for the answer. She had no idea.

"Not far," Sigurd answered. "Just beyond the next bend in the road."

"Can you make it?" Allana asked.

"I think so. Stay close, Allana. Being with you again gives me strength."

Sigurd and Bogard carried an unconscious Javik into his tent with Allana and Barinosh close behind.

Allana removed the moss poultice and inspected the wound.

"It's beginning to fester, Barinosh. Are there any Argani in Othis?"

"Yes, I know one of the money handlers there."

"Go to him and ask about a healer. This wound will take more care than my knowledge encompasses. Ride quickly."

"I go my lady." Barinosh strode from the tent and rode toward the gates of Othis.

"Sigurd, have a servant bring me some hot water and salt. I must cleanse this wound."

Sigurd was not used to following a woman's orders, but Allana's commands seemed to have the authority of an experienced war leader about them. He left to see to the preparations.

Bogard knelt beside Javik's cot. "I didn't think his wound was that serious," he said.

"It must be closed soon or he will lose his leg. I've seen this kind of infection before, and it must be treated promptly. I fear our ride here may have delayed us too long. The Argani have great medical knowledge and ways of closing wounds besides the hot iron."

"I've never heard of the Argani. Tao Shan told us of many strange people, but I don't remember them," Bogard said.

"They come from a land far across the great sea, and they don't stray far from the coast. Many people consider them to be sorcerers because of their great knowledge and their ability to brew potions. They have been persecuted by some nations, and they seek out places where they can live in peace."

Margan entered the tent to check on Javik with Berda and Karl close behind him. "How is Javik? Sigurd said he was wounded."

"He has a sword cut on his leg. I've sent Barinosh into Othis to search for an Argani healer."

"A wise move. Let me look at it." Margan knelt next to Javik and inspected the wound.

"It is serious, but I don't think he'll lose the leg unless it becomes festered."

"That's what I fear." Allana put her hand on Javik's forehead. "Get me some cold water, Margan. I fear he's running a fever."

Margan and Karl left to do her bidding while Berda moved closer.

"That is a nasty wound, but it will make a magnificent scar," Berda said.

Allana bristled. "Sigurd said the same thing. All you men think about is your masculinity. Can't a man be a man without scars?"

Margan returned with a pail of water as Berda backed out of the tent to avoid another outburst from Allana.

Allana soaked a cloth in the cold water and draped it across Javik's forehead.

"It's good he's sleeping now," Margan said. "Sleep heals many wounds."

"It helps, but this wound needs more than sleep."

It seemed like hours before Barinosh returned accompanied by a short, thin, dark-complected man on a donkey. His black beard and peculiar hairstyle marked him as an Argani as much as the silk robe and odd fur hat. They dismounted in front of Javik's tent, and the Argani untied a large wooden box from the donkey's saddle. They entered the tent to find Allana still administering to Javik's fever.

"This is Avra. He claims to be a healer of great power, and I must believe him because it cost me ten gold crowns to get him here," Barinosh announced.

Allana rose, and Avra bowed before her.

"Lady, my powers as a healer are well known in Othis. You

may ask anyone," Avra said.

"You are welcome here, Avra. Please look at this man's wound," Allana said.

Avra bent over Javik's leg and probed around the wound with his fingers as he murmured to himself.

"Does he have any fever?" Arva asked.

"Yes, he is very hot," Allana answered.

"Good, good. His body is fighting back. Who used the tree moss on him?"

"I did," Allana answered again.

"You probably saved his leg." Avra stood up and addressed Allana. "I can close the wound and give you a potion to break his fever, but it will cost you another ten crowns."

Allana looked at Barinosh who exhaled angrily before producing another ten crowns from his purse and placing them in the Argani's hand.

The little man inspected the coins and deposited them inside his robe. The large box opened in sections very cleverly arranged to put everything in full view. An array of highly polished, steel tools of frightening aspect sat in the left sections. There were saws and large knives, curiously shaped tongs of several varieties. On the right side lay an assortment of bronze rods with oddly shaped ends. He rummaged through the center portion of the box to find a beaker and pestle and placed them on the small camp table beside the bed. From a row of jars on one side of the box's center, he selected a jar of brown nodules and poured a few into the beaker. He ground them into a powder and added enough water to make a paste. Constantly mumbling under his breath, he spread the paste on the wound.

"Now it must be closed," he announced.

"Shall I bring some coals for the cauterizing rods?" Barinosh asked.

The Argani looked at the old man in disgust. "You barbarians! This wound will close without such drastic measures."

Once more he dug into his chest and produced a needle and some thread-like material. He carefully threaded the needle and began to sew the leg muscle together.

"I've never seen anything like that," Barinosh gasped.

"Nor I," Allana said.

"It is a technique my people learned long ago. His body will absorb the thread I use here in a few weeks. By that time, the muscle will have started to heal itself."

"Then you will cauterize the skin over it?" Allana asked.

"No, Lady. I will use other thread for that." The Aganii finished with one thread and pulled another darker and coarser thread from his box. He sewed the skin together over the muscle making sure to apply more of the salve as he did so.

"There," Avra pronounced his satisfaction with the work. "In two weeks you may cut these stitches and pull them out, but make sure the skin has begun to heal nicely before you do. He must not stress that leg until it is fully healed. No riding and no combat. I assume he is a warrior, and those types love battle."

"I will see that he remains quiet," Allana said.

"And no women," Avra cautioned. "Making love is as much stress as combat."

Barinosh laughed at the Argani's admonishment, but Allana frowned at him, and he quickly resumed a stern manner.

"Show me how to remove your stitches," Allana said.

"It is a simple matter. Cut here and pull from here." Avra indicated the places to cut and pull. "Make sure you get all the thread. If any remains in the wound, send for me at once."

"I understand," Allana nodded.

Avra produced another jar of white powder and poured a large portion into a paper envelope. "Mix as much of this as will fit in the center of your palm in a mug of water and make him drink it at sunrise and sunset. His fever should be gone before the powder is gone. If not, send for me again."

"Should I bandage the wound?" Allana asked.

"It would be a good idea. This sort usually insists on being up and about as soon as they're conscious. Keep dirt out of the wound at all costs if you want to save his leg."

"I'll take good care of him. Thank you Avra," Allana said.

"My pay is my thanks, Lady. Good day." The Argani bowed then turned to repack his box. In a few moments he was riding his donkey back to Othis.

"I've never seen anything like that before," Sigurd said as he entered the tent and inspected Javik's wound.

"The Argani have strange ways," Barinosh said.

"Let's hope they are effective ways," Allana sighed. "Now, out, all of you. I will see to Javik."

The lamp in Javik's tent burned all night. Allana insisted on having food brought to her and would not allow a cot to be set up or a bedroll to be placed on the floor of the tent. She stayed awake nursing Javik until morning.

A low-lying mist covered the camp area as the sun rose above the nearby mountains. Allana dozed in spite of herself, and Javik's voice awakened her.

"I'm thirsty," he said.

Allana roused herself slowly and dipped a mug into the pail of water she had been using to cool his fever.

"How are you this morning?" she asked as she helped him rise to one elbow and held the mug to his lips.

"My leg aches, but I think my fever is down." Javik looked at his wounded leg to make sure it was still part of him.

Allana felt his forehead. "You still have some fever. You must drink this." She took the powder envelope and dumped some into her hand before adding it to the water. It fizzed and bubbled furiously for a few seconds then stopped.

"What is it?" he asked.

"Medicine to make you well. Drink." She held the mug to his lips once more, and Javik drank, but he quickly pulled back.

"Blah! That tastes terrible."

"Drink it anyway. It will cure your fever."

Javik downed the rest of the mug in one gulp and screwed up his face in reaction to the bitter taste.

"How much more of this must I drink?"

"Until the powder is gone." Allana held up the large envelope and saw Javik wince in reaction to its size.

"I have to get up. The bandits may already be in pursuit. We have to move on."

"You may get up, but you are not to ride or stress your leg. Look at it, and you'll see why."

Javik unwrapped the bandage, looked at his wound and gave a low whistle. "You've stitched me up like a tent."

"Not I, but an Argani from the city. He says it is his people's way."

"I can see why he doesn't want me to stress it. I could rip apart like an old apron. Has Sigurd been on the lookout for the

Turrek?"

"Karl checked before sunset last night, and he said no one was in sight. Noka was to check this morning, but I don't think he's left yet."

"Let me see if I can stand." Javik swung his legs off the cot and winced in pain as his feet hit the ground. "I'll need to lean on you to get up," he told Allana.

She moved to his side, and Javik used her for support as he stood up using only his right leg.

"I'll try some weight on it now," he announced as he gingerly shifted to an even stance. He gritted his teeth as the weight came down on the injured leg. "I can stand, but I doubt I can walk. I'll try, though."

Javik took two steps using Allana as a crutch and stopped. He was sweating by now and breathing heavily.

"It puts too much strain on the stitching. I'll need crutches." Javik hopped back to the cot and sat down.

"I'll have a servant make you some," Allana said. "Are you hungry?"

"I'm starving, but you look tired. Were you here all night?"

"Yes, I wanted to be sure your fever was under control." She placed a hand on his forehead.

Javik relished the cool touch and imagined them in an intimate embrace before Allana pulled her hand away. Javik grasped her wrist and placed her hand back where it had been.

"My fever will go quickly if you keep your hand there."

Allana wrenched her wrist from his grasp. "Nonsense! You still have some fever, but it's not as high. I'll see if anyone's cooking yet." She left the tent a bit too hastily, Javik thought.

The men checked every day for pursuit by the bandits, but

none came. Javik's fever subsided, and he was able to walk without the crutches after only a week, though Allana would not let him ride until the stitches were removed. By the end of the month, he was his old self again.

That night around the campfire, Allana brought up the subject closest to her heart.

"We must ride to Agam to see Oliga. He promised Vargon he would have Gorgos if he attacked the Queen, and I intend to hold him to his promise."

Sigurd spoke next. "From what I've heard in the city, Oliga is not one to remember promises to bandits. Even if he did promise Gorgos to Vargon, the bandit king is dead, and his heir is the new king, not his widow."

"Sigurd's words are wise, Lady," Barinosh said. "We must have a friend at Oliga's court to help plead our case. I think Charlan, Count of Ollon, would help us. He controls the sea trade, and he would like to have Gorgos in friendly hands. Particularly so if you resume the governance of the island and make it thrive again."

"Where is this Charlan?" Javik asked.

"His capitol city is Harrish, a seaport of Ollon. He owes allegiance to Oliga, but he is a powerful man in his own right. Oliga dare not anger him," Barinosh said.

"Then we are off to Harrish in the morning," Javik said.

"How far is this city?" Noka asked.

"Four day's journey from here," Barinosh responded.

"Javik, we will need supplies for this journey. How much money is left?"

Sigurd spoke. "Buy what you need, Noka. I have enough gold to pay for it."

"I will pay for the supplies," Allana said. She turned to Barinosh. "Are my accounts established in this country?"

"Aye, Lady. The Argani have you credited with 2,000 gold crowns."

"2,000 gold crowns!" Berda exclaimed. "That's a fortune."

"Only a fraction of my lady's holdings," Barinosh said. "When our pearl ship returns this summer, she should see a profit of twice that, if the market holds."

"Fortunately, I put my gold with the Argani. The Turrek do not understand paper, so Barinosh was able to take it out of their fortress with him. My jewelry is still in the bandit stronghold, and I fear it's part of Tumak's treasury now," Allana said. She looked off longingly toward the forest as if expecting the gems and gold to walk out at any moment.

"There's not much I can contribute to our cause," Javik said. "What little gold I have must last me the rest of my life, or at least until I can win more in battle."

"You have the secret of your hand cannon," Karl offered.

"I swore to Tao Shan never to reveal the secret of the powder," Javik replied.

"No need to do that," Berda said. "We could make the powder and sell it."

"And become tradesmen?" Sigurd snorted.

"The only secret is the proportions of the mix. Those of us who know the secret could make the initial mix then let servants package it and deliver the product. We could even employ people to sell the powder," Javik said.

"We'd still be tied to our factory like merchants," Sigurd insisted.

Noka broke in. "I wouldn't mind running the factory, and I

know the secret of the mix."

Javik looked at Sigurd and shrugged in resignation. "Why not?"

"It's settled," Sigurd said. "You will be our merchant. You were never that good with a sword anyway."

Noka bristled, but he kept his tongue knowing Sigurd's complete lack of tactfulness.

"That will be our contribution to the resurrection of Gorgos," Javik said to Allana. "It's settled then, we leave for Harrish in the morning."

Chapter 13

Harrish was no comparison to Agam. Its walls were half as high, but they hid the city completely except for an ornate palace rising high above the center of the city. The palace's golden domes reflected the setting sun into the traveler's faces forcing them to shade their eyes. The harbor stretched out just west of the city filled with boats of all sizes and descriptions. The men turned toward the city gate, but Allana spurred her horse on to the cliff overlooking an emerald green sea. Javik and Barinosh rode up beside her.

"Is that Gorgos, Barinosh?" Allana asked. Her eyes were fixed on a long, blue-gray shape rising from the ocean near the horizon.

"Yes, Lady. That is your home," Barinosh replied.

"I want to go to it. Will you get a boat and take me there?"

"I can, Lady, but it would be dark before we reached Gorgos, and the approach is dangerous at night. We should wait until morning."

Allana fidgeted in her saddle, and sighed in resignation. "You're right. We will go in the morning."

"What about Count Charlan?" Javik asked.

"He can wait. I must see where I came from and what it's like before I speak with him."

Javik turned to ride back to the others, but Allana called to him. "May we camp here tonight, Javik? I want to be as close to Gorgos as possible."

Javik smiled as he rode up beside her. "Yes, we can camp here. I'll go bring the others. Are you coming with me?"

"No, I'll stay here and wait for you," Allana said.

"I will stay with you, Lady. Who knows what brigands prowl these lonely moors," Barinosh said.

The camp was soon set up much to the distress of Noka who complained of the distance to the nearest water and the difficulty of digging latrines in the hard, rocky soil. Allana was completely preoccupied, and not even Margan's most stirring ballads could divert her thoughts from seeing her homeland. She tossed fitfully that night and hardly slept.

The next morning, Allana, Barinosh, Javik, Bogard, and Noka rode to the harbor leaving Sigurd in charge of the camp. Barinosh soon purchased passage to Gorgos for the party, and they were off on the first sea voyage for all but Barinosh. Half way to the island, four of the travelers were leaning over the gunwales of the boat. Barinosh laughed heartily at the plight of his friends.

"I wish I'd skipped breakfast," Bogard said between trips to the rail.

"It would be worse for you if you had," Barinosh laughed. "It's better to have something to lose when you're seasick. Keep your eyes on the horizon and learn to anticipate the motions of the boat. The waves come in regular patterns, and you'll soon get used to it."

Javik helped Allana to a small bench near the center of the boat.

"You'll feel better here. The boat's motion is not so violent near the center," Javik said as he eased the woman into her seat and propped her against the mast.

"Oh, Javik, I'm going to die before I ever see Gorgos," Allana sighed.

Barinosh came over to comfort her.

"You will do much better on the return voyage, Lady. Look, we're almost there." He pointed to the island.

Gorgos now filled most of the horizon, but there appeared to be no place to land a boat. Sheer cliffs rose as far as they could see. The mountains rose high above the cliffs, and their tops were shrouded in gray clouds. Javik thought they were only about half the height of those in Berglaundia. As they neared the cliffs, thousands of sea birds wheeled and soared over the large rocks near their base.

"I've never seen so many birds before," Noka said with a note of awe in his voice.

"They nest here each spring," Barinosh explained. "They raise their young over the early summer, then, they're off to the deep sea until the following year."

The crashing sound of the waves on the rocks grew louder as they neared the cliffs. To everyone's relief, the boat steered away from the breakers and toward some lower cliffs to the South. Soon, they could see some green expanses sloping down to the sea and ending in a long, white beach. Animals scampered across the fields, and here and there, a stone hut dotted the landscape. Curls of smoke rose from holes in the thatched roofs. The island was already awake and working.

The boat rounded a spit of land and steered into a deep green harbor. The remains of a great city rose from the docks.

Some buildings had been repaired enough to allow habitation, but most were only empty shells. The slips were empty except for a small trading vessel. They docked at a long, stone quay jutting into the harbor near the center of the ruined city. Allana stepped off first with help from Javik and Barinosh. She stood there for a moment surveying the situation.

"It must have been a beautiful city," she said.

"It was, Lady," Barinosh replied. "It was the finest of all the ocean's ports. Your father was the richest king of all, but the Voldunee destroyed him for that wealth."

"I see no fortifications for the harbor," Bogard said. "Did they destroy those also?"

"No, Gorgos relied upon its navy for protection. We never thought an invader would be able to get past our fleet, but the Voldunee created a distraction causing the navy to split into two task forces. They attacked immediately, once the defensive force was weakened. I escaped because I led the force sailing to meet the diversionary threat. When I returned, this was all I found." Barinosh swept his hand across the bleak vista of the desolated city.

"You said some of my people are here. Take me to them," Allana said.

"They are simple fishermen, Lady. They will be out on their boats now and won't be back for several hours," Barinosh answered.

"I want to see where they live. Surely the women will be home tending to their children."

Barinosh led the group off toward some houses bordering the docks. The smell of fish was nearly overpowering, and Noka had to visit the edge of the wharf once. The old man stopped at the second house and knocked at the doorsill.

"Mistress Branna, are you home?" he called.

A pudgy woman with curly black hair appeared from the darkness at the back of the house wiping her hands on a dingy gray cloth. Her face seemed to light up at the sight of Barinosh.

"Barinosh! It's good to see you. You've been gone a long time." She looked at the other people in the group, and her face took on a bewildered expression. "Who are these people?"

"Mistress Branna, this is Princess Allana." Barinosh swept an arm toward his queen and smiled broadly.

"My Lady," the woman gasped as she dropped to one knee before Allana. "We all thought you were dead."

"Rise Mistress Branna. I am not yet queen, and I don't even remember being a princess. May we come in?" She helped the woman to her feet.

"My home is not worthy of you, Lady," the woman said as she stuffed the dirty cloth into a pocket under her apron.

"Nonsense! It appears to be a fine house," Allana said. Behind her, Bogard looked at Javik with an incredulous expression, and Javik only shrugged his shoulders in response.

"We'll wait for you here," Javik said.

The older woman led Allana inside the improvised house. It had once been a business of some type along the waterfront, but expediency demanded a new use when it was one of the few structures left standing after the Voldunee attack. The lower floor was now devoted to the fishing business with bins of dried fish along one wall and nets, weights and floats hanging on the opposite wall. She led Allana through the stink to a large courtyard filled with racks for drying fish. Wooden stairs led up to a second floor and the family living quarters on the second floor. A single room served all functions needed by the family. Two small children played with their homemade toys in the middle of the floor, but they scurried off behind beds as the women entered.

"These are my children," mistress Branna said. "Come out Tina, Marcus. Meet your Queen."

Allana knelt on the floor and held her arms open to the dark haired urchins. The two moved slowly toward her with wary gazes, glancing to their mother from time to time and holding hands for reassurance.

"What lovely children," Allana said. "Come and let me know you better."

Their clothes were ragged, but they were clean and well groomed. They finally succumbed to Allana's charm and fell into her arms.

"You must be Tina," Allana said to the little girl.

"Yes, Lady," Tina responded.

"And, you must be Marcus."

"Yes, Lady. Do you have any sweets for us?"

Allana laughed as mistress Branna scolded Marcus.

"It's alright," Allana assured her. "I have no sweets, but I will give your mother a coin to buy you some." She selected a gold crown from her purse and gave it to the mother who reacted with shock.

"Lady, this is too much," she protested.

"Buy something for your family also. How does your family fare under Count Charlan?"

"We do well enough, Lady, but I remember better times under your father. The taxes are heavy now but we manage."

Allana embraced the woman. "With any luck at all, you will

soon be under my family's rule again. Tell our fellow Gorgons that I have returned, and my goal is to restore the island to its former prosperity. There is hope for the future."

"Bless you, Lady, bless you. We will all pray to Godon for your success."

Allana joined the men downstairs with tears in her eyes.

"Was it that bad?" Javik asked.

"No, it's just sad that no one has bothered to rebuild this city."

"Lady, there is no reason to rebuild Thatos. The trade your father developed now goes to Harrish. We must find some new way to bring prosperity to Gorgos," Barinosh said.

"We will think on that. Take me to the palace, please. I want to see where I was born."

Barinosh led the group up the ruined streets to a large complex of ruins atop a hill. It was a hard climb, and Javik's leg began to ache half way up, but he kept going.

"This was the royal palace of Gorgos," Barinosh said as he spread both arms wide and turned around. "It rose high above the city and gleamed in the sun like gold."

Noka scuffed away the dirt to reveal a mosaic floor. "Look at this. It's beautiful."

He dropped to his knees and began to sweep away the white dusty covering with his hands. The more he cleared, the more magnificent it became. Here and there pieces were missing, but the general theme of the work was clear.

"This was a map of the world known to Gorgos," Barinosh said.

"Look, Javik! It shows lands beyond the great sea," Noka almost shouted.

"Those are only legends, Noka," Barinosh said. "Some of our great navigators of ancient times claimed they found lands far across the sea, but no one dared follow after them to prove them right or wrong."

Noka stood and beat the dust from his hands on his tunic. "Still, it is marvelous to think about it."

Bogard spoke. "I once heard of an island far away famed for building ships. Was that Gorgos?"

"Yes, we made some of the finest ships in the world, but the shipyards were destroyed and the yards at Harrish now turn out most of the ships used in this part of the great ocean. Using Gorgon workers, I might add," Barinosh replied.

Allana walked back among the crumbling walls to an area near the rear of the palace. "I seem to remember this place," she said as she surveyed the remnants of the walls. They were painted with scenes of the sea, and though the paint was faded from the sun, the images were still visible.

Barinosh joined her and looked around to orient himself. "This would have been your nursery, Lady."

Allana ran her hands along one wall as if coaxing a story from the plaster. "I can feel the happiness of former times here, Javik. When I rebuild this palace, this will be my room again."

Javik moved behind her and enfolded her in his arms. He whispered in her ear, "Perhaps it could be our room?"

Allana turned and smiled at him. She lifted a hand to his cheek. "Yes, our room, Javik."

They rented horses from a blacksmith and rode up to the mountains. Noka rode to the edge of the high cliffs and looked over at the soaring birds and the rocks below. He called Javik to his side.

"What is it, Noka?"

"Look at the space between the rocks down there, Javik. It's full of bird droppings."

"So?"

"So it would be a wonderful source of saltpeter. I'd wager there are niter deposits in the caves in these mountains also. We could manufacture the magic powder here. It could be the resource to bring Gorgos back its former glory."

"You may have something there, Noka. We'll discuss it this evening." They rode back to the others.

"I'm hungry," Bogard said. "I lost most of breakfast on that damned boat."

"There's an inn in the city," Barinosh advised. "Let's go back."

Allana nodded her consent, and they dined on excellent fish and passable wine before returning to the mainland.

Chapter 14

That night around the campfire the travelers discussed the future of Gorgos.

"There aren't many options," Javik said. "Trade and shipbuilding have been taken over by Harrish, and there's not much in the way of good farmland. Fishing seems to be their only source of income."

Sigurd turned to Barinosh. "The island has mountains. Is there any gold in them?"

"The mines were exhausted before Allana was born. There may be more, but the shafts can go no deeper."

"We could look for other metals," Noka inserted. "Perhaps we could find copper?"

"There are some copper mines," Barinosh said. "They were still producing at the time of the attack, but the shafts may have collapsed."

"With few trees we'd have to import lumber and firewood," Sigurd said.

"Only lumber," Barinosh said. "The mountains have deposits of the black stone that burns. The Gorgons call it kaol."

"And iron?" Karl asked.

"Yes, but those mines were also abandoned years ago," Barinosh said.

"What about tin for making bronze?" Noka asked.

"Yes, there's tin also. We used to cast bronze heads for our ship's rams," Barinosh said.

"Don't forget the precious bird droppings you mentioned, Noka," Sigurd said with an air of disdain.

"I think that's the most important element," Noka said. "The kaol could be used as the charcoal, and the bird droppings could be processed into saltpeter some way. All we would need is sulphur."

"That we have in abundance," Barinosh added. "There are vast fields of it on the other side of the island."

"With all of this mineral wealth, why are the people so poor?" Javik asked.

"We worked the mines with slaves. Free people will not risk the hazards of the mines," Barinosh explained.

"If you paid enough, they might do it," Berda added.

"A man's life is cut in half in the mines. How could you pay him enough to compensate for that?" Barinosh snorted.

"Perhaps if we only required each man to work for one year in the mines? Would that shorten their lives?" Karl suggested.

"Perhaps, perhaps not, I don't know, but some might be willing to risk it if the wages were high enough," Barinosh said.

"We'd have to sell our powder dearly, indeed, to make any money for ourselves," Sigurd said.

"Don't forget the sale of hand cannons," Noka reminded them. "We would have all the materials we need for a forge, and Barinosh says there was once a foundry on Gorgos. If the furnaces are repairable, we could cast our weapons instead of forging them."

"After seeing them in action I wish they were big enough to use against a ship. They would be a formidable weapon at sea,"

Barinosh said.

"Why couldn't we make them large enough for that?" Noka mused. "Iron might be too heavy for ships, but we could see if bronze would do the job."

"All of this talk is useless until we have Charlan's permission to take over Gorgos and the money to pay for all of these dreams," Javik, the voice of reason, broke in.

"Charlan can't be collecting much in the way of taxes from Gorgos as it sits now," Allana entered the conversation. "We can offer him an opportunity to more than double his tribute, and I am the rightful ruler of Gorgos in any case. Tomorrow you will seek an audience with him, Barinosh. I will need some new clothes, so I will visit the bazaar while you do that. Javik, you will accompany me to the audience along with Barinosh. Now that everything is settled, we should all get some sleep."

The next morning, Barinosh entered the palace of Count Charlan. He was ushered into the Count's presence after only a short wait.

"Barinosh, it's good to see you again. I trust you and your mistress fared well after the war?" The Count smiled broadly as he took the old man's hand in a warm embrace.

"We did, Sir. Princess Allana is now free of the bandits and is camped just outside the walls of Harrish."

"My guards told me there was a camp containing some young warriors, but they seemed to be peaceful. The only thing they feared was the monstrous dog. Is he a war dog?"

"Yes, Sir. He belongs to Javik, the beloved of Princess Allana. He's a formidable animal. I've seen him bring down a man on horseback."

The count whistled slowly. "I've also heard they bear new

and unique weapons with more power than the strongest crossbow."

"Aye, they do. They use a secret powder known only to three of them. I've seen these weapons in action also. They struck fear into the hearts of the Turrek, and that is no mean feat."

"Truly! When can I expect a visit from Princess Allana?"

"She would see you as soon as possible to discuss the island of Gorgos."

"Bring her tomorrow at noon, and we will talk. Now, come have a cup of wine with me, old friend."

Charlan wrapped one arm around Barinosh and steered him toward a table laden with wine pitchers and golden cups.

* * * * *

Allana walked through the bazaar of Harrish with Javik close by her side. The vendors assailed her on every side with silk, jewels and all manner of baubles. She smiled at each one, but walked on past most, stopping only at a few to handle the material or inspect a necklace more closely. Small children pestered her for coins, and Javik shooed them away until she told him to throw a few coppers their way. The urchins pounced on the coins like vultures on carrion, but they left them alone after that.

Javik was dazzled. The bazaar held every item imaginable. There were clothes, jewelry, exotic foods, shoes, cloth of all varieties, artwork, sculptures, brightly feathered birds in wicker cages, monkeys frolicking on a piece of tree trunk, and everywhere the calls of the merchants mingled with the sound of music and the cries of the animals. The smell was like nothing he'd ever experienced before, spices mingled with roast meat, incense and perfume. Allana seemed to be taking everything in stride. She passed up most of the vendors, but she stopped in front of a shop where a lovely woman was modeling a flimsy gown.

The display had attracted a large group of men eager to catch a glimpse of something more than the gown. Two of them were bidding on the item.

"Five gold crowns!" the older man cried. He was dressed in a fashion strange to Javik. He wore a white silk turban and a long blue robe of equally high quality silk embroidered in exotic designs of red, blue and green.

"Six!" the other man countered. He was a warrior dressed much like Javik. A woolen cap sat on a wealth of deep brown hair, and his tunic was leather with no decorations. His boots shone with the effort of much polishing, and Javik looked at his own boots dull and tarnished from travel. A plain handled sword hung at his left side, and an ornate dagger stuck out of his broad belt.

"Seven!" the turban bid.

"Ten!" The voice was Allana's.

"Too much for me." Turban waved a hand at the auctioneer indicating he was finished, but the warrior bid again.

"Fifteen!"

Allana shook her head. "It's yours, sir," she said.

The warrior paid the auctioneer and moved to Allana. "This gown is my gift to you, lovely lady." He bowed low before her.

"I may not accept your gift, sir. I don't even know you."

"My name is Artun, and I come from a land far to the North seeking the loveliest of women. My quest is now complete."

"You are good at flattery, warrior Artun. Please meet my

beloved, Javik, son of Tolda."

Artun saluted Javik and offered his hand. Javik took it warily keeping a good eye on the man's sword and dagger.

"A pleasure to meet you, Javik."

"And mine also," Javik responded. "Which land to the North do you call home? I can't place your accent."

"I am from Ruzza. Perhaps you've heard of it?"

"I have. I once bought a piece of amber from one of your countrymen. What brings you here?"

"A long journey by boat."

Allana laughed, but Javik wasn't in the mood for humor at the moment.

"Are you traveling on, Artun?" Allana asked.

"I'm afraid the purchase of your gift has depleted my purse, Lady. I was hoping to find work in your employ."

"We have no funds to pay for mercenaries," Javik said.

"Javik, don't be so cruel," Allana scolded. "We will need every man we can get to rebuild Gorgos."

"Gorgos? Is that the island yonder?" Artun asked.

"Yes, it will be my home, and our small band of adventurers plan to take on the task of restoring its former glory. The pay is nothing now except food and a tent to sleep in, but future rewards could be great if you are worthy."

"Lady, I would serve you only for the privilege of looking at you each day. Your words would be my food and your beauty my pay." Artun bowed and kissed Allana's hand.

Javik was barely holding back his anger. This man was an adventurer, and probably not to be trusted, and Allana was falling for his flattery. He whispered in Allana's ear.

"May I speak with you privately?"

Allana nodded and spoke to Artun. "Please excuse us for a moment, Artun."

The pair moved away a few steps, and Javik spoke in a low voice. "Allana, I don't trust this man. He flatters too much, and we know next to nothing about him. We have all the men we need right now, anyway."

"I don't trust him either, Javik, but he has winning ways, and we may need those skills before we're done. Are you jealous of him?"

"Nonsense!" Javik blushed bright red, and Allana laughed like the sound of a silver bell.

"I believe you are jealous, Javik. We have enough good men to keep an eye on him for a while. Let's see what he's made of besides pretty phrases before we turn him out. I'll pay his way."

"Very well, I do this to please you. I hope you know what you're doing."

"Trust me, Javik." Allana gave Javik a short kiss and turned back to Artun.

"You will join our band, Artun, but understand that Javik, here, is in command. You will obey him as you would me. Is that clear?"

"Clear, Lady, and thank you for your confidence. You will never be sorry for this."

"I hope not," Javik muttered under his breath.

The merchant came out of his shop and placed a package in Artun's hands. Artun passed it to Allana.

"Your gown, Lady."

"I will wear this to see Count Charlan. Perhaps it will bring us good fortune."

The three walked on through the bazaar with Allana buying

a few more items to compliment the gown. Each package was passed to Artun who gladly served as the pack animal.

They arrived back in camp to find Sigurd and Berda engaged in fencing practice. Sigurd was getting the better of the match at the moment, but Berda's look of determination meant the braggart would have to keep up his guard to win. A deft move by Sigurd forced an awkward parry, and Berda soon faced the point of a sword at his throat.

"That's two in a row, Berda. Do you want another match?" Sigurd bellowed.

"Enough, Sigurd. I'm too tired now," Berda answered as he sheathed his sword and reached for a cup of wine on the small table nearby.

"Sigurd is our best swordsman," Javik said to Artun.

"Really?" Artun put down Allana's packages and drew his sword.

"May I try you?" Artun asked Sigurd.

"And who is this?" Sigurd asked.

"This is Artun of Ruzza," Javik answered. "Allana took him on as part of our band at the bazaar today."

Sigurd joined Berda in a cup of wine and wiped the sweat from his brow with a white cloth.

"Well, Artun, you might as well learn your lesson immediately. On guard."

The two warriors circled each other warily watching for any sign of a weakness. It seemed a long time before Artun lunged at Sigurd like a bolt of lightning. Sigurd barely managed to parry and gave ground quickly.

"A fine attack, Artun. Where did you learn that?" Sigurd asked.

"At my father's sword point," Artun laughed in response.

This time, Sigurd attacked, and a furious exchange ensued with each warrior backing away at the end.

"Your father taught you well," Sigurd said. He was almost out of breath from the effort, but he kept his point high.

"And you learned from a master yourself," Artun returned the compliment. "Is Javik as good as you?"

"Almost. There's little to choose between us, and I would hate to face him in a serious duel."

"Then I won't try him," Artun said as he lunged once more at Sigurd. This time, Sigurd parried high, and Artun circled his blade below Sigurd's too quickly for any counter move. His sword point rested on Sigurd's stomach.

"You win," Sigurd said. "That was a very quick move. You must teach it to me."

"We will practice again, Sigurd. Here's my hand." Artun offered his hand to Sigurd who took it with a broad smile.

"Have some wine, Artun. I bought this from a vendor passing into the city this morning. It's a very good vintage."

As Allana was putting away her purchases, Barinosh arrived.

"What did you find out, Barinosh?" Allana asked as he bowed to her.

"Charlan will see you tomorrow at noon. We drank together, and he gave me the feeling he's not pleased with his revenues from Gorgos. He seems to think the current governor is stealing from him, and he's anxious to hear your proposal."

"Good, good. We will have some leverage." Allana smiled contentedly as she unwrapped the gown and held it up to herself.

Chapter 15

The next morning, Javik went into the city and hired a carriage for their trip to the palace. He and Barinosh polished their armor to shining perfection, and donned their best boots before pulling the carriage up to Allana's tent. They were not prepared for the sight greeting their eyes as her tent flap opened.

Allana strode out looking radiant and as regal as any queen Javik could imagine. Her hair was piled up on her head and held in place with several golden combs. Bracelets circled each wrist in a profusion of gold, while three necklaces accented her low neckline. As she moved, the gown flowed with her, clinging sensually to her hips and thighs. The top bloused just enough to cover the movement of her breasts, but when she stopped, the gossamer cloth outlined their shape perfectly. It was as if the gods had painted the gown on her body. The scent of a thousand flowers wafted across the space between her and the men, nearly overpowering Javik with barely contained lust.

"You're beautiful," Javik gasped.

"Close your mouth, Javik. You act like you've never seen a queen before," Allana laughed.

"You are a vision, my Lady," Barinosh added.

"Thank you both. Help me into the carriage."

The warriors stood on either side and supported her gently

as she entered the coach. They mounted their horses and took up positions on either side. Javik gave the coachman the order to move off.

The city gaped in awe as the carriage made its way down the broad road to the palace. It was just wide enough for the coach, and the warriors rode with Javik in front and Barinosh in the rear. Allana was visible from the waist up, and drew whispered praise as she passed the watching groups of people interrupted in the process of completing their morning chores.

The palace guards saluted smartly as Javik rode past into the courtyard. It was a modest palace from what he'd seen up to that point. It was far below the King's palace in Berglaundia, but it had a charm all its own. Stone statues of sea gods and strange ocean creatures lined the courtyard. At the end of the stairs leading up to the palace, two large statues of naked goddesses in sensual poses greeted visitors.

Javik and Barinosh dismounted and moved to the coach door to assist Allana. As she stepped to the ground, the clatter of many feet on the marble steps caused the men to turn quickly with their hands on their swords, but it was only a sedan chair sent by Count Charlan for Allana. As if she expected such treatment as her due, Allana stepped into the chair and motioned for the bearers to move on. Javik and Barinosh followed.

The gardens at the top of the stairs were beautiful. Flowers of every color bloomed in profusion, and fountains sparkled in the sunlight singing bright songs of cool breezes. The smell was even finer than Allana's perfume. The entourage strode into the palace, down a hallway and stopped at a large door. The guards nodded at the sedan chair and opened the heavy wooden doors. As Allana's chair was carried in, a seneschal pounded the floor with his staff and announced.

"All bow to Princess Allana of Gorgos!"

Javik was now on Allana's right side, and she whispered to him. "At least they're using my title. We can hope for the best."

Allana stepped from the sedan chair and walked toward Charlan with Javik on her right and Barinosh on her left. Charlan sat in a plain chair on a slightly raised platform and smiled broadly as she approached. A stately blonde woman in a fine dress sat next to him, and Allana guessed it was his wife. Allana knelt before him, and Charlan jumped to his feet immediately. He lifted her to her feet and stood staring into her eyes.

"You are even more beautiful than I was told you were."

"Thank you, my lord. I'm surprised you've heard anything about one so unimportant as myself."

Charlan laughed softly. "You underestimate your own beauty and the fame of the warriors traveling with you. I understand they wield awesome power."

"Power that could be at your service if we could come to an agreement on Gorgos," Allana answered. "This is Javik, son of Tolda, he knows the secret of the weapons."

Javik remembered his etiquette and bowed to Charlan. "My Lady speaks the truth, Sir."

Charlan extended his hand to Javik, but not with the palm down. Javik understood he meant to shake his hand and took it in a firm grip.

"It's a pleasure to meet you, Javik. If your weapon is as strong as your grip, it is formidable indeed."

"I'm sorry, Sir. I didn't mean…"

"Don't apologize. I'm not used to a warrior's greeting at my court." He leaned closer to Javik and whispered, "As you can see, it's sometimes hard to tell the males from the females here."

Javik stifled a smile with great difficulty. He'd noticed the dress and bearing of many of the courtiers as they approached Charlan's throne, and he'd already come to the same conclusion.

The blonde lady rose from her chair and joined Charlan. "Please present me, husband."

"Countess Brianna, Princess Allana, Javik, son of Tolda, and Barinosh, Admiral of the Gorgon Fleet."

The three bowed before her, and she nodded her recognition as she moved to Javik.

"You seem quite young to possess such great powers. How old are you?"

"I have seen 18 winters, Lady."

"Yes very young, indeed." Brianna eyed Javik from head to toe almost causing the young warrior to blush.

Javik stole a glance at Allana and noticed a stern expression come over her face as Brianna offered a hand to Javik.

Javik kissed the highly perfumed fingers noticing the heavy gems on each finger.

"Thank you, Lady," was all Javik could manage.

"Brianna, please see that these warriors are entertained while the Princess and I talk. Come, Allana, we have much to discuss." Charlan led Allana from the room as the courtiers bowed in deference to their lord. Javik and Barinosh followed suit. When they were gone, Brianna spoke.

"Come sit by me and tell me of all your adventures, Javik. You too, Barinosh," she added hastily.

A servant brought another chair for Barinosh, but set it on the countess's left side much farther away. Brianna indicated the closer chair for Javik.

* * * * *

Allana accompanied Charlan into a conference room where several older men sat around a table. They rose and bowed as Charlan entered.

"Gentlemen, allow me to present Allana, Princess of Gorgos." The men bowed to Allana.

"This is Bradish, my chief counselor," Charlan indicated a gray haired man in a blue velvet robe.

"My Lady," Bradish said as he kissed Allana's offered hand.

"This is Timlik, my treasurer," Charlan led her to a younger man with a full black beard and a wealth of even blacker hair.

"My Lady," Timlik followed suit.

"And, this is Wargall, the commander of my merchant fleet." Wargall smiled at Allana and kissed her hand.

"I did not know any of the royal family of Gorgos survived the Voldunee," Wargall said.

"Admiral Barinosh can verify that I bear the royal mark, but you may see it if you doubt my legitimacy," Allana replied.

"That would be a wonderful sight, indeed, but under the circumstances, I'll take the Admiral's word for it," Wargall smiled even more broadly.

The other men stifled laughter out of respect for their guest.

"You are a gentleman, Sir," Allana answered as she took the chair indicated by Charlan. The others sat also.

Charlan spoke first. "I assume you've come to claim Gorgos in the name of the royal family."

"I come to ask your recognition of such a claim, my lord.

Gorgos would still be part of your territory and owe allegiance to you."

"Well, that solves one problem," Bradish said. "You would be satisfied, then, as governor of Gorgos under Count Charlan?"

"Yes, Sir. I ask no more than that."

"My current governor will not be happy to be replaced. He's built himself a very nice villa on the leeward side of the city."

"I will purchase it from him," Allana said.

"He may name a high price, Lady," Timlik said.

"I'm sure we can arrange terms. If not, there may be other ways to resolve the issue." Allana smiled knowingly at the treasurer.

Charlan jumped in. "You need not waste your favors on him, Princess. I was about to replace him anyway. His collection of taxes from the island has been quite poor lately. I will purchase his house and rent it to you."

"You are most generous, Sir." Allana spoke the words knowing what Charlan had in mind. State visits to Gorgos would be required, and Allana could show her gratitude in a proper manner on those occasions. Charlan was ignorant of her own plans for Gorgos, and that was just as well at this time.

"How would you propose to increase the taxes from Gorgos? The current governor has beaten and tortured the people there unmercifully, and he still only manages a pittance," Timlik said.

"I would gather no taxes at all, Sir," Allana answered.

The men gasped and leaned forward in their chairs. Wargall recovered first.

"Lady, Count Charlan is unhappy with the current revenue,

why would he accept none at all?"

"My people would pay no taxes, but I would pay an annual tribute to the Count. What taxes do you collect now?"

Timlik consulted a scroll before answering. "A bit less than 5,000 gold crowns, Lady."

"I will pay a tribute of 10,000 gold crowns at the end of my first year and 20,000 every year after that."

Again the men gasped. Charlan jumped on it at once.

"Done, Princess, the island is yours to govern, but should you fail in meeting your obligation, what is the forfeit?"

"Why, you may have your island back, my lord, along with all of my personal wealth."

"I'd rather have another forfeit," Charlan said with a lustful look on his face.

"My lord, you already have a wife," Allana said. The other men quickly suppressed laughter over her reaction to his obvious intentions.

"And, I don't mean to get rid of her," Charlan countered quickly. "As long as you pay the original 10,000 crown tribute annually, you may stay as autonomous governor of Gorgos. If you fail four state visits each year will be my forfeit."

Wargall looked at his lord in disgust. *This man's lechery would be the downfall of the kingdom yet,* he thought to himself, but he held his voice.

Allana smiled. She knew she could deal with this lecherous fool and still remain true to Javik. She'd learned much from Varuda about handling his ilk. "I must accept your generosity and your forfeit, my lord."

"Good, good, then it's all settled. Are there any objections?" Charlan looked at each man, in turn, and each one shook his head in the negative. "Good, let's join the court, so I may announce the new governor of Gorgos and celebrate a promising future with a Princess back on her throne."

Chapter 16

Charlan escorted Allana back to the audience hall with his council behind them. The courtiers bowed low as they approached the thrones, but Allana's eyes were focused on Javik. He was speaking in an animated manner to Brianna who seemed to be hanging on his every word and looking at him like a cat about to pounce on a mouse. Barinosh gave her a worried look as she caught his eye, and she knew it was time to break up the tet-a-tet.

Charlan stood before his court and pulled Allana to his side.

"Nobles of my realm, I am pleased to announce my appointment of Princess Allana as the new governor of Gorgos. Welcome her to our company."

The assembled court applauded politely, distracting Allana for a moment while she bowed in response.

"Bring wine and food. We must celebrate our good fortune on the return of the royal family of Gorgos," Charlan called. Servants ran to do his bidding, and Allana turned to Javik.

"Javik, won't you and Barinosh join me in our celebration?"

"Certainly, please excuse me, Countess," Javik said as he rose to join Allana.

"We are honored," Barinosh said with a definite air of relief in his voice.

Brianna's frosty gaze told Allana she was not a welcome

intrusion.

Allana led the two men to the long tables at one end of the room where servants were laying out food and standing by with pitchers of wine to fill the silver goblets stacked on one table. The courtiers lined up to partake of the luncheon buffet, but Charlan led Allana, Barinosh and Javik to a table containing cups already filled and plates already stacked high with food. Brianna joined them.

"You must try this wine, Allana. It's a product of our special vineyards. Brianna loves it." He passed a goblet full of dark red liquid to her.

Allana tasted the wine and was surprised at its dryness. "It is a fine wine, indeed. You have good taste, Countess."

"My taste in wine can't compare to your taste in men, Princess. Javik, here, is a fine warrior."

"Thank you, I am honored to sample your fine wine. It's a pity one cannot share men the same way."

Brianna laughed at the obvious warning. "Men are more like stud horses, Princess. They don't mind servicing an entire herd of mares."

"I have no horses of my own right now, but if I did, I'd be very careful in selecting the mares to stand for any of my studs. They would not be allowed to run amok and do as they pleased."

Javik was becoming very uncomfortable with the women's conversation and turned his attention to the food.

The wine was excellent, but the food was amazing. Everything was cut into bite-sized pieces and skewered on slivers of a wood he hadn't seen before. He turned to Barinosh.

"I've not seen wood like this before. What is it?"

"It's called bamboo here in Tulla. It grows in great profusion at the foot of the mountains. The peasants make all sorts of things with it."

Javik selected a dark blob of something from a tray proffered by a servant and pulled it from the bamboo sliver with his teeth.

"This is good, Barinosh. I've never tasted anything like it before."

Barinosh took several of the morsels and downed one quickly.

"Yes, the snails are quite good."

Javik almost choked, but controlled himself in time.

"Snails? These are snails?"

"Yes, a special breed they cultivate here for food. They cook them in butter and spices. I love them, but they are quite expensive."

Javik lay his remaining snail down on the table, and Barinosh scooped it up.

"Somehow, the knowledge of what they are has ruined my appetite for them," Javik said.

"All the more for me," Barinosh responded.

The meal went on for another hour with Allana making sure she stayed between Javik and Brianna. Finally, she took her leave of Charlan, and the trio returned to camp.

* * * * *

"What news?" Sigurd called as the carriage stopped near the campfire.

"Gorgos has a new governor," Javik called from horseback.

Sigurd helped Allana alight from the carriage as the rest of the band came up to hear the news.

"I'll tell you all about it after I get comfortable. I'm tired of being a Princess right now, and I want to change into something a little less provocative." Allana pulled at her gown to indicate her meaning and strode off to her tent.

Javik and Barinosh took off their breastplates and sat down by the fire.

"Allana was marvelous," Javik began. "She was the most beautiful woman there, and all eyes were on her."

"All but two," Barinosh interrupted. "The Countess's eyes were fixed upon Javik."

The men laughed heartily as Javik blushed a bright red.

"Javik, you have all the luck with women," Noka said.

"I should have been there to take some of the pressure off Javik," Sigurd said.

Again, the men laughed.

"I wish you would have been there, Sigurd. You could have taken some of the daggers Allana was staring at me after she saw me talking with the Countess," Javik said.

At that point, Allana arrived, and the men grew quiet.

"What macho, male conversation did I interrupt?" Allana asked.

"Javik was telling us about how the Countess fell in love with him," Bogard said with a playful expression.

"Then I shall tell you how I enchanted the Count," Allana said just as playfully.

"Oooohhh," the men responded.

"After seeing you in that gown, I would believe any story you tell," Sigurd said.

"Well, all joking aside, I am the new governor of Gorgos," Allana said.

The statement was met with a round of applause.

"Do we have to bow to you now?" Karl asked.

"None of you ever need bow to me though I be Queen of the World. You rescued me from the Turrek, and I shall always be grateful for that. I owe Javik and Tao Shan much more because they freed me from slavery, but I love the rest of you no less."

Another round of applause met her statement.

"What are your plans now?" Bogard asked.

"I will go to Gorgos and begin to rule there. Those of you who wish to join me are welcome. I can't promise gold or glory now, but anyone who helps me will receive a fair share of our profits. I plan to make the island prosperous again by bringing in skilled people in all fields of endeavor. We will begin with the mines. I want them back in operation as soon as possible."

Barinosh broke in. "My Lady, we have no slaves to work the mines."

"I will not have slavery on my island. Each man will be required to work one year in the mines. In exchange for his labors, he will be granted freedom from all taxes for three years."

A murmur of approval ran through the men, and Allana continued.

"We will use the minerals from the mines to revive the industries of Gorgos and gain wealth for expansion into other fields. Javik, will you manage the production of your magic powder?"

"Of course, I go wherever you go."

"And I, also," Noka said.

"Good! I think the powder will make us all rich," Allana said.

"We also need to make hand cannon and sell them," Noka added.

"Yes, we will do that also, but it may have to wait for our treasury to fill. I promised Charlan 10,000 gold crowns tribute in a year. We will need to work fast to avoid my forfeit."

"What forfeit?" Javik asked.

"Taking Charlan to my bed."

"Well, we'll make sure that never happens even if I have to face half of his guards to stop it," Javik blustered.

"Don't worry about it. If we work together on this, earning the tribute will be easy. Now, who will join me in this adventure besides Javik and Noka, and Barinosh, of course?"

Mikka spoke. "I promised Lord Browdat I would look after Javik until he found you, Allana. Now that he has, I need to get back to my wife and family. I will leave in the morning for Berglaundia. This has been a magnificent adventure, but I'm a warrior, and it looks like you will need more than mere talent with weapons to complete your plans."

"Thank you, Mikka. Please tell Lord Browdat that I am grateful to him for allowing you to accompany Javik." Allana rose and walked to the big warrior. He stood to meet her, and she embraced him. "I will miss you, Mikka. Safe journey."

"I will return home with Mikka," Berda said. "I long for the familiar sights of our village, and I miss my home."

"Not as much as you miss Clara," Karl said.

Berda blushed a deep red while the others laughed good-naturedly.

"Her too. I hate to leave you, Javik, but I promised her I'd return before fall."

"You've been a big help, Berda, but I understand," Javik said.

Allana moved to Berda and embraced him also.

"You and Mikka will make good company for each other on the journey," Allana said.

"I'll stay with you, Javik," Karl said.

"What about you, Sigurd?" Allana asked.

Sigurd shifted uneasily on his makeshift log seat

"I don't know about this part of the adventure. I don't mind facing battle or fierce beasts, but I'm not sure I'm up to fighting with account scrolls."

"We'll need someone to design the defenses for Gorgos," Barinosh said. "Once the island becomes prosperous again, it will attract raiders."

"Well, I might be helpful at that, and I would like to stay near Allana, if only to see the day Javik asks for her hand. Perhaps she'll turn him down and there will be hope for me."

Another round of laughter rippled through the men.

"If Sigurd and Javik are here, you'll need someone to keep them from killing each other, Highness. I'll stay with you," Bogard said.

"You will always need a minstrel, Lady," Margan said.

"Your pay will be small for a long while, I fear," Allana said.

"I am also welcome at Charlan's court, and the nobles there pay handsomely for flattery. Besides, I learn a great deal while I play, and you will also need a spy in that hotbed of intrigue."

"A good point, Margan," Allana said. "I'm pleased you plan to stay. And you, Artun?"

"Lady, I have nowhere else to go, and I would rather starve while basking in the radiance of your beauty than feast like a king under a blazing sun."

"What horse manure," Karl laughed.

"Don't be cruel, Karl," Allana scolded. "Artun was only

trying to be a gentleman."

Artun reached for his sword, but Allana's words calmed his anger.

At that point, the dinner bell rang, and the group broke up for the evening meal. Afterward, Allana took Javik aside.

"Come walk with me, Javik. I want to speak with you."

The two walked toward the beach with Mordah loping along behind. The setting sun perched precariously on low, purple clouds just above the horizon, bathing the ocean in a red-orange glow. The salt air seemed to stimulate their senses as they walked, and the soft sound of the waves breaking on the sand was like a lullaby.

"Javik, do you still love me?"

Javik stopped and looked at Allana a bit surprised.

"Of course. I love you more now than I ever have, but there was no time for that with the Turrek close behind us. Then, I was ill with my wound, and now you have so many things on your mind. I don't want to be a bother."

Allana laughed gently as a breeze through the willows.

"Javik, you are such an idiot in some ways. Don't you know how I've longed for you all this time we've been apart?"

Javik looked into Allana's dark eyes and saw his fondest dreams coming true. He swept her into his arms and felt her warmth against his body. She melted into him as if they were becoming one person. Her head tilted back, and she closed her eyes as his lips pressed against hers. He felt her hand on his neck pulling them together in passion's embrace. As they broke off the kiss, he heard her breath grow more labored and looked down at her still open mouth and closed eyes. He kissed her again, this time allowing his tongue to explore her mouth. He felt his heart opening like a new flower to this marvelous and beautiful woman.

"Oh Javik, I love you, I love you, I love you," Allana murmured into his ear.

He laid her gently on the sand and began to unfasten her clothes. The growing lust made his fingers clumsy, but she didn't seem to mind. Soon they were entwined in love's embrace and completely unaware there were any other people in the entire world.

* * * * *

Javik awoke to find Allana asleep in the crook of his arm. He was about to kiss her when a wave washed over their feet, shocking Allana into consciousness with a sharp scream.

"Javik! We're getting wet," she shrieked as she sat up abruptly.

"So we are, but we're also covered with sand. Let's wash it off in the ocean."

"Our clothes, they'll be washed away."

"I'll move them to higher ground," Javik said as he scooped up the clothes and dropped them higher up on the sand.

"Come on, the water feels good," Javik said as he took her hand and pulled her into the surf.

The water was cool but not cold, and they quickly grew used to it. They washed off the sand and kissed even more passionately as the waves pushed them toward the shore. Javik caught Allana just as a large one knocked her over. He stood in the water holding her in his arms.

"You are the most beautiful woman the gods ever created, and I love you more than my own life," Javik whispered. "Go with me to Harrish in the morning, and we will be married."

Allana looked away from Javik as she dropped to her feet. "We can't do that, Javik."

"Why not? We love each other; what's to stop us?"

"My kingdom. I want a royal wedding, Javik, and I can't have that until I'm truly Queen of Gorgos."

"But, you're practically queen now."

"No, I'm only the governor appointed by Charlan. He could remove me tomorrow. I have to build up my island and make it capable of standing on its own. Then, I'll declare independence from Tulla and be a true queen. Please be patient with me, my love. Even though we may not be married in the formal sense we will have all the things a man and wife could desire."

Javik looked into her eyes and knew he could deny her nothing. If she thought it best to delay their marriage, he would be patient.

"Very well, but we must marry within five years. My son will need a father by that time, and I want him to also have you as a mother."

"I promise, Javik. Within five years, we will marry."

They kissed again as another large wave knocked them into the surf.

Chapter 17

In the morning, the group said goodbye to Mikka and Berda, and Allana called another council meeting.

"Barinosh, I want you to find the remnants of our people and try to convince them to return to Gorgos. Tell them they will pay no taxes for two years if they come back. We'll need all the artisans you can muster and men to work the mines. Tell the miners they will only have to work for one year to earn their wages, and those wages will be free of taxes for as long as they work the mines. Whatever you need to promise, I will agree to when you return."

"I will go tomorrow, my Lady," Barinosh answered.

"Lady," Artun broke in. "I have some experience with mining. May I help you by supervising those operations?"

"Yes, Artun. You may have that job. I need someone to go into Harrish and recruit men for rebuilding the city. People will need places to live when they arrive. Who can do that?"

"My servant, Obla, has some knowledge of building," Sigurd answered. Before he became a slave, he was a master builder in Sentius."

"See if he will do that job in exchange for his freedom," Allana said.

"I paid over 150 gold crowns for Obla. You're very free with my slaves, Allana."

"I'll pay you for the loss. If he's as good as you say he is, I'll pay you double that."

"Agreed," Sigurd said as his face lit up in a broad smile.

"Noka, you will supervise the manufacture of the magic powder."

"Allana, I think we can use the bird droppings for saltpeter, but I'm not sure about how to convert it. It may take a while to perfect the process without some professional help. We may need an alchemist."

"Look, your Argani healer is here," Sigurd said pointing toward the dark little man on his donkey.

Avra rode up to the assembled group and recognized Javik immediately.

"It appears there is no need for my visit, Lady. Your young warrior seems to be mending quite well," Avra said.

"I'm doing very well, thanks to your distasteful potion," Javik said as he helped the man dismount. "Have you come all the way from Othis just to check my wound?"

"Yes, and since you seem to be doing very well, I'll return to that city as soon as I've had a chance to rest a bit. Do you have any tea, Lady?"

Allana called to a servant to bring tea and turned back to Avra.

"We were just discussing our need for an alchemist on Gorgos. Do you know of any Argani who might be willing to help us?"

"At what price, Lady? I know several men who might be enticed to that lonely island if there were enough gold in the bargain."

"The gold would be small, at first, but he would share in the profits of our magic powder and live tax free on Gorgos."

The little man rubbed his beard and thought for a moment before speaking. The gleam in his eyes betrayed his interest in the arrangement.

"I've heard tales of your magic weapons, but I've never seen one in action. Perhaps you could demonstrate one for me? It might be the very thing that could convince a doubtful candidate."

"Certainly," Javik said, and he proceeded to his tent returning with his own hand cannon.

Avra watched carefully as Javik loaded powder and balls into the weapon and lit his match from the fire.

"I'll need a target," Javik said. The area up from the beach was flat and covered only with scrub grass. The trees were over two hundred meters away.

Sigurd stopped a nearby servant and took the broad brimmed had from his head.

"Here, use this." He tossed a coin to the servant and took a piece of firewood from the small pile next to the fire. He strode a few dozen meters toward the beach and pushed the piece of wood into the sandy soil, placing the hat on the end of the stick.

Javik took careful aim and blew the hat off the stick.

Avra shook his head to clear his ears.

"It makes a frightful noise, but what damage does it do? The wind might have blown the hat off the stick."

Javik smiled as Sigurd returned with the hat, poking his fingers through the three holes in the crown. He handed the hat to Avra.

"It can also penetrate a breastplate at that range, old man," Sigurd said.

Avra inspected the hat and smiled his satisfaction.

"I am your man, Lady. I have some knowledge of alchemy, and you know I'm a good healer. You may have both services for twenty percent of the proceeds from the sale of this powder."

Javik cleared his throat before answering. "We have only seen your skill as a healer, Avra. How do we know you are an alchemist?"

"I will show you," Avra said. He moved to his donkey and carried his wooden chest near the fire. He opened it to reveal the same items they'd seen before, but removed a tightly stoppered jar from the center of the case.

"Gather around me closely, for this will be difficult to see in the bright sunlight," Avra said.

The group moved in closer, and Avra uncorked the jar. A soft glow began to build inside the jar as the men drew back in total surprise.

"What is that?" Bogard said with a note of awe in his voice.

"A simple salt I make from tin. I've often needed some light in dark places, and I discovered this material after reading several scrolls from our people's archives on alchemy. It's come in quite handy many times."

"How long will it burn like that?" Noka asked.

"I've had this jar for several years, and it still glows brightly."

"You are truly the man we need," Allana said, "but what of your business in Othis?"

"It's rumored that King Oliga will soon persecute the Argani. He owes several of us considerable sums of money, and he does not wish to repay it on our terms. I will speak to my people. I'm sure many of us will join you on your island."

"You will all be welcome," Allana said. "Come as soon as you can. We should be ready in a few days. I plan to move to the island as soon as possible."

"I will join you within one cycle of the moon, Lady." Avra bowed low, packed his chest on the donkey and rode off toward Harrish.

"The Argani will be a great asset to our cause, Lady. They are a formidable people, though not in military prowess. We can learn much from them," Barinosh said.

"Karl, what can you do for our group?" Allana asked.

Karl thought for a moment then responded. "My family farmed, and we will need our own food supply on Gorgos. Perhaps I can find a way to make the island self-sufficient."

"Good, we all have tasks to perform. Tomorrow we move to Gorgos."

The move took several days of ferrying people, animals and material from Harrish to Gorgos. The old governor moved out of his villa, but Allana set up camp in the ruins of the old palace, leaving the old governor's place to a very happy Sigurd and his servants.

Artun managed to find several residents familiar with the old mines. Within a few days, he was off to the mountains to explore the remnants of the mineral operations.

Karl spoke with the few farmers on the island and learned that, in older times, many crops were grown on terraced fields cut into the sides of the mountains. He made plans to revive the terraces and their irrigation system.

Noka found a fisherman willing to risk the rocks, allowing him to secure samples of the bird droppings for Avra's experiments. The Argani set up a laboratory in one of the few repairable buildings in the city after spending considerable gold on the restoration.

Sigurd drew up grand plans for the fortification of the harbor and the restoration of the city, but his designs would have to wait for workers as well as gold from the pearl ship or sales of the magic powder.

Things were beginning to look up for the island, and the people felt a new energy from the activity. The beauty and kindness of the former princess who now governed them was also a major incentive. Many spoke of the return of the monarchy, but in hushed whispers lest Charlan's spies hear them.

Immigrants arrived by the boatload, and Javik stayed busy processing them. He soon had a staff of six men helping him. A few were Gorgons displaced years ago by the Voldunee raid, but most were Tullans fleeing taxation. Many of the men agreed to work the mines for a year in return for the tax relief, but some were artisans. Javik assigned those people to one of his fellow administrators to assist in rebuilding the economy of the island.

Barinosh returned after several weeks of travel, and Allana called an immediate council meeting to hear his report. They met in a part of the old palace recently restored by the efforts of several former residents of the island. The mosaic floor still showed a few blank spaces in its depiction of the gods, but the walls were repainted with images of Allana, Javik, Sigurd, and the rest of the ruling group. A blank space was left for Barinosh's picture, since none of the artists felt confident in rendering his image from memory. Other craftsmen created furniture in the old style to fill out the room. Allana greeted

Barinosh warmly.

"Welcome home, trusted companion," she embraced the old man.

"It's good to be back. I'm very tired of the deck of a ship under my feet and only a hammock for a bed."

"Tell us what you've found out," Sigurd urged.

"I found many of our people, my Lady, but many foreigners also elected to join us in this great adventure. I did the best I could to keep undesirable persons away, but I'm afraid I was not entirely successful."

"We've had to make a prison our first building priority, and Bogard has taken over as warden. Sigurd has trained a watch force, and pays them out of his own pocket until I can provide the gold."

"I'm sorry, my Lady."

"Don't worry about that. You couldn't help it. Go on," Allana said.

"Everywhere I went, people were excited about paying no taxes in return for their labor on our reconstruction. I was afraid you would not be able to feed and house so many."

"It has been a problem," Javik said. "Karl has been rebuilding the farming terraces, but there will be no crops for several months. We've been forced to import much of our food at great cost. Fish make up most of our meat, but the people grow tired of that diet. We've brought in more chickens, pigs, sheep and cattle. Even the goats are nearly depleted."

"I fear you may also be developing enemies, my Lady. The rulers of Philisia to the North and Karran to the South are very curious about the revival of Gorgos and may see it as a possible conquest. They don't seem to think Tulla would fight for so small a territory, and they would annex Gorgos if they see a source of wealth here. There are also rumors the Voldunee may return."

"Let's hope we will be in a position to defend ourselves before that happens," Allana said.

"It will take at least a year to build any kind of defense for the city or the seacoast," Sigurd answered. "Do you think we have that much time, Barinosh?"

"It's hard to say, but I don't think anyone will act as long as we are rebuilding. Charlan would protect us as long as there is any hope of tribute, and I doubt anyone would dare oppose him on the sea. His fleet is our best protection now, but we must build our own fleet in case he decides to turn against us."

Noka spoke next. "We could use some brave seamen to help harvest the bird droppings from the rocks. Have you managed to convince any to join us?"

"Yes, many are coming and in their own boats. They will be here after they finish catching whatever fish are running this time of year in their seas. You should have no problem there."

"All we need is time," Avra said. "I've arranged for loans from several of my people, but they will come due in a year, and we are still working on a means of extracting saltpeter from the bird droppings. I think I'm close, but I've thought that before."

"I have some hope for one of the old gold mines," Artun added. "We may be able to begin producing some gold in a few weeks. The kaol mines are up and working, but they were almost ready for larger scale production when we arrived. The copper and tin mines will be ready in a month, and we can begin to export brass and bronze."

"The pearl ship should be arriving soon," Barinosh said. "We should realize a handsome profit from that voyage."

"It can't get here soon enough for me," Allana said. "We are nearly out of funds now, and I don't think the Argani will loan us any more money."

"My funds are almost gone also," Sigurd said. "I could ask my father for more, but that means a long ride home and time away from my duties here."

"Stay here, Sigurd," Allana said. "We need you here more than we need money."

Allana rose to signal the end of the council.

"My friends, I thank all of you for your efforts. You have my gratitude if not the gold you all sought on coming here. We must work even harder if we want to realize our dreams. We will meet again in six days."

Javik noticed Allana looking much more fatigued recently and remained behind to speak with her.

"My darling, you must take some time to rest. I fear for your health if you continue working as hard as you have been."

Allana smiled warmly at her love and placed a hand on his cheek.

"You are so sweet, Javik. I don't see how I can relax considering our plight."

"Will you come sailing with me for a while? The sea air will do you a lot of good."

"Javik, I didn't know you could sail."

"One of the fishermen taught me, and he has a small boat he said I could use whenever I wished. Come with me, Darling. I'll pack us a lunch, and we can get away from these problems for a while."

"I have so many people wanting to see me. I don't see how I can leave them waiting."

Javik moved to the door and summoned Allana's secretary.

"Marima, come here please."

The rather portly woman rose from her desk with difficulty and moved to Javik.

"Yes, Lord."

"Our Lady is not feeling well. Cancel her appointments for the rest of the day. I must take her to see a healer in Harrish."

Marima looked past Javik at Allana. Her mistress seemed to be very healthy, but she understood when Allana raised a hand to indicate she shouldn't protest the order.

"I will do as you say, Lord." Marima bowed and returned to the throng of waiting petitioners.

Javik returned to Allana. "Change into something less conspicuous. We must look like peasants if we want to make it to the docks without recognition. I'll get the lunch."

Javik secured a wicker hamper full of cheese, bread, cold meat and wine and changed into peasant clothing he'd secured at the bazaar the day before. He returned to find Allana dressed in a common gown with a scarf around her hair. Her usual high coiffure was not in place, and her hair hung well past her shoulders. It reminded Javik of the first time he'd seen her running through the forest near his village.

"I'm ready. Do I pass your inspection?" Allana turned to model her outfit.

"You're still ravishingly beautiful, but I think we can make it. Come, the sea awaits."

Javik led Allana through the back alleys of the growing city to a small house near the seashore. A sturdy woman was busy stirring a large cauldron and watching her children play on the beach. Javik greeted her.

"Mistress Domma, I've come to use your husband's small boat."

"Bless me, it's the Lord Javik, but who is this with you, Sir?"

"Princess Allana, may I present Mistress Domma," Javik said as he gestured toward the older woman.

Domma wiped her hands on her apron and brushed her hair back from her eyes before she bowed low. "I'm honored to have you at our house, your highness."

"Rise, good wife Domma," Allana said as she moved closer to the woman. "Lord Javik has promised me a quiet sail. I hope your boat is a sound one."

"One of the best, your highness. Come this way."

Domma led them to a sailboat lying tilted to one side on the beach. Javik placed the hamper in the boat and pushed it out into the surf. He helped Allana embark and waved to Domma as he pushed it into deeper water. Soon the sail was up and the little craft was skimming across the harbor toward the breakwater.

Allana leaned back against the gunwale and let her hand drag through the water.

"I'm glad you asked me to do this. I've needed some time away from my duties. Where are we going?"

"I've found a small cove not far from here, and I think it would be an excellent spot for a picnic." Javik looked at Allana and smiled. Her eyes were closed, and he thought he could see the old vigor returning to her face as the sun baked away the gloom associated with the great burden on her shoulders. She opened her eyes as he steered around the breakwater and reset his sail to run before the wind.

"When did you find time to learn how to sail?" Allana asked.

"I took the time. I often watched the boats gliding gracefully out to the fishing grounds, and I envied the fishermen. I wanted to know what it felt like to be a creature of the wind and the sea, so I approached Domma's husband one morning before he set out. He agreed to take me out in this boat after he returned from his fishing. I fell in love with sailing, and he's taught me a great deal over the last few weeks. I'm still a novice, and I don't dare wander far from shore, but I thought you might enjoy this."

"I do. It's very relaxing."

"We're on the leeward side of the island here, and the water's smooth. It gets quite choppy once you hit the ocean's waves just around that far headland." Javik nodded toward the end of the steep cliffs far ahead.

"Will we be going that far?"

"No, my cove is just a little further. The entrance is a bit tricky, but I've done it before."

They sailed on for several more minutes, and then Javik swung the little boat out from shore before turning straight toward the cliff face.

"Javik! We're going to hit the cliff," Allana said as she sat bolt upright.

"Don't worry. There's an opening here. You'll see it once we get a little closer."

Allana studied the cliffs carefully and finally breathed easier as the narrow opening came into view.

"You'd never know that was a cove from any distance out," Allana said.

Domma's husband says it's a secret place known only to a few fishermen. He said smugglers used to use it many years ago. There's a beach at the end of the inlet.

The sail grew slack as the boat entered the inlet. Javik produced a paddle and began to use it to propel the boat after dropping the sail entirely. Around a slight bend, the shore came into view. Javik beached the boat and helped Allana to shore before planting the anchor firmly in the sand.

Allana looked around in awe. The cliffs rose fifty meters above them on all sides stark and devoid of vegetation. A few sea birds wheeled above them, and their cries echoed down the walls of the inlet. The white sand rose gently toward the place where the cliffs came together. The only other sound was the water lapping gently on the shore. The smell of the sea was strong here, and she noticed several starfish and broken shells littering the beach.

Javik pulled the hamper from the boat and marched back a bit from the water. He sat the hamper down and produced a blanket from its interior. Spreading the blanket on the sand, he motioned for Allana to join him.

They sat down with the hamper between them, and Javik produced the lunch. They ate heartily and washed the food down with a good wine. Allana lay back on the blanket and stared at the small patch of blue sky high over their heads.

"We are the only two people in the world here, Javik."

Javik leaned over and kissed her. "This will be our own paradise forever. You will command that no other person set foot here on pain of death."

Allana smiled up at him and placed a hand on his cheek. "Thank you, Javik. Thank you for finding me that day in the forest. Thank you for rescuing me from the Turrek. I owe you so very much."

"I know how you can repay me," Javik said as he bent to kiss her again.

* * * * *

They made love on the beach and swam in the little cove afterwards. As they dried off, they drank more wine and finished the cold meat and bread. They dressed, and Javik loaded the hamper in the boat. He was about to push off when Allana spoke.

"Let's explore our paradise. I think there's a cave back there." She pointed to a spot where the cliffs came together and a darker area Javik hadn't noticed before. The sun was directly over their heads now, and the new angle cast an unfamiliar shadow. They walked back to the area and found an opening just large enough to squeeze through sideways.

"It's not dark inside," Javik said. "It isn't a cave. I can see light only a few meters away."

"Let's explore it," Allana urged with an air of excitement in her voice.

"Let me go first. I'll let you know if you should follow."

Javik edged through the opening and found the passage opened up considerably on the other side.

"It's much wider in here," he called back. "I can walk toward the other opening easily. Let me see what's there before you come in."

He made his way to the light and found the passageway opened onto a small canyon. The floor of the canyon was littered with large boulders. There was no sign of any life, not even moss or lichens. It was as if the boulders had just fallen from the cliffs on either side. He was about to go back when Allana appeared beside him.

"Not much here, is there?" she said.

"What were you expecting?"

"Something mysterious - a magic land hidden from the eyes of man or an ancient temple containing vast treasures."

"You're much too romantic. There's nothing here but rocks."

"Look, Javik!" Allana pointed to a space between two of the boulders.

Javik followed her finger to what appeared to be a bone wedged between the rocks. He climbed to get a better look and found the remains of a human skeleton.

"It's a skeleton," Javik called back to Allana. He must have fallen into this canyon from above." He looked up at the top of the cliffs expecting to see people leaning over the edge, but it was vacant.

A glint of gold caused Javik to give the bones closer inspection. A large ring with an even larger red stone clung to the dead finger of the unfortunate soul. Javik reached into the crevice and pulled the ring from the bony finger. He inspected it carefully.

"No clue as to who it might be except for this ring." He passed the ring to Allana who also inspected it thoroughly.

"I've never seen a ring like this before. Look at the curious inscription inside the band." She held it up for Javik to read.

"I don't recognize the writing. We'll take it back and see if Avra can decipher it. We'd better get back before you have a revolt on your hands." Javik slipped the ring on one of his fingers.

Allana laughed as she worked her way back through the passage and up to the boat. Javik launched the craft and paddled out to the sea before raising the sail and tacking back to the harbor and home.

Chapter 18

As Javik beached the boat, the sound of an explosion caused him to look up at the house higher on the hill Noka and Avra were using as a laboratory. A rising cloud of gray smoke told him they were now successful at extracting saltpeter from the bird droppings.

"What was that?" Allana asked.

"I think we have a process for making the powder now. Let's go see."

He led Allana up to the house and around to the back where a joyful Noka was patting Avra on the back quite heavily.

"You've done it, Avra! You've done it!" Noka shouted.

"All the island knows about it," Javik said as they approached the happy pair.

Noka turned and stared at Javik and Allana.

"What have you two been doing dressed up as peasants?" Noka asked.

"We've taken a small vacation from our duties," Allana answered. "I see your work has finally paid off."

"Yes, Lady," Avra said as he extracted himself from Noka's congratulatory embrace. "We can now begin to produce your magic powder, Javik."

"Good, but we need to start making hand cannon to use it," Javik said.

"I've already spoken with a recent arrival named Votter," Noka said. "He's an expert blacksmith. You know him, Javik. You sent him to me."

"Yes, I remember. He said he was an expert at both forging and casting. I thought he might be the person we needed for the hand cannons."

"He's building his shop now at the site of the old ram foundry. He can't wait to get started on the weapons," Noka said.

"We need to discuss sales of the hand cannons more before we do anything," Allana said.

"Why? I thought we were going to use that as our main source of income," Javik said.

"I know, but I've been having second thoughts about that lately. Perhaps we should keep the weapons to ourselves? It is our only advantage against powerful neighbors or seafaring marauders."

"I will assemble the council after dinner," Javik said. "We need to make a decision on this matter as soon as possible if we are to meet our tribute obligation to Charlan."

Allana and Javik arrived back at the palace and changed into more suitable clothes. They were barely dressed when Barinosh rushed in.

"Lady, the pearl boat is back, and their catch is larger than anyone could expect. I just came from the docks, and I can tell you the quality of the pearls is the finest I have ever seen."

"What wonderful news," Allana said. "Will their sale pay our tribute?"

"Yes, easily, but we must not sell them all at once. We must keep the price as high as possible if we want to realize our full gain.   Dumping this lot on the market too soon would drive down the price drastically."

"How long will it take?"

Barinosh stood for a moment doing mental calculations before answering.

"I'd say a year, or more, if we want the best prices."

Allana's face fell, and she exhaled sharply.

"I was hoping the pearls would be our salvation. Everything else seems to be taking so long."

"We can discuss all of this at the council meeting this evening," Javik said. "You've brought good news, Barinosh, even if it wasn't quite as good as Allana expected."

The governing council of Gorgos consisted of Allana, as governor, Javik, as her chief advisor, Barinosh, as her trade and immigration counselor, Sigurd, in charge of the watch and military preparations, Karl, in charge of agriculture, Artun, minister of mines, Noka, minister of armaments and supply, Avra, who served triple duty as healer, chief scientist and finance minister, Bogard the jailer and Margan, who provided a means of easing tensions whenever they arose. The news of the pearl boat was welcome to everyone, but when Barinosh explained the need to hold back the sales, spirits dropped somewhat.

"Well, it looks like my gold mine had better start producing as quickly as possible," Artun said.

"Didn't you find a way to make the powder?" Karl asked Noka.

"We did, but it will be a few months before we can begin large scale production," Noka answered. "Besides, Allana is having second thoughts about selling hand cannons."

"What?" Sigurd turned his attention away from the excellent wine in his goblet.

"Yes, Sigurd. I think we must keep the weapons for our exclusive use. It's the only advantage we have until our fortifications are completed."

"True, Lady, but if we do not have the money for Charlan's tribute, will it make any difference?" Barinosh said.

"We must find another way to earn the tribute. I wouldn't feel comfortable with our weapons in the hands of other forces who may turn hostile at any time," Allana answered.

"My people have given you all the money we dare," Avra said. "If Oliga begins his persecution, they will need their funds when they're forced to leave Tulla."

"They would always be welcome here," Allana said.

"Lady, Gorgos would be an excellent home, but it would still be part of Tulla and subject to Oliga's rule. If he pursued us here, how could you protect us?" Avra asked.

"We'd need a fleet for that," Barinosh said.

"Didn't Gorgos once build the best warships on the ocean?" Sigurd asked.

"Yes, but the shipyards are in ruins and the builders either murdered or scattered to the four winds," Barinosh answered.

"More people arrive every day," Javik said. "Perhaps some of the shipbuilders will return? Ships manned with sailors using hand cannons would be formidable indeed."

"Aye, they would, but it would be better if the hand cannons could sink ships. I fear ships using the sticking fire thrown from their catapults would destroy ours before they could bring the enemy in range of the hand cannons," Barinosh said.

"That's easy. We'll just build a huge hand cannon and

mount it on our ships," Sigurd jested.

"Not a bad idea," Noka mused. "Avra, do you think we could forge a large enough barrel to do that?"

"Hmm, I doubt if forging anything that large is practical, but it could be cast," Avra responded.

"The ram foundry!" Bogard shouted.

"Yes," Barinosh said. "We used to cast large pieces of bronze for our ship's ramming heads. We should be able to make large hand cannon."

"Bronze may not be strong enough," Avra said. "Your hand cannon are forged steel."

"We could give it a try," Noka said.

"With such ships we would be the terror of the seas," Sigurd mused. "We could raid freely and bring back enough booty to pay your tribute several times over."

"Become pirates?" Barinosh protested. "I won't have any part of piracy."

"I think it would be great sport," Karl said. "We used to raid for gold and horses back in Berglaundia. I suppose that was a form of land piracy."

"A very honorable way to live," Sigurd said as he raised his nose in the air a bit.

"You land people don't understand anything about piracy. First of all, piracy takes place on the sea. When you raided on land, the people you attacked didn't drown because of your raid. Second, pirates are hunted down by every seafaring nation. They would soon discover the source of our piracy and attack here to wipe it out. We wouldn't last long as pirates. Even Charlan would be against us."

"Not if we were his pirates," Javik mused.

"Tell me, Barinosh, are Charlan's ships ever attacked by pirates?" Javik asked.

"Quite often. The pirates know his ships carry the finest cargoes, and his battle fleet can't escort all of his merchantmen."

"Then, we could provide a means of eliminating the pirates," Javik said.

"How would that work?" Noka asked.

"We could track the pirates to their lairs and attack them there. We eliminate the pirates, gain Charlan's gratitude and reap the reward of claiming the pirate's ill-gotten gain for ourselves."

Barinosh laughed. "A good plan, Javik, except for the fact that these pirates often enjoy the protection of powerful lords. Their homeports would be heavily fortified, and their lords would sorely miss the tribute. You'd have to face their navies as well as the pirate ships."

"But, if ships armed with large hand cannon would be as formidable as you seem to think, we'd have little to fear," Javik countered.

"True, true," Barinosh said as he resumed a thoughtful pose.

"I like the idea," Allana said. "Noka, work with Artun and Barinosh on the design of a hand cannon large enough to sink a ship. Barinosh, find a suitable warship and purchase it. We will test our theory."

"What shall I use for money, Lady?" Barinosh asked.

"Sell enough pearls to fund the effort, even if we don't get the best price. I think we've found the answer to our prayers. Charlan will demand the lion's share of what we get from the pirates, but there may be enough left to help our cause considerably."

* * * * *

Artun's mines were producing copper and tin for export now, but the gold mine was only yielding meager amounts of the precious metal. Votter managed to get the foundry back into operation using the kaol from another of the mines. Noka and Avra were into quantity production of powder, and the design for a ship's cannon was complete. Barinosh found an older warship from Charlan's fleet and was able to purchase it for a reasonable price.

At last, the prototype cannon was ready for testing, and the council watched from a nearby hill as Noka loaded the shining new weapon. The long, ornate tube of bronze sat on a heavy wooden frame. It pointed out to sea from just behind the cliffs on the west side of the island. Avra weighed out the powder charge, and a servant poured it into the barrel using a scoop on the end of pole. Next, the servant tamped a wad of excelsior over the powder following that with an iron ball slightly smaller than the tube's bore. Noka and Avra argued long and hard over the fit of the ball in the barrel. Avra felt it should fit snugly, but Noka insisted the ball be smaller allowing some of the gases to pass around it and relieve the pressure on the tube.

Avra and the servant ran for the cover of a low stone wall as Noka lit a match on the end of a long pole. Laying flat on the ground for maximum protection in case of a disaster, Noka touched the match to a hole at the end of the barrel.

The noise was deafening. Hundreds of sea birds rose from the cliff face and began to wheel above the surf loudly protesting the disturbance. A cloud of gray smoke billowed from the mouth of the cannon and drifted back toward a cowering Noka. Avra and the servant slowly rose from their hiding place. It was a moment before the cannoneers noticed the wild cheering from the observers on the hill. Javik was pointing frantically out to sea as he ran toward Noka.

"Did you see it, Noka?" Javik shouted.

"Javik, I was too busy praying for my life to see anything. What happened?"

"The ball traveled half way to Harrish. See that fishing boat?"

Noka looked out to sea at a small boat nearly half a league away. "You mean that one with the blue sail?"

"Yes, that one. You nearly sank it," Javik said as he laughed and enfolded his comrade in a bear hug.

Sigurd joined the frenzied celebration. "Noka, with this weapon, Gorgos will rule the sea."

"If it doesn't sink the ship it's mounted on. Look at this," Barinosh said pointing to two ruts in the turf.

"What caused those?" Allana asked as she came up.

Avra studied the marks. "The cannon moved in reaction to the explosion, Lady." He measured the distance using his feet. "A good meter, I calculate."

Noka was busy inspecting the cannon. He tested the heat from the barrel and found it cooled off more quickly than the tubes on the hand cannons. Using a small mirror, he reflected sunlight down the barrel and found a whitish coating from the powder. Noka rubbed his finger on the coating and sniffed the residue.

"How does it look?" Javik asked.

"Seems to be in good shape. No cracks I can see, and the barrel cools down quickly. I don't know about this residue. It might corrode the bronze if we don't clean it out. I'll have to make some kind of swab to do that. I think it's safe to try a few more shots. This time I should aim at something."

Noka looked around for a suitable target and spotted an old stone barn several hundred meters away toward the mountains.

"We can use that old barn," Noka said. He turned to a servant. "Make sure no one is living there and keep anyone well back from it. Take as many men as you need."

The servant gathered several of his companions and headed for the barn. After a careful search, he signaled Noka the target was ready.

It took all the men present to turn the cannon toward the new target, but it was soon lined up to Noka's satisfaction. The council stood by waiting for the shot, but Noka insisted they move away in case the weapon broke up.

Once more, the match with the long pole was used, but Noka stayed upright to see the results of his shot firsthand.

The iron ball flew through the air and tore a gaping hole in one side of the barn.

"By the gods, that would sink any ship I know of," Barinosh said with a note of awe in his voice.

"Good aim," Sigurd congratulated Noka.

"It's easy here on land. I don't know about firing from the pitching deck of a ship," Noka said.

"You'd soon get the hang of it," Karl said.

"I think you'd have to be very accurate to save the cost of the iron balls," Artun added.

"They're not cheap," Avra said, "and there's no hope of using them more than once at sea."

One of the servants approached carrying a misshapen lump of iron.

"This is the ball, master. It was inside the barn."

Noka inspected the mass of metal. "I doubt that this would happen with ships. The stones of the barn are much harder than wood."

"It might go all the way through the hull," Barinosh added.

Allana pointed to the new set of ruts from the latest shot.

"You'll have to find some way of controlling the movement to keep the thing from blowing itself overboard," she said.

Avra stroked his beard as he surveyed the latest marks. "Yes, we must do some work on a proper mounting for the weapon aboard a ship, but I think we can do it. Possibly if we used wheels?"

The cannon withstood several more shots with no ill effects, but the barn was reduced to rubble. The group moved off to other duties while Noka, Avra and Barinosh discussed mounting the new weapon on a ship.

Chapter 19

Thatos rose from its ashes and rubble in new glory every day. As the summer waned into fall, testing of the new warship proceeded at a rapid pace. The mount for the cannon proved to be a real challenge, but a new émigré from Philisia provided the best design. He was a stonemason and used to moving large blocks of stone out of quarries. The system of ropes and pulleys not only snubbed the reaction of the weapon quickly, it also allowed for the rapid movement of the cannon to another direction of fire. Noka devised a system for changing the elevation of the barrel using a wedge under the back end of the cannon. He also spent a great deal of time training prospective gunners and sorting out the best men for the crew.

Production of hand cannon also began in earnest. Sigurd trained the island's small army in their use and also conducted sessions for the sailors who would man the warship. Barinosh saw to the restoration of the ship, and when it was ready for its first voyage, he asked Allana to attend the departure ceremony.

Allana and her council assembled near the stern of the small warship, and they were surprised by a canvas panel covering the rear of the hull where the name should be. A large crowd assembled for the occasion, and Barinosh approached Allana to speak privately before mounting the small platform next to the stern.

"My Lady, it is customary to offer a sacrifice to the sea gods on the first voyage of any ship. Will you please break this jug of wine on the hull?"

"I'd be glad to, but don't you want me to make a speech?"

"I will speak first, then you will address the people once you know the name of the ship."

"Why so mysterious about its name?"

"You will know my reasons soon. It's time now."

Barinosh mounted the small platform and signaled for silence. The crowd noise fell to a whisper as he spoke.

"People of Gorgos. This ship represents the future of our island, and our governor, Princess Allana, has graciously consented to offer the traditional sacrifice of wine to insure its success. My lady, if you please."

Barinosh helped Allana to the platform as he took hold of a rope attached to the canvas.

Allana raised the jug of wine and spoke.

"My people, may the sea gods always smile on our ship, the..." She turned to Barinosh and whispered. "What is its name?"

Barinosh pulled the rope, and the canvas fell away. He shouted as the name was revealed, "I give you 'The Queen of Gorgos'!"

Allana's jaw dropped for a moment, but she recovered quickly. She was about to speak again when a shout rose from the assembled mob.

"Hail Allana, Queen of Gorgos! Hail Allana! Hail Allana!" It seemed the shouts would never stop. Allana gave Barinosh a dirty look and smashed the jug against the hull. Red wine and shards of the jug flew everywhere spattering both Barinosh and Allana with crimson dots.

"I'll have you flogged for this, Barinosh." Allana spoke in a harsh tone but pulled the old sailor into an embrace as she spoke. The people were still shouting, and Allana turned to them raising her arms for silence. Slowly, the cries died away.

"My people, you have been very patient these past months. I promise you that whatever treasure this ship brings home to Gorgos will first go to paying any person owed wages from my treasury. You all know of the tribute demanded by Count Charlan. If the sea god is kind, we will pay the tribute and know prosperity again very soon. Thank you for your loyalty."

A great cheer rose from the crowd as Allana stepped from the platform. Javik was there to meet her.

"An excellent speech, Princess. You almost make me want to be one of your subjects."

"You are my subject in many ways." Allana gave him a knowing smile and took his arm to make her way through the adoring throng.

The next day, Barinosh set sail with Noka aboard as master gunner. As they cleared the breakwater, Noka noticed the harbor fortifications rising on either side.

"Sigurd is doing a good job with the defenses of Thatos," he said.

"Yes, he seems to have a good understanding of the power these things wield." Barinosh patted the cannon.

"Are you sure naming this ship 'The Queen of Gorgos' was a good idea?" Noka asked.

"Why not?"

"Anyone wanting to find her will know where to look."

"They'd find us in any case. I place great confidence in our new weapon's ability to deter pursuit."

"We will soon find out. Where are we going?" Noka asked.

"I know of a den of pirates some two day's sailing north of here. They use some deserted islands for refuge and prey upon any ship venturing within sight. We will disguise ourselves as a merchantman and draw them into a fight. I think we'll be able to give them a nasty surprise."

"How many are they?"

"Two ships, and they attack as a team. We'll have to be on our toes to defeat them, but I think our men are ready."

"Let's hope so," Noka said as the ship began to pitch in greater amplitude now that it was encountering the open sea.

Barinosh placed great confidence in his ship. It was only thirty meters from bow to stern, and less than ten meters wide, but it was of sturdy construction with a deep keel. The single mast held a square sail for use in running before the wind. A bank of twenty oars on either side provided propulsion at other times. At present, the wind was favorable, and they moved under sail. At the bow, a large bronze ram rode just beneath the water line. The large dragonhead that usually graced the prow of Tullan warships had been removed to allow the cannon a full circle of fire. In the stern, a small cabin rose above the deck. The roof of the cabin was modified to serve as a fighting deck for sailors with hand cannon, but the rudder bar took up the center part of the deck. Two strong men were needed to manage steering the ship.

The old sailor looked up at the sail billowing in the wind. The crest of the royal house of Gorgos graced the huge canvas, two snakes, each consuming the other in a circle around a black field with a golden conch shell in the middle. He'd served that house well in the past. He prayed he could serve it as well now.

The first day out, the crew practiced gunnery until they could load and aim the weapon easily and fire it four times in the space of one cycle of the sandglass Noka held for timing purposes. He pronounced his satisfaction with their efforts, and the crew stacked bales of rags around the cannon to hide it from the pirates.

On the second day, the pirate islands came into view. The ship was being rowed now, but the second shift crew of rowers was called up to man the battle stations. They stayed low on the high rear deck to avoid detection. Some crewmen stood ready to climb the rigging and fight from a platform near the top of the mast. Half the men were armed with hand cannon, and half carried crossbows. As they passed the first island, two ships appeared behind them.

"They're after us, Barinosh," Noka said.

"A merchantman would try to outrun them, but their ships are too fast. They know they can overtake almost any other ship in these waters, so they'll be overly confident. We'll act like we're running, then turn and attack them as soon as they're in cannon range. Tell me when to give the command," Barinosh said.

Noka judged the distance between his ship and the pirates and waited as the gap closed. When he felt the maneuver would bring them in range, he called to Barinosh.

"Turn now, Barinosh. Gun crew, to the cannon," Noka shouted.

As the ship turned, the crew moved the bales away from the cannon and loaded for the first shot. Noka watched the pirate ships as the gun swung toward them.

"Steady men, we'll fire when the anchor head crosses the first ship's bow. That should give us enough lead. Hold it, hold it. Fire!"

The roar of the cannon seemed to make time stand still. Noka watched as the smoke cleared and the ball arced through the air directly at the first ship's bow. The crew pulled the cannon back into firing position and reloaded automatically. The ball crashed into the bow of the pirate ship blowing away its prow.

"Good shot! We'll take the second ship at the waterline as we pass her," Noka shouted as he lowered the barrel to the correct elevation and the crew swung the cannon into line. Crackling fire from the hand cannons punctuated the air as the ships passed. Noka could see men falling on the decks of the pirate ships, but concentrated on his aim as the ship rolled up bringing the cannon to bear. The range was very short, and he touched the gun off just as the barrel reached the other ship's waterline. When the smoke cleared, the men cheered to see water pouring into the pirate ship.

Arrows and crossbow bolts from the first pirate ship were now raining down on The Queen of Gorgos as Barinosh turned to bring the cannon to bear on it again. The speed of the pirate ship as considerably slower now due to the damage to its bow, and he easily overtook it. The gun crew swung the cannon to the other side and reloaded. Noka fired at the waterline, but misjudged the roll. The ball tore through the pirate's oarsmen leaving a haze of blood.

Noka's crew reloaded as the ship turned again to attack the second pirate.

"She's sinking, Barinosh. We don't need to waste powder on her," Noka shouted.

"Aye, we'll go back to the first one."

By this time, the first ship was making all the speed it could muster back toward its homeport. Barinosh fell in behind it and the oarsmen kept pace allowing Noka optimum range. Several more balls tore through the pirate ship's hull before the oars stopped and a white flag appeared at the stern of the cripple. Barinosh pulled alongside and hailed the pirate captain.

"Throw your weapons on the deck where I can see them and have your men come out on deck."

A heavily accented voice replied. "Who are you, and what manner of magic do you possess?"

"We are from Gorgos in Ollon, and we have great magic. If you try to trick us, we'll blow you out of the water and leave you for the sharks."

"Allow me to pick up the men from my other ship. I give you my word we will not trick you."

"Do you trust the word of a pirate?" Noka asked Barinosh.

"Not one bit, but I have no desire to see even a pirate as food for the fish," Barinosh replied.

"You may pick up your men in the water, Captain, but we will be watching. Any false move, and we will sink you at once."

The crew watched as the pirate captain plucked several men from the sea. The survivors were not as numerous as Barinosh expected, and many were badly wounded. The deck of the pirate ship ran red with blood after the men were aboard.

"Row back to your home port," Barinosh ordered. "We will follow."

"Aye, captain," the pirate acknowledged.

The ships rounded a headland on the second island, and a small village appeared at the end of a shallow cove. The pirate ran his ship up on the beach, and Noka saw the extensive damage to the bow more clearly. He wondered how the ship managed to stay afloat, let alone make headway.

Barinosh anchored his ship a bit offshore but advised Noka to keep the cannon trained on the largest house. Women and children ran down to meet the men and began a wailing chorus of grief upon seeing the carnage. He called to the pirate captain.

"We will come ashore. Line all your able bodied men up on the beach. You may take the wounded for treatment. Any trouble, and we'll blast the village to ruins."

"We understand. We will wait for you," the pirate answered as his men formed a line on the beach.

The Gorgons now outnumbered the pirates, but Barinosh worried that even more of their kind lurked inside the houses waiting to attack. Two boats lowered from the Gorgon ship filled with sailors armed with hand cannons. Barinosh stood in the bow of the lead boat. After discharging their cargo, the boats returned for another load. Barinosh walked up to the pirate captain.

"I am Admiral Barinosh of Gorgos," he introduced himself.

"I am Captain Laval of these islands with no name," the pirate answered. "You had the right to defend yourself, but please know that we sail under letter of marque from the King of Karran. Any mistreatment of my men or this village would be ill advised."

"We mean you and your people no harm as long as you pay a tribute to Princess Allana of Gorgos for attacking one of her ships."

"Gorgos is part of Ollom, and there is no such person. The royal house of Gorgos was wiped out years ago," the pirate replied.

Barinosh bared his arm to show the tattoo. "Do you recognize this? My Princess bears the royal mark on her rump, and I wouldn't want her to be against me. You've seen the power of this ship. Soon she will have many more like it.

Laval seemed to sag a bit at Barinosh's remarks. "What are your demands?"

"We ask 10,000 gold crowns. Deliver that sum, and we will leave in peace."

"A princely sum, Captain. We don't have that kind of wealth."

"You may bring it to me, or my men will search every house and building for whatever gold or valuable we can find. I might add that they aren't very particular about how they leave a place after they search it. They're also very careless. A candle or a lamp might be knocked over by accident."

"You drive a hard bargain, Captain. I can give you only 1,000 gold crowns, but we recently took a merchantman loaded with spices. You may have her cargo for the rest. My treasurer valued it at over 10,000 gold crowns."

"Fair enough. Have your men bring the gold and the spices to the beach. We will load our ship and be gone on the tide. By the way, we'll hold ten of your men here on the beach as guarantee of your honesty. Any trickery, and they will die instantly."

"I understand," the pirate said as he bowed to Barinosh.

In short order, the chests of gold and the bales of spices were stacked on the beach. Barinosh's men ferried the cargo to their ship as the gun crew stood a silent watch aboard and men with hand cannon stood facing the hostage pirates. When the last bale was loaded, Barinosh approached the pirate captain.

"I thank you, sir, for your honesty in dealing with me. You have kept your word, and I will keep mine." He bowed to the pirate as he signaled his men to retreat. They boarded their boats and rowed back to the ship as the pirates watched from the shore. Noka put a last shot over their heads as they sailed away.

Chapter 20

Javik was busy supervising the process of screening immigrants when Avra approached.

"May I have a word with you, Javik?" Avra asked.

"Certainly." He turned to his aide. "Keep going, you know what we're looking for."

"Yes, Lord Javik," the man replied.

Avra led Javik outside the house the island used as a temporary holding area for immigrants and down to the docks.

"I need your advice on a matter before I take it up with Princess Allana," the Argani said.

"Go ahead," Javik assured him.

"Several of my countrymen are afraid Oliga will soon begin persecuting us. It's happened before in other countries. Some of them have been forced to move several times during their lives, and they're weary of it. They plan on moving to Gorgos if Oliga starts anything. They know it's part of Ollon, but they trust Princess Allana. They've heard she's a fair woman and welcomes all who will help her rebuild the island. She's said she would welcome my people. Is she sincere about that?"

"I know she is, but we're in no position to oppose Oliga at this time. Perhaps in a few more months when we have more cannon and the fortifications are complete, but not now. He would have an easy time of it if he wanted to invade Gorgos and enforce his edicts."

Avra thought for a moment before continuing.

"You're right, Lord Javik. We can only pray that Oliga will delay his actions long enough.   Still, you give me some encouragement to speak with our Princess. Thank you."

Javik suddenly remembered the ring and stopped Avra from leaving.

"I've been meaning to talk to you about this ring, Avra." He removed the ring from his finger and passed it to the Argani. "It has an inscription on the inside in a strange language. I thought you might know something about it."

Avra held the ring up to the sunlight and turned it slowly as he read the inscription.

"It is an inscription in our ancient language. This ring belongs to Moshish, the smuggler. Where did you get it?"

"I found it on a skeleton."

"Where is this skeleton," Avra asked with the note of urgency in his voice building.

"Behind a cove on the East side of the island. It looked like he'd fallen from the cliff above a narrow canyon. Why?"

"Moshish was a famous smuggler who used Grogos as a refuge. Our Princess's father gave him sanctuary in return for the payment of a large sum in tribute. He vanished years before the island fell to the Voldunee, and people have been looking for his secret cave ever since then. It is said he stored untold riches in that cave, but its location is still a mystery."

"If we have his body, we may have the solution to that mystery," Javik said.

"The ring could have been on anyone's finger. Who knows what villain might have slain Moshish and taken it from his dead hand, but it would be worth looking into. Could you take me to this cove?"

"Yes, but only small boats can enter. The passage is very narrow."

"Describe the canyon to me."

"It's very narrow, only about ten meters wide, and the walls are quite steep. The floor is littered with large boulders, and the walls rise nearly fifty meters above the floor. I saw no life there at all."

"Hmmm, we'll need climbers we can trust and equipment for scaling the cliff walls."

"Bogard is a good climber, and I've had a little experience," Javik said.

"Good, I'm afraid I'm too old for that sort of thing. When could we go?"

"I'll speak with Bogard tonight. We should be able to sail in the morning."

"I'll find you after breakfast, and I'll be ready to sail."

"Until then." Javik returned to his work, and Avra walked away wringing his hands in the manner he always did when money was a good prospect.

* * * * *

Bogard agreed to the adventure, and the two were ready when Avra appeared at the palace. They used the same sailboat Javik and Allana employed for their picnic, and it wasn't long before they beached the craft on the soft sand of the hidden cove.

"Through that small cave, over there," Javik pointed out the opening.

The men squeezed through and entered the little canyon.

Javik led them to the skeleton.

Avra inspected the remains of the mysterious man.

"This is Moshish. I recognize the skull."

"How can you tell one skull from another," Bogard said as he laughed at the idea.

"Notice this small hole." Avra pointed to a round opening in the skull about ten millimeters in diameter and perfectly round. "I once treated him for a particularly evil spirit possessing his mind. I drilled this hole to let it out."

Javik winced a bit at the thought of someone drilling a hole in his head, but Bogard seemed to take it in stride.

"I've heard of such things, but I never knew anyone who survived such an operation," Bogard said.

"You have to be very careful and know which potions to use on the wound. Otherwise, the demons enter again, and your work is for naught. This is Moshish, I'd swear to it. I'll wager his secret cave is nearby."

Bogard looked up at the cliff face on both sides.

"I don't see any caves from here, but the sun angle isn't good. I think if we climbed to the top, we might have a better chance of spotting something."

"I agree. Let's climb," Javik said.

The two men roped themselves together and began the climb. Bogard secured metal rings in the chinks of rock as they climbed and tied off their rope at each one. They were nearly two thirds of the way up when Bogard called back to Javik.

"I've found an old climbing ring here. Someone's been here before us."

"They've probably looted the treasure too," Javik replied. "We might as well go on, though. We're almost there."

The men reached the top of the canyon wall and climbed out on a short expanse of scrub and mossy ground between the next mountain and the canyon. Bogard turned to look back at the gorge.

"Look at this, Javik." Bogard pointed to the rim of the canyon. "The wall here appears to have fallen away some time back. Notice how it curves in for several meters."

"I see it." Javik looked over the rim to see Avra standing directly below them. "This slide probably killed Moshish. His skeleton is directly below us."

"Then his cave must be up here somewhere," Bogard said as he began to explore the area. "I'll go right, and you go left."

Javik moved off to the left searching for any clue to the cave's location. It wasn't long before he heard Bogard's call.

"Javik, I think I've found it. Come here."

Bogard stood before a large flat stone propped up against the side of the mountain. He pointed to a rut in the ground now overgrown with lichen.

"See, this stone has been moved many times, but not recently. I think the cave is behind this stone."

Javik inspected the rock. "It's a different kind of rock than the rest of the mountain." He looked around. "It came from that cliff, over there." Javik pointed to the location.

"Do you think we can move it?" Bogard asked.

"Let's give it a try."

The two men pushed with all of their might but couldn't budge the huge stone.

"If we had a lever, we might be able to do it," Bogard said.

Javik thought for a moment, and then responded.

"The boom from our boat should do it. I'll go get it." Javik rappelled down the canyon wall and worked his way back to the boat after asking Avra to help him. The two men carried the boom back through the cave and set it at the foot of the canyon wall. Bogard dropped a rope, and Javik tied the boom in place ready to hoist it up.

"I'll come up and give you a hand," Javik shouted to Bogard and began to climb to the top once more.

Using the boom for a lever, the stone moved easily. Javik looked inside.

"I can't see anything from here. We'll need torches if we go in."

Bogard called down to Avra. "There are torches in the boat, Avra. Bring them here, and I'll lower a rope."

Avra waved his arm to indicate his understanding and vanished into the cave. He returned carrying two torches and tied them to Bogard's rope.

With light available, Javik and Bogard entered the cave. It was not large, but the men could stand up easily. Just inside the entrance they found timbers and a windlass.

"I was wondering how a smuggler would get his booty from the canyon floor to this cave, now I know," Bogard said as he examined the items.

"The timbers must fit into the rocks somewhere, but I didn't see any place they could," Javik said.

"Probably well hidden. We'll look for them later." Bogard walked back into the darkness with Javik close behind.

A low moaning noise told them air was moving somewhere deeper in the bowels of the cave. There were no stalactites or stalagmites, and it was very dry and dusty. Their feet scuffed up small clouds as they walked. Javik noticed footprints in the dust ahead of them.

"Look, the footprints of the last visitors are still here," Javik said.

"Hmmm, a small man from the size of the prints." Bogard measured the print against his own foot, and it was almost two centimeters shorter than his boot.

"Perhaps these footprints will lead us to the treasure?" Javik said.

The men followed the footprints deeper into the cave. It branched several times, but the footprints told them which branch to follow. The last fork in the cave ended at a large, steel door with a heavy padlock.

"We won't get this open without some serious tools," Bogard said as he surveyed the hinges and the lock. "It's in remarkably good condition. I'd expect iron to be rusted if it's been here as long as Avra says it has."

"It's very dry in here, no water to rust it," Javik said. "Well, it must have a key, and if Moshish is laying on the canyon floor, it's probably near him somewhere. We need to look for it there. Besides, these torches are almost gone. We'll need some new ones."

The men climbed back down the canyon wall and began to search around the skeleton with no luck.

"It might have been covered with dirt by now," Avra offered as he knelt and began to dig around the bones. The other two joined in the digging, and Javik was the one to find the key.

"Here it is, along with some old coins and the remains of a dagger."

"His purse must have been jolted loose by the fall," Bogard said. "I'll get more torches, and we'll go back up."

"I wish I were younger," Avra moaned. "I'd love to be there when you open that door."

"Would you feel comfortable if we hoisted you up?" Bogard asked.

"I'm too heavy for you two," Avra protested.

"Nonsense, you can't weigh more than eight stone," Javik said. "We can lift you easily."

"I'm willing to try it," Avra said.

Bogard fashioned a harness from some rope and tied it on the Argani. The men climbed the canyon wall again then hauled up the torches. Javik lowered the rope back to Avra.

"Fasten this to the harness as we showed you. Let us know when you're ready."

Avra tested the knot several times before he signaled his readiness.

As Javik and Bogard lifted the little man off the ground, he let out a frightened moan.

"Be careful, young lords. Don't let me fall."

"Use your feet to push away from the wall," Bogard called down as they continued to hoist away.

Avra's eyes were wide as plates by the time he reached the top. Javik and Bogard helped him over the edge, and the little Argani sat for a moment composing himself.

"I hope what's in that cave is worth the ten years of my life I lost coming up here," Avra said as Javik unfastened his harness.

Once more, they stood before the iron door, but this time Javik turned the key in the lock. It opened grudgingly, and he stood back a bit before opening the door.

"Are we ready?" Javik asked.

"Just a moment!" Avra called moving Javik to one side. "Let

me look at this door a moment."

The little man inspected the iron and the stone around the door carefully then dropped to his knees and began to clear away the dust. He uncovered a large square stone exactly where Javik had been standing.

"As I feared. The door is a trap. Give me some rope, Bogard."

Avra tied the rope to the door's handle and led the men back around the last fork in the cave. He tugged on the rope, and they could hear the iron hinges protesting before a loud bang from the door hitting the cave wall.

Avra peered cautiously around the corner and signaled for the men to follow.

"Be careful not to step on that stone I uncovered. There was no trap on opening the door, so it must trigger whatever trap Moshish built here. Stay behind me."

Avra moved cautiously through the door checking the floor and walls carefully with each step. Several times he indicated stones in the floor to avoid. After only a few meters, it ended abruptly in a stone wall.

"What now?" Bogard asked.

"There is a trigger," Avra said. "We must find it."

The little man began another search as Javik inspected the wall.

"This wall has moved in the past. I can see the cracks, and notice how the torch flickers when I hold it close to this edge."

The other two watched as Javik moved the torch to the spot. The flame danced and was drawn to the crack between the walls.

Bogard put his ear to the wall. "I can hear the wind louder in there."

"I can't reach up there," Avra pointed to the ceiling. "Will one of you see if there's anything on that ledge."

Javik reached up to the ledge and was startled when a chain rattled down on him.

"It's a hoist," Bogard said as he pulled on the chain.

Slowly, the stone wall in front of them moved upward revealing a room filled with old chests, crates, bales and large pots of all sizes and shapes.

"This is Moshish's treasure," Avra gasped.

"What do I do with this door?" Bogard said. "If I let go, it will fall back down."

Avra searched the area near the opening and found two large pieces of wood. He handed one to Javik.

"There should be places in the wall where these can block it in its up position."

They found two neatly carved out square holes just large enough for the wood. Bogard lowered the wall on the stops carefully, but they seemed to hold it easily. He joined the other two in the room.

They began to open the containers. There were spices, cloth, leather, herbs, roots and various powders. Avra identified many items as powerful medicines or narcotics. Rare woods and a chest full of semi-precious stones came to light. It wasn't until they were well back into the room they found the gold. One chest was filled with gold crowns. Two men could hardly lift it. Two crates near it held gold bars, and behind that were three chests full of jewelry. Javik selected a particularly beautiful necklace and put it in his purse.

"This is for our Princess," Javik announced, and the other men nodded approval.

"There must be millions here," Bogard gasped.

"Enough to bring prosperity to Gorgos for a while," Javik added.

"Our Princess will be able to pay the tribute and satisfy all of her creditors from this treasure alone," Avra said.

"We'll need more men and more boats to haul this out of here," Bogard said.

"After I disarm Moshish's traps," Avra said.

The men laughed more out of relief than the humor in Avra's remark.

Chapter 21

The Queen of Gorgos returned with cargo and gold extracted from several pirate bands worth nearly fifty thousand gold crowns, and the treasure from the cave valued out at nearly 800,000. For the first time in a generation, Gorgos was prosperous again. Allana's council met to discuss good news for a change. Allana spoke first.

"My friends, we have the money we need to pay the tribute plus all of our debts and still leave a handsome treasury. What shall we do with it?"

"We should invest at least half of it with my people," Avra suggested. "The income from such a sum will produce over 30,000 gold crowns a year."

"A good suggestion," Allana agreed.

"We must build a fleet of warships to defend our island now that there is something here for the pirates to take," Barinosh offered.

"I agree," Sigurd said. "Our fortifications will not be finished until next spring, and the ships are our best means of defense until then."

"Nothing on the seas can stand against our cannon," Noka said. "No catapult has the range of our guns. With only one cannon, we were able to defeat the most dreaded pirate ships. I think if we add more guns to the ship we would be invincible."

"We'd need wood to build ships," Karl said. "Wood is expensive, and we grow very little here on Gorgos."

"We could buy ships and convert them here," Barinosh said.

"Which is more economical?" Allana asked.

"I'll look into it," Noka offered.

"Cannon production is doing well," Artun said. "All of the mines are producing to capacity, except for the gold mines. We still haven't found a good vein of gold in any of them."

"Will we need slaves soon for the mines?" Javik asked.

"Javik! I've told you before, will not have slaves on this island," Allana scolded.

"We must face facts, Allana," Javik said. "In only a few more months the immigrants will complete their one year obligations. We must either pay enough wages to induce men to the mines or bring in slaves."

"We will see what wages we can pay at that time, and how many men accept the work. I refuse to even consider slaves until there is no other alternative," Allana said.

Avra stepped in to smooth the waters. "We have some time to debate that point. Slaves are easily obtained given our power at sea. The fortifications are my major concern. How many cannon could we mount on the walls?" he asked Sigurd.

"As many as you like. My plans now call for thirty facing out to sea from the port of Thatos. There are only two other places on the island suitable for landing ships, and we must also fortify those spots, eventually. In the meantime, we could use ten or twelve cannon at each point in earthen revetments."

"That's several month's production, at our current rate," Noka said.

"Let's just hope our enemies will hold off that long,"

Barinosh said.

"Then more ships it will be, and the sooner the better," Allana said with an air of finality. "Barinosh, purchase three more ships and convert them for our defense. We'll wait for Noka's analysis before we go farther, but I think four ships should be adequate for now."

"I agree, Lady," Barinosh said.

"Javik, go to Charlan and arrange a state visit. I want to deliver the tribute to him as soon as possible."

"I'll arrange it," Javik said.

"Do we need to vote on investing half our treasury with the Argani?" Allana asked.

"We all agree on that," Bogard said, and the others nodded their approval.

"Then we are finished." Allana rose and men left to go about their duties. Javik stayed in the council room.

"Allana, now that we have some gold, I'd like to take some to my family."

"Certainly, Darling. How much would you like?"

"I think 1,000 crowns should be plenty. I'll set up your meeting with Charlan then leave for Berglaundia as soon as that's done. I should be back in less than two months."

"Who will take care of immigration while you're gone?"

"My choice would be Eric, the Zargaian. He's a good man, and knows what we want. I'd feel comfortable with him in charge."

"Then Eric it will be. I'll sign the order today." Allana thought for a moment. "Since you're going back to Berglaundia, you need to take some gold to Tao Shan and Grazhda."

"Gladly, how much should I take them?"

"I owe each of them 500 crowns, and I promised to pay that back with interest. I want you to take 1,000 to each of them."

"I think that should repay them adequately," Javik said with a hint of sarcasm in his voice.

"I would not be here without their help. I owe them much more than that." She bent to ruffle Mordah's fur and frowned. "Mordah doesn't seem himself lately. Is he ill?"

"I need to let him run more. He doesn't care much for city life. He'll get plenty of running time on the way back to Berglaundia, but I'll take him up to the high pastures and let him chase some goats. That seems to revive him," Javik said.

"That sounds like an excellent idea, but can he wait for an hour, or so?"

"I suppose so. What did you want me to do for you?" Javik asked.

"I also have need of some exercise right now." Allana led Javik to her private rooms and instructed the guard she was not to be disturbed.

* * * * *

Autumn in Gorgos was not the brilliant display Javik and his friends were used to back home. The island was far enough South that fall and winter were only minor variations of summer. The curtains in Allana's room billowed gently in the cool breeze from the sea. Javik watched as she shed her gown and beckoned him to the bed.

Javik fumbled a bit with his clothes, but soon joined her on the silken sheets. The smell of the salt air mingled with her perfume creating a golden fog inside his head. Her touch sent bolts of lightning through his body. The opiate of bliss overcame the cares of government as they fell into a world of love.

* * * * *

The next morning, Javik's personal servant, Farras, offered to accompany Javik on his journey.

"That's very good of you, Farras, but you have a wife and children here on Gorgos. Won't they need your attention?"

"Master, if you will pay me in advance, they will have all they need. We have other family here on Gorgos if they need more."

"Then you may go with me, and I'm glad for your company. Prepare three horses, one for each of us and one to carry the supplies. We'll take food for three day's travel. We can purchase more on the way. I'll need clothes and all of my weapons. You may select whatever weapon you wish for your own. We will leave as soon as all is ready. I plan to spend the night in Harrish, see Charlan in the morning and be off by noon."

"Very good, master. I will see to it." Farras bowed and left the room. Javik's next visitor was Avra.

"I've prepared a letter of credit for you." He handed Javik a roll of parchment. "I made it out for 3,500 crowns. You don't need to use all of it, but I thought some extra for an emergency wouldn't hurt."

"Thank you, Avra, but where could I convert this to gold in Berglaundia?"

"None of my people are in your homeland, I fear, but go to the house of Gallam in Ullum. He will give you gold."

"I know the House of Orgama there, and Varuda should know where to find him," Javik said.

"If he is not there, any Argani will honor this paper. I wish you a safe journey, Lord Javik."

Javik embraced Avra. "You've been such an asset to our island. Please just call me Javik. I can't get used to a title yet."

"As you wish, Javik, but addressing you by your name alone is very hard for me also."

"Then call me whatever you wish. I'll always know we are friends in any case."

Allana and the others gathered at the dock as Javik prepared to board the ferryboat to Harrish. Even Mordah seemed to sense the sadness of the occasion as he whimpered at his master's heels.

"Zhou be with you, Javik," Noka said as he embraced his old roommate.

Sigurd took Javik's hand in a farewell grip. "Be careful of the Turrek," he advised.

"I'll travel with a caravan to be sure," Javik assured him.

"Say hello to everyone for me," Karl said.

"I'll let your parents know you're a rich man now," Javik said, and the men laughed together as they embraced.

Bogard took Javik's hand in a firm grip. "Will you see that my parents know about me?"

"Gladly, but where's Artun?" Javik asked.

"He's busy at the mines today, but he told me to wish you good luck," Margan said as he took his turn embracing Javik.

"I'll miss your songs," Javik said.

"I'll make up some new ones after you return and tell me of all your adventures along the way," Margan said.

Allana was the last to say goodbye. Barinosh was at sea once more in search of ships suitable for conversion to cannon use. She presented Javik with a small case.

"I had this made for you when we first came to the island, but I've kept it until some suitable occasion. I think now is the right time."

Javik opened the case revealing a silver pendant of the Royal crest of Gorgos on a heavy silver chain.

"It's beautiful," he said as he slipped it over his head.

He took Allana in his arms and kissed her passionately to the applause of the other men.

"Come home safely to me," Allana whispered in his ear then leaned over and ruffled Mordah's fur behind his head. "Take care of him for me, Mordah."

The huge dog responded by shaking its fur back into place then licked Allana's hand as if in acknowledgement of his charge.

Javik boarded the ferry before tears could overwhelm his composure. He waved to all until they were mere specks on the dock.

The audience with Charlan was an easy matter, and Javik and Farras were on the road to Othis the next morning after sending a servant back to Gorgos with the information.

As the two rode with Mordah trotting along at the horses' side, Javik probed Farras.

"Why did you choose service, Farras?"

"I grew tired of the smell of fish, Lord."

"Surely you had a better life as a fisherman?"

"As a fisherman, I lived in a hut by the beach. As a servant, I live in a palace."

"True, but what about your self-image? Didn't you feel more like a man while you were a fisherman?"

"Lord, I feel more like a man right now than I ever have in my life. Look at me. I have a fine horse, good clothes, and a crossbow. I'm riding with a brave warrior into an adventure fraught with the possibilities of danger. What more could a man ask for?"

"He could be a warrior in his own right."

"True, perhaps I'll earn that position during our journey?"

"Serve me well, Farras, and I'll see that you are given warrior status someday."

That night they made camp, and after their meal, Farras dared ask his master a sensitive question.

"How long have you and Princess Allana been lovers?"

Javik laughed at the servant's bravery in asking. It amused him more than offending.

"To tell the truth, only since coming to Gorgos."

"But, the other servants say you've known her for years."

"About three years, to be exact, but we were apart for over half that time. I found her in the forest, would you believe?"

"No! Then what Margan sings is true. The servants all know the song of Allana and how she escaped her slavery and found you."

"Margan always sings the truth."

Farras stirred the fire and added another log.

"He sings of your father and his bravery."

Javik leaned back against his saddle and smiled as he gazed into the embers of the campfire.

"He was a fine man, Farras. I miss him."

"Would you like some wine, Master?"

"Yes, bring two cups and we'll share a flask."

Farras left the fireside and returned with a goatskin bag and two pewter cups. He poured two full measures of red wine and passed one cup to Javik.

"To Gorgos," Javik said as he raised his cup.

"To Gorgos," Farras replied.

The two men sipped their wine until the fire began to die and slipped off to sleep without need of blankets.

* * * * *

The next day they reached Othis and found a comfortable inn until a caravan formed to cross the land of the Turrek. That evening, Javik sat in the common room with Farras eating dinner when three men entered.

They were dressed in rough clothes and their beards and hair were unkempt. The swords at their sides were curved and ornately decorated as were the daggers stuck in the silken sashes around their waists. They smelled of long days on the trail.

Mordah was contentedly gnawing on a large shank of lamb, and the noise of his powerful jaws cracking the bone echoed from the rafters.

"Must I share my evening meal with a mongrel dog?" one of the new arrivals said to the landlord. He said it loud enough for Javik to hear clearly.

Javik did not respond, but Farras whispered to him. "Those men are Turrek bandits. Perhaps I should take Mordah outside?"

"No, Farras, it's too chilly outside. Mordah can stay here."

"But Master, there are three of them and only two of us."

"You forget Mordah. He evens out the odds considerably." Javik reached down and patted the gray wooly head busily cracking the bone.

The Turrek seethed over Javik's disregard and rose from his table. "I said, I want that dog outside."

"I heard you," Javik replied. My dog stays here with me. He'll be finished soon. Have some wine and wait if you don't like the noise. I'll buy." Javik signaled the landlord to bring more wine to the Turreks.

"I don't want wine, I want peace and quiet while I eat." The Turrek walked to Javik and stood over him. He noticed the crest on Farras's tunic and the pendant around Javik's neck.

"I see you serve the whore of Zargaia who claims to be a princess of Gorgos," the Turrek said, pointing to the crest on Farras' tunic.

"This man serves me, and Princess Allana is my beloved. She is a princess of the blood, and I will not have her called a whore."

The Turrek laughed heartily. "Did you hear him? He won't have her called a whore."

The other two joined in the laughter as the first man turned back to Javik.

"Know this, stranger. I am Tumak, king of the bandits, and I know all about this princess. She lay with Vargon to save her skin and would have been my wife but for the use of powerful magic by some of her pimps."

"She's told me of you, Tumak, and also of Vargon. If you really want to know, I am the one who rescued her from your filthy hands. You've seen my magic, and if you don't want to feel it now, sit down and eat your dinner."

"No one speaks to Tumak in that manner." The Turrek drew his sword and stepped back waiting for Javik to stand and defend himself.

Mordah dropped his bone and stood facing Tumak with barred teeth and a low growl rumbling from deep inside his chest. The fur on his back bristled.

Javik slowly rose from his seat and wiped his mouth on a napkin. "There is no need for this, Tumak. I don't want to kill you."

Farras placed his hand on his dagger ready to help his master should the other two Turrek intervene.

"Look to your own life, scum." Tumak lunged at Javik who sidestepped his thrust easily.

Javik drew his sword and faced Tumak as the common room occupants moved to a safer distance.

Once more, Tumak attacked, and Javik parried smartly reposting toward the Turrek's face. His sword cut a streak of red across the bandit's cheek, and Tumak parried strongly forcing Javik's sword away from its target. The men backed away from each other and circled warily.

"The first scratch is yours, pimp, but the last thrust will be mine. If I'm to kill you, I would know your name."

"I am Javik son of Tolda and son of Browdat, beloved of Princess Allana the true Queen of Gorgos."

"I'll put that on your tombstone, but I don't think King Oliga would be too pleased to hear the whore using that title. He thinks Gorgos belongs to him."

"Not for much longer," Javik said as he attacked fiercely driving Tumak back against a table. The bandit lost his footing and fell to the floor. Javik moved to finish him when he heard Farras shout.

"Look out, Master!"

Javik turned to see the other two bandits racing toward him.

A gray streak pounced on the first one knocking him to the ground. He screamed in agony as the animal tore at his throat. Farras jumped in front of the second bandit with his dagger, and the two fell to the floor battling for advantage. Tumak regained his feet and lunged at Javik.

Javik parried and let the bandit run past him turning to be ready when he recovered. The fire in Tumak's eyes told him the Turrek was beginning to succumb to his emotions. Javik knew his next attack would be more frenzied than the others. It would be his best chance to make the kill.

Tumak paused a moment. "You have some skill, pimp, but it's time to end this lesson."

Javik smiled as he saw the rage burning even more brightly in Tumak's eyes. The bandit's attack was clumsy and too brash. It was an easy matter to evade the point and strike at a vital spot on his chest. He felt his sword grate on ribs and watched as the expression on Tumak's face changed from one of rage to surprise. The sword fell from the bandit's hand as he gripped Javik's blade and pulled it from his chest. He staggered backwards falling down on a heavy wooden table. He pulled his hand away from the wound and inspected the blood.

"You've killed me, pimp. Now the Turrek will forever curse you. Your blood will be the only remedy for this act. Your blood and the blood of all those you call friend. My men will have sport with your whore while you watch."

Javik thrust his sword into Tumak's chest again, and this time, the words were choked off in a flow of blood from the bandit king's mouth as he fell to the floor.

Javik turned to see if Farras needed help and was pleased to see the servant wiping his dagger clean on the man's tunic.

"Are you hurt, Farras?" Javik asked.

"Only a scratch or two, Master."

Mordah was his next concern, but the huge dog was back to his bone, crunching away oblivious to the mangled mess that was once a Turrek bandit.

The landlord looked upon the carnage and began wringing his hands in fear.

"These were powerful men, Sir. I fear more will come to avenge them once they know of this matter."

Javik placed several gold coins in the man's hand. "See to their burial. I apologize for the disturbance to your guests."

"No need, Sir. It was a wonderful fight. I've never seen a dog kill a man before. He may have whatever he wants while you're with us."

Javik laughed at the landlord's fears and turned to his servant. "Farras, take their weapons and gold."

"Yes, Sir." Farras emptied the men's purses and took charge of their weapons.

The next day, a caravan arrived from Zargaia, and Javik made arrangements to travel back with them.

Chapter 22

The *Queen of Gorgos* tied up at the dock of Harrish and immediately drew a crowd for two reasons. First was the highly polished bronze cannon on the foredeck, but second, and not at all least, was Allana and her entourage filing down the gangway and out toward the palace.

A squad of six guards carrying hand cannon led the way. Six dancing girls cavorting in time to the music of four flutes, six tambourines and the songs of eight other women followed. Allana was next in a gold trimmed sedan chair carried by four brawny servants. Behind her three more servants carried chests of gold coins on their shoulders guarded by Artun and Barinosh. Bringing up the rear were six more guards with hand cannon.

Charlan watched the procession approach from a balcony outside his bedroom. Bradish stood beside him.

"Your new governor has a flair for the theatrical, I see," Bradish said as a smile spread across his otherwise stern face.

'Isn't she magnificent?" Charlan said unable to take his eyes off the sedan chair hoping for even the slightest glimpse of the beautiful lady.

"The people may come to believe she is the Queen of Gorgos if she keeps up with this type of thing. You know that's the name of their ship?"

"I know - our fleet has a **Queen of Ollon** though Brianna is only a countess. I see no harm in it."

"Perhaps not, but be careful with this woman. I fear she has great ambitions."

"Tonight I will see if those ambitions include testing my metal in the bedroom." Charlan nudged his chief advisor playfully and moved to meet Allana.

The bearers sat Allana's sedan chair down before Charlan's throne as the treasure bearers laid their chests before him and opened them to reveal the coins inside.

Allana stepped from her sedan chair aided by Artun and Barinosh and knelt before Charlan. She noticed Brianna's throne was vacant and reminded herself to be on guard.

"Welcome Princess Allana," Charlan said as he rose from his throne and lifted Allana to her feet.

"I bring your tribute, Sir. Our island has prospered far better than I ever hoped."

"Finding Moshish's treasure was a big help, I imagine," Charlan said as he lifted some coins from the first chest and inspected them. "These crowns bear my grandfather's likeness. They are old, indeed."

"I thought you might appreciate some of the older coins in the horde. Your tribute is paid mainly in these more valuable items."

"Very considerate of you. This is truly a happy occasion, and I've prepared a banquet for tonight to celebrate our success. I'm sure you wish to rest and refresh yourself until then. I've had rooms prepared for you and your servants." Charlan clapped his hands and several women appeared. "These ladies will show you the way. The festivities will begin at sundown."

"Will the Countess be joining us then?" Allana asked.

"No, the Countess is in Zargaia on family business and will not return for several weeks. I'm sorry she has to miss the festivities, but it can't be helped."

"Then until sundown." Allana bowed to Charlan and followed the servants to her quarters.

That evening the dinner was the usual lavish spectacular expected of Charlan. The entertainment included exotic dancers from lands far across the sea and a tumbling act that had everyone holding their breath watching its dangerous tricks. Allana was engrossed in the proceedings and did not notice Charlan slipping a bit of white powder into the wine served to Barinosh and Artun. They were both sleeping soundly in a few minutes.

"I fear your retainers are poor company," Charlan said pointing to the sleeping men.

"Your wine is powerful, My Lord. I'm beginning to feel it myself. Would you excuse us? We need to be back on Gorgos early tomorrow."

"Of course. My servants will see to your men. May I walk you back to your quarters?"

Allana knew what Charlan had in mind, but she felt confident in her ability to handle his advances.

"You may, Sir."

They walked back through the palace with two of Charlan's servants carrying torches to light the way. When they reached Allana's rooms, she was surprised to see Charlan's guards at the door.

"What happened to my guards?"

"I took the liberty of assigning my own guards to your door

so your people could share in our celebration. I hope you don't mind. I could have your men back in place, if you like."

Allana silently congratulated Charlan on his cleverness. Even if she asked for her own guards, she doubted they were in any condition to be effective. With Barinosh and Artun asleep, she was on her own.

"No, your men will do. Goodnight, My Lord." Allana bowed to Charlan who took her hand and lifted it to his lips.

"Allana, I would ask the favor of one last cup of wine with you before we part. Your balcony has a lovely view of the harbor, and there's a full moon tonight."

She smiled inwardly at the obvious excuse to enter her bedchamber, but she also felt it was time to dampen the Count's ardor for good and all.

"A lovely idea. Please come in."

The room was almost dark. Only a few candles burned giving the room a soft, gray tone. The large window leading to the balcony was open, and the silver disc of the moon hung above the harbor like a giant shield. A small table on the balcony held two silver cups and a glass pitcher of red wine. Charlan led her to the table and poured two cups of the liquid.

"This is beautiful," Allana said as she took the goblet. She sniffed the contents and noted nothing out of the ordinary, but she reminded herself not to drink any of it. She lifted the cup to her lips and pretended to drink. She noticed Charlan appeared to be doing the same.

"Not as beautiful as you, my Princess. You outshine the moon with your radiance, and your body draws me to you like a heavy tide draws a boat to shore. I fall at your feet a servant to your whims, a lackey to your desires. Use me as you will."

Charlan dropped to one knee and bowed his head in mock servitude.

Allana was delighted with the ploy. It had been a long time since any man said things like that to her, and she doubted she'd ever hear them from Javik. It was almost enough to tempt her into letting him have his way, but she kept her composure. The false protestations gave her a new idea for dealing with him.

"Do you truly mean that, Lord?"

"As truly as I breathe the air made sweet by your fragrance, as truly as my eyes reflect the grandeur of your beauty. Command me!"

Charlan walked toward her on his knees, and she thought he did it most gracefully. A quick inventory of the room told her she had everything she needed.

"My Lord, I fear you may not like my commands."

"The foulest command from you is like the sweetest pleasure from any other woman."

"Very well, would you strip naked for me now?"

"Gladly, Princess, gladly." Charlan lost no time removing his clothes. He stood naked before her in the moonlight with his manhood already aroused. He moved toward her, but she held him at arm's length.

"Not yet, Lord. First, we must tie you to the pillar, yonder." She pointed to a slender column on one side of the balcony.

Charlan looked at the pillar and back to Allana with an uncertain smile. "I usually tie up the Countess. Are you sure that's what you want?"

"Oh yes, Lord. There are things I must do to arouse my libido. Otherwise, I'm little better than a hole in the wall for my lovers."

"Very well, how do you want me?"

Allana moved him to the pillar and turned him to face it. She remembered the heavy silken cords holding back the draperies and secured two of them. One tied the Count's hands to the pillar over his head, while the other tied his feet.

"The cords are soft, and you tie very gently," the Count said.

"I wouldn't want the bindings to harm you, My Lord," Allana cooed. She pulled Charlan's leather belt form his tunic and swung it through the air sharply making a soft cracking sound. Charlan's eyes grew wide with fear.

"What are you going to do?" he asked.

"I must prepare both you and myself for our adventure in the realm of the love goddess, Lord. You're a brave man. It won't hurt very much."

Before he could protest any more, Allana brought the belt down against his buttocks in a gentle swing, barely making a mark.

"Ooooh!" Charlan reacted, but he soon smiled at her. "It does have a certain stimulating effect."

"Yes, Lord. It does." Allana hit him again only harder this time.

"Not so hard, my darling, please?"

"But, I'm only beginning to be aroused. We must continue." She brought the belt down even harder.

"Aaaaah!" Charlan screamed, and Allana stood back to wait for the inevitable.

The guards burst into the room ready to defend their lord and took in the sight of their sovereign tied to a post naked and being whipped by a woman. They fought to maintain straight faces.

"Are you all right, Lord?" one asked.

"Get out of here, you fools, and if you speak a word of this to anyone, I'll have you flogged to death."

"Yes, Lord." The guards turned to leave, but Allana thought she heard a muffled snicker from one of them.

"I'm afraid they've spoiled it for me, Lord," Allana said with as disappointed a look as she could muster under the circumstances.

"No, no, you may continue, Lady. Please go on. They won't come in again."

"It's too late, Sir. The intrusion combined with the wine has taken away my lust. We'll just have to try another time. I'm sure you understand." Allana untied the Count.

Charlan had no choice but to agree with her. He cursed himself for not giving the guards better instructions, but the woman's use of the belt was a total surprise. He'd know better next time.

"Of course, I know how it is with these things. Once the mood is broken, there's no going back." Charlan dressed and bid Allana goodnight.

Allana could hardly contain her laughter. She changed into her nightclothes and was about to dump the wine over the balcony railing, when she heard a loud knock at her door. She opened it to find Artun, sword in hand along with two of her guards.

"I just woke up, Lady, and I ran here to see if you were safe. I found Charlan's guards here and replaced them with our men. Are you all right?"

"I'm fine, Artun." Allana began to laugh merrily to Artun's total surprise.

"What's funny, Lady? Barinosh told me to be wary of Charlan, and when I found I'd been drugged, I feared the worst.

"You should have been here, Artun. It was hilarious." Allana described her session with the Count, and Artun joined in her laughter.

As they enjoyed the image of Charlan being spanked, Artun slipped his arm around Allana and tried to pull her close to him.

"Artun! What are you doing? I just put off one unwanted lover."

"Allana, I've been in love with you since I first saw you in the bazaar. I dream of you each night. I think of nothing but you during the day. You are my goddess of love. Don't deny me a kiss to cool my fevered brow."

Allana sighed in resignation. Artun wouldn't fall for the belt trick now, and she doubted he'd be satisfied with a kiss. Suddenly, a solution hit her.

"Very well, Artun, but first, we will drink a toast to my defeat of Charlan tonight." She led him to the wine she knew contained some sort of potion. She was sure it was concocted to make her oblivious to Charlan's advances, but she hoped it was not an aphrodisiac. She poured out two cups and passed one to Artun.

"To my conquest," Allana said.

"To mine," Artun answered as he drained his cup.

Once more, Allana pretended to drink and set her cup down beside the pitcher.

Artun drew her into his arms again.

"Now I'll have that kiss," he said as he pressed his lips to hers.

Allana felt his tongue probing her lips but kept her teeth firmly closed against his intrusion. His hand groped for her breast, and she felt his arousal grow stronger. He pushed her toward the bed, but half way there his hand dropped away and he grew limp in her arms. Charlan's potion was powerful, indeed. She moved to the door and called the guards.

"Lord Artun has fainted. He was so relieved to see I was not harmed. Please take him to his quarters."

"But Lady, he instructed us to guard you."

"One of you stay here with him while the other goes for help, then. Take him outside so I may get some sleep. We start for Gorgos early in the morning."

* * * * *

The next day, Allana's procession formed just after she ate breakfast alone in her room. Charlan was there to see her off as if nothing happened the night before. Allana bowed to him.

"My Lord, you must come visit me soon. I'm much better equipped to entertain visitors in my own palace," she said giving him a knowing wink.

"I can imagine, Princess. We will plan a visit soon." He bent and kissed her hand before Barinosh and Artun helped her into the sedan chair.

As they made their way back to the dock, Artun came up beside the chair and spoke to Allana.

"My Lady, I apologize for my forwardness last night. I think the wine made me bold."

"No Artun, it was the wine that saved me from your attack. I forgive you, but see that it doesn't happen again or Javik may h ave something to say about it." She extended her hand from the chair, and Artun kissed it with a proper demeanor.

Chapter 23

When the caravan reached Ulum, Javik left Farras and Mordah in camp and rode into the city to the House of Orgama. Varuda would know where to find this Argani Avra spoke of. He walked in the front entrance and was surrounded by beauty immediately. The scent of the place was enough to arouse an ogre, and the lovely women in filmy costumes almost made him forget why he'd come. He soon made it known he was not a customer, and that he was there to see his friend, Varuda.

"Varuda gets all the handsome ones," one girl moaned as she resumed her seat on a nearby lounge chair.

Varuda soon appeared in a gown that did little to hide her attractions. Her mask was still a shock to Javik, though he'd seen it before.

"Javik, it's good to see you. How is Allana?" She embraced Javik who fought the urge to do more.

"She's now governor of Gorgos, and doing well."

"Not queen yet?"

"Give her time, that's all she needs. I came here to seek out an Argani named Gallam. I need to use my letter of credit to obtain some gold. I'm on my way home to visit my family for a few days."

"I can have one of my servants take you to him, but stay and have a meal with me. You can tell me all about your adventures since leaving here."

Javik agreed readily after two days of caravan food.

As they ate, a servant came in and whispered in Varuda's ear. She nodded her head in agreement, and the servant left. Javik told her of all that happened since he last saw her, and was about to ask for the servant to lead him to Gallam when Varuda rose and took his hand.

"There is someone here who knows you, Javik. She's a very important customer of mine who spends a great deal of money in my house. I'll take you to her."

"Her? A woman?" Javik asked.

Varuda laughed merrily. "We serve women here as well as men."

"You mean, women who like women?"

"Yes, and those who like men as well as those who like both. Come with me. She only wants to speak with you. No need to be afraid."

"I fear no woman," Javik boasted.

"You have much to learn about women, Javik," Varuda said as she led him to a door guarded by a large man in the livery of Ollon.

"This is Javik of Gorgos," Varuda said.

The guard nodded and opened the door.

Javik was shocked to see the Countess Brianna lying on a bed naked with two other women, also naked.

"I'll leave you here, Javik," Varuda said as she closed the door.

"Welcome, Javik!" Brianna called as the other women moved off the bed and behind some curtains to the left.

"I certainly didn't expect to see you here, Countess, and definitely not in this condition."

"Javik, you disappoint me. I thought you were a real warrior and wise in the ways of the world. Haven't you ever seen women with women before?"

"No, and I don't find it a very pleasant sight. What did you want to talk about?"

"Talk? I want you to join me here." Brianna patted the bed next to her and beckoned to Javik with the other hand.

"I'm sorry, I have important business to attend to here in Ulum. I must be on my way." Javik turned to leave, and Brianna leapt from the bed to intercept him.

"I've wanted you from the first day I saw you, and I'm not used to being turned down by men. Is there something about me you find distasteful?"

Javik looked her over. She was beautiful, and her body was tempting, but he knew that if he once gave in to her there would be no end of it.

You're a very beautiful woman, Countess, but I love Allana, and I will be true to her. Now I must leave."

Javik moved her to one side easily, but she grabbed his arm before he could leave.

"My husband appointed your Allana as governor, and he can discharge her just as easily. He listens to my recommendations on such things."

"Does he know of your activities here in Ulum?" Javik asked.

"Charlan knows I have desires he cannot satisfy. He only asks me to take care of them far from Ollon. Don't think you can threaten me with the possibility of exposing my activities here. It would be an empty threat. I, however, can make good on my threats."

Javik considered the Countess's words carefully. He really didn't know her or Charlan very well at this point, but he'd seen Charlan's expression when he was around Allana. The Count was probably trying to seduce Allana at this very moment. Would Allana refuse his advances, or would she succumb until Gorgos was strong enough to defend itself? What would Charlan do if Allana turned him down? Making love to Brianna would be an easy thing to do, and Allana would never be the wiser, but Brianna would keep on demanding his attentions even after he and Allana were married. There had to be some way out of this mess, but he didn't see it.

Brianna noticed Javik's hesitation and pressed her case even harder, but with a different tack.

"Javik, I can make all of your love dreams come true. I know things Allana can never know. Come to bed with me. After all, how will Allana ever know about it?" She began to undo his sword belt.

"You know Allana used to own this house?" Javik asked.

"I know, that's how I heard of it. One of her servants told me about it. She doesn't own it now."

Suddenly, a thought struck Javik. His father once told him of a dreaded pox common to women who had many lovers. It was his only hope.

"No, Allana would never know until you came down with the pox."

Brianna stepped back. "What pox?"

"I contracted the lover's pox while visiting a place in Wallandia much like this one. I've avoided making love to

Allana until I could be cured of it. I understand the Argani have a potion capable of freeing me from this curse, but it's much too expensive. I'm sure you could afford it, though. Why should I not enjoy the pleasure of your love?"

Javik dropped his sword belt to the floor and began to undo his tunic.

Brianna backed away from him even farther.

"Now wait, Javik. Let's be sensible about this. Why should we both pay for the potion when only one fee is needed? I will give you the gold for the cure, and we can meet again when you are free of the curse."

Javik feigned gratitude. "That's very generous of you, Countess. The potion costs 200 crowns."

Brianna choked back a gasp and retreated to a writing desk.

"I have that much here, but it will deplete my funds considerably. I'll give you a letter of credit for that amount. Any Argani will honor it. It's well worth it to have you in my bed. How long does this cure take?" she asked.

"I'm told several weeks," Javik said as he refastened his tunic and picked up his sword belt. "I will know by the time I return from Berglaundia. I'll purchase the potion today, and begin the treatment immediately. I'm very grateful to you."

"You can show your gratitude when you return to Gorgos. I will be in touch with you then."

Javik moved to enfold her in his arms and kiss her, but Brianna pushed him away quickly.

"We will kiss next time, Javik. Have a safe journey."

"Thank you, My Lady." Javik bowed to her and left the room.

Varuda was waiting outside the door.

"That was quick for Brianna," she said.

"We did not make love. You know I love only Allana," Javik replied.

"Nothing like that has stopped her before. How did you manage it?"

"I told her I had a pox."

Varuda stopped and put a hand to her mask in shock. "You don't, do you?"

"Of course not. It was the only way I could think of to get out of there."

Varuda's shock turned to laughter. "I can imagine the look on her face now. That's hilarious."

"The best part is, I told her the potion needed to cure it cost 200 crowns, and she gave me the money." Javik waved the letter of credit in Varuda's face.

Varuda burst out in a new wave of laughter and bent over holding her side.

"Javik, you are as good at deception as any mountebank I've ever known. You not only convince the Countess you have an imaginary pox, you milk her for the gold to buy the non-existent cure."

"The gold will help my family in Berglaundia. Now, have your servant lead me to this Gallam."

* * * * *

Javik presented his letters of credit to the Argani who read them over thoroughly.

"I know Avra; how did he come into possession of so much gold?" Gallam asked.

"The letter is only for 3,500 crowns," Javik said.

"Yes, but to stand good for that much, he must have at least ten times that amount at his disposal."

"He has much more than that on Gorgos. The island is prospering again under its new governor, and Avra serves her and me both."

"He mentions he is now treasurer to the Queen of Gorgos. I thought the island was still part of Tulla."

"It is, he likes to use that term instead of governor in order to flatter her."

"Ahhh, could this governor be the Lady Allana who used to own the House of Orgama here in Ulum?"

"The same. She is a member of the royal house of Gorgos, but her island is in no position to declare itself independent of Tulla. We must rely on the protection of Charlan, Count of Ollon, and therefore, she must remain his governor."

"A wise decision. You will need several chests to carry this sum, and a strong packhorse, if you're not using a wagon."

"I assume you have appropriate chests for sale?" Javik asked.

"At a most reasonable price. Only two crowns each. A special price for you."

Javik doubted his price was special, but it fit within his expectations. "I'll return in the morning, and we will count out the coins then. Until morning, Gallam."

"Until morning, Lord Javik."

* * * * *

Javik purchased a wagon to carry the gold and watched as Gallam's servants counted out 500 coins in each chest. Farras secured the chests in the wagon and covered the bounty with other parcels to hide it from the casual observer. Farras tied his horse behind the wagon and mounted to the driver's bench. Soon, the men were on their way to Berglaundia.

Chapter 24

Barinosh worked quickly. Within a few weeks, six ships sat in the harbor at Thatos waiting to be converted to men-of-war. The shipyard could only handle two at a time, but they worked around the clock on the project of creating a Gorgon navy.

Sailors from all along the coast heard of the new fleet and rushed to Gorgos to offer their services. Barinosh kept busy screening them and left most of the conversion supervision to Noka.

The first part of the conversion process involved removing the bow and sternposts to allow the cannons full fields of fire. Rudders moved by a system of chains and a wheel replaced steering oars. The wheel was now located amidships to allow room for a stern cannon. A fighting platform for men with hand cannons sat atop the single mast. The rams were retained since ramming was still a useful tactic.

Powder production increased when deposits of saltpeter were found close to the sulfur fields. The bird droppings were still collected since Karl found them to be a good source of fertilizer for his terraced agriculture.

Fortifications progressed daily, and more cannon were added to the earthen defenses along the approachable coastline. Sigurd now commanded a sizeable garrison and drilled them constantly.

Artun was behaving himself, but the mines were producing on a reduced scale now that the demand for cannon material was diminishing a bit, which was good considering that the manpower for them was tapering off also.

Gorgos neared its maximum population, and immigration would soon need to be cut off. Crime was beginning to grow, and the first executions took place on a gibbet erected at the end of the main pier.

Allana moved freely among her people, but she longed for Javik's return. Council meetings now included people who were not part of the original group. She found herself delegating more and more authority to people she'd only known for a few months. In spite of her misgivings, things were going well, and she was beginning to feel confident in her ability to declare independence from Ollon and Tulla at the end of the next year.

Margan returned from several weeks of travel on the mainland and sought an immediate audience with Allana. She granted it readily.

"Margan, it's good to have you back on Gorgos," Allana said as she embraced the crippled minstrel.

"I fear I don't bring good news, Princess. Clouds are beginning to gather on the horizon."

Allana slumped into a chair and indicated another one for Margan. A servant brought wine, and Margan took a full cup while Allana declined.

"Tell me the worst. It's been a day of bad tidings. I've signed two execution warrants, and Avra says we may have some kind of plague on our hands."

"I've been through Philisia and Karran before ending up at Charlan's court. Philisia is preparing for war, and the rumor is they will invade Tulla next spring."

"Why should that concern us? They would invade by land over the plains common to both countries."

"Their navy is also planning for war, and I've heard they will attack Gorgos."

"They'll have a surprise here. Do they know about our cannon?"

"Yes, but they feel their fleet is large enough to land a big army on the island in spite of the cannon. They don't think you'll have enough ships to defend the beach by next spring."

"Sigurd is busy building earthworks and cannon emplacements on the beach. If they wait until spring, we will be ready."

"They have a large navy, Allana. You may need more ships than you plan for now. They could send as many as twenty warships and thirty transports if they chose to."

"Hmmm, we **will** need more ships. I'll send Barinosh out again immediately, and we'll expand the shipyards to accommodate more dry-docks. What of Karran?"

"They too covet your island, but they have only a small navy. They rely on Ollon for sea defense, but they could raise a formidable army. They've sent emissaries to Philisia to explore a possible alliance. They would propose defeating Ollon, taking Gorgos and strangling the rest of Tulla into surrender."

"Oliga would never let such an alliance go unchallenged. He doesn't want to lose Ollon."

"I think you're correct. Charlan has already been to Agam to discuss contingencies with Oliga. I wasn't able to learn the entire plan, but part of it involves placing a large garrison on Gorgos and using Thatos as the base for naval operations against the Philisian fleet. Charlan needs your cannon equipped fleet to defeat Philisia, but his benevolence toward you will change once his realm is secure. He still wants you in his bed, but as a slave, not a princess," Margan said.

"So, we face not only Philisia but also Charlan once Philisia is defeated. We might be able to defeat Charlan's navy, if that were the only threat , but if he should manage to land a large force on Gorgos, we'd be hard pressed to defeat them with the small army we have now. He's probably planning on us losing a few ships in the battle against Philisia's fleet so that our conquest would be an easy matter. We need an ally."

"You sound like you have a plan," Margan said.

"A wise man once told me, 'the largest meal is eaten one bite at a time.' We could reduce Charlan's navy easily and take on part of the Philisian fleet at the same time," Allana answered.

"How?"

"By employing the pirates. Barinosh knows of several groups capable of challenging warships. We will offer them a fat price for any Ollon man-of-war they capture."

"Just the Ollon ships? Why not also Philisian vessels?"

"One opponent at a time, Margan. Charlan is my greatest worry, and I can't attack him directly as long as Gorgos is part of Ollon. If Philisia invades, we can attack her ships with impunity while still using the pirates against Charlan. We may be able to weaken Charlan enough over the winter to force him into rethinking his plan for using Gorgos as a base."

"A clever scheme, but dangerous."

"We live in dangerous times, Margan. I only pray Javik

returns before we have to act."

"Where is Javik?"

"He's gone back to Berglaundia to take some gold to his family. He said he'd return as soon as possible, but winter is coming to that country, and the passes may be snowed in early. I'd hate to face a war without him."

"Javik will return soon. I can't imagine him being away from you long, now that he's found you."

"I hope you're right, Margan. I hope you're right."

Chapter 25

Javik and Farras rode past ripe grain fields as they neared Holliga, Javik's village. The men were already busy harvesting the golden treasure.

"What abundance!" Farras said with a note of awe in his voice. Your homeland is rich as well as being beautiful. I've never seen such splendor as the explosion of colors in the forest, and now, grain fields larger than the whole island of Gorgos."

"Grain is our only wealth here, Farras. Gorgos has many other sources of income."

"Still, I marvel at the sight," Farras said.

One of the men working the harvest recognized Javik and ran to greet him.

Mordah began to growl menacingly, but Javik soothed the war dog.

"Javik! Is that really you?" the man called out.

Javik recognized Nickos, Karl's father. He dismounted to embrace his friend's parent.

"It's good to see you in good health, Nickos. How is your family?"

"All fine, but tell me of my son."

"He's in charge of all agriculture on the island of Gorgos. We now call him Lord Karl."

"Lord Karl," Nickos savored the words. "My son, a lord, I

can't believe it."

"Come to the common house tonight, and I'll tell all of my adventures since leaving a year ago last spring."

"I'll be there." Nickos embraced Javik again and ran back to the other men waiting to hear his news.

The pair rode through the stockade gate to be met by the welcoming shouts of the guards who watched him approach and recognized the huge gray dog. Soon, Dana and Goldar appeared from inside their longhouse.

"My son," Dana ran to greet her boy as Goldar beamed his approval.

Javik embraced his mother. "I've brought you many surprises, Mother. I can't wait to tell you all, but I think it best to hold most of my news for a meeting at the common house tonight."

"Yes, of course, Son. Come greet your third father," Dana said.

Javik clasped hands with Goldar, but the big war leader enfolded him in a manly embrace. "You look fine, Son."

"I am fine, though I've had a few scrapes since you last saw me." He was about to go on when a loud voice broke his chain of thought.

"By Zhou! It *is* my son, Javik," Browdat bellowed as he joined the group and smothered Javik in his embrace.

"I'm a very lucky man to have three great fathers," Javik said.

"Come to my house and tell me of your adventures," Browdat demanded. "The lady Frieda will want to fatten you up a bit." Browdat tapped on Javik's lean stomach for emphasis.

"I think his mother has first priority in that area," Dana laughed. "Why don't you and Frieda join us tonight for the evening meal? We'll go to the common house immediately after dinner so Javik may tell the whole village of his exploits."

"Fine, fine, we'll be there. I'll go and make the arrangements now. May I bring a keg of qush?"

"I wish you would," Javik said. "I haven't had any good qush since leaving Holliga. Oh, Mother, may we also invite Tao Shan?"

"Certainly, I'll send a servant to inform him," Dana said.

"If you don't mind, I'd like to invite him myself as soon as my servant and I are settled in."

"Very well, bring your wagon and horses to our house, and we'll see that you and your servant are taken care of properly," Goldar said.

Javik turned to Farras and pulled him forward. "This is Farras of Gorgos. He's served me well since we landed on Gorgos."

"You are welcome in our house, Farras," Goldar said as Farras bowed to him.

"Thank you, Lord Goldar," Farras replied.

Farras soon had everything in order at Goldar's longhouse, and Javik left for Tao Shan's house in the forest.

A boy in a green uniform met Javik at the door and bowed low. "How may I serve you, Sir?" he said.

Javik smiled at the lad. It hadn't been that long ago that he was in the boy's position.

"Tell Tao Shan, your master, Javik is here to see him."

"Yes, Sir. Won't you come in?"

He led Javik to the central arena area and bid him wait while he knocked on Tao Shan's private quarters. The old mentor answered the door and immediately noticed Javik. He brushed the boy aside. "That will be all, Tuggan. I know Javik well."

Tao Shan moved to Javik and offered his hand. Javik took it wanting to embrace his old mentor, but thought better of it with the student watching.

"You really look like a warrior now, Javik," Tao Shan said.

"Thanks to your teachings. I must tell you that I've used several in my journey to Gorgos and back."

"How is Allana?"

"She's governor of Gorgos, and soon to be Queen, if all goes well."

"And, you and she?" Tao Shan placed his fingertips together to indicate a joining.

"Not yet, we're still not married, but we are together again."

"Then you are…?" He repeated his gesture.

Javik laughed as he finally caught the significance of the action.

"Yes, we are that, at last."

Tao Shan slapped Javik's back heavily in response.

"Good man! Now, you must tell me all of your adventures," Tao Shan said.

"I came to invite you to dinner with us at Goldar's house tonight. I'll tell you all after dinner."

"I never decline the Lady Dana's cooking. I'll be there."

Javik left Tao Shan and returned to the village. As he entered the longhouse, he saw Dana rolling a ball across the packed dirt floor of the longhouse toward a blonde toddler all smiles and giggling merrily at the game.

"Is that my son?" Javik stared at the boy for a moment

before moving toward him with outstretched arms. The child ran to the protection of Dana's apron, his face beginning to cloud over with fear.

"Why does he run from me?" Javik asked.

"You're a stranger to him, Javik. He must get used to you," Dana said as she soothed the boy.

"He's grown."

"They do that. Come, we'll watch him play for a while. Maybe you'll be able to hold him tomorrow."

"What about dinner? Aren't you needed in the kitchen?"

Dana laughed. "Now that Goldar is my husband, I have servants. All I do is give orders these days."

"Tao Shan is anticipating your cooking."

"He will not be disappointed. Come, get to know your son."

Javik watched Garen and Dana play ball. After a few moments Dana rolled the ball to Javik. Garen started to move toward his father but stopped well out of arm's reach.

"Hello, son." Javik said. He rolled the ball toward the boy who quickly turned to roll it toward Dana.

"Go say hello to your father, Garen," Dana said as she rolled the ball back to Javik.

Garen turned to the stranger and frowned before running to Dana's arms. "No!" was his response to the request. "No say hello to man."

"Garen, that's your father. He's a brave warrior. You should be proud of him," Dana scolded.

"No!" Garen said as he buried his face in Dana's bosom.

It took several more minutes of play before Garen would consent to approaching Javik at close range, but soon he accepted his father at least as someone who had a right to be in the house.

As he came to know his son better, Javik felt the pride of a parent for the first time and vowed his son would not be without a father any longer than necessary.

Dinner was a grand affair filling the central room of Goldar's longhouse. Besides Browdat and Frieda, his parents and Tao Shan, Polla's father and mother were there along with Berda and his wife and Karl's family. Javik answered some questions, but saved his tales for the common house gathering. During the meal, Farras approached Javik.

"Lord Javik, when do want to present your gifts?" Farras asked.

"Lord Javik? Is it Lord Javik now?" Browdat bellowed.

Javik rose and addressed his stepfather. "Sir, I am a lord of Gorgos, but here in Berglaundia, I am only Javik son of Tolda, Browdat and Goldar. I think those three distinguished men are title enough for me here."

The guests applauded his speech, but Javik signaled for silence.

"Farras has reminded me of one of the reasons I returned." He turned to his servant. "Have the chests brought in, Farras."

Farras bowed and left the room returning with five other servants bearing wooden chests. They set them in front of Javik who opened the first one to surprised exclamations on revealing the contents.

"I bring you some of the gold of Gorgos. This chest," he indicated one as yet unopened, "is for my Mother alone." More applause greeted this announcement as the guests assumed the chest held the same amount of gold.

"From these other chests," he indicated the rest, "I will repay the kindness shown me by all those I hold dear in this village."

Farras opened another chest, and Javik took out five sacks of fifty crowns each and gave them to Farras. "These are for you, Berda. This is your share for helping us rescue Allana and my belated wedding present to you and your bride."

More applause as Javik pulled out another five sacks of fifty crowns. "These are for you, Lord Browdat, to repay your kindness to my mother and I."

Farras took the coins to Browdat who was speechless for the first time in Javik's memory.

Farras opened another chest, and Javik produced five more sacks. "These are for Mikka. I understand he is away on a raid, but will you see he gets them, Father?" Goldar nodded as Farras carried the gold to him.

"The rest are for you, Challa and Gilda, for caring for little Garen."

Once more the guests showed their approval of the gift.

"Finally, these are for you, Tao Shan. Allana sends this as her repayment of your loan."

Tao Shan rose as Farras directed the servants to place two chests before the mentor.

"I have no need of this gold, but I would ask Javik's permission to put it aside as the fee for my mentoring of Garen."

"Gladly, but I hope to do much of that task myself," Javik replied.

"I only ask one year with him. It was enough to get you through Mauhad, and it should be enough for him."

"Even if I train him well, a year in your house will make a better man out of any lad," Javik said as he embraced his old mentor.

After a final round of qush the guests left Goldar's house for the common house where Javik enthralled the village with his exploits in rescuing Allana and battling the Turrek as part of the caravan guard. The warriors were less fascinated by the story of Gorgos, but the women asked dozens of questions about the fashions in the cities along the way. The session went on well into the morning hours.

The next morning, Javik took Mordah into the forest so the dog could hunt up a meal. He took along his bow and hunting knife besides his dagger. Mordah was on a scent as soon as they cleared the village and ran off baying happily. Javik followed the sound of his cries and was surprised when they stopped. He walked on to find Grazhda in a small clearing with Mordah lying at her feet panting contentedly.

"Your beast has a powerful spirit, Javik. It was all I could do to keep him from devouring me." The old hag cackled merrily.

"He's saved my life twice since I found him. I don't think he would have harmed you without my command."

"He knows magic when he sees it, and he doesn't like it. His previous master must have been an evil man."

"He was a Sentii war leader."

"I guessed as much. Have you seen your son?"

"Yes, he's growing nicely."

"He'll be a fine boy. Remember your promise to let me have him for a year."

"I will remember. I hope to be back before that time."

"Gorgos will be Allana's to rule alone by then."

"Why do you say she'll rule alone?"

"A greater kingdom calls your name, Javik." Grazhda stooped down and began to pet Mordah. The war dog responded by moving his head to accommodate her.

"My place is beside Allana. I can think of no greater kingdom than our life together."

"Your love will never die, but a time will come when you must leave her on Gorgos and fulfill your destiny elsewhere."

"I'd never leave her, even for the greatest kingdom in the world."

Grazhda cackled merrily. "A rash statement. The gods care nothing for the loves of men. They will have their way regardless of mortal wishes."

"My father taught me that men have power over their own lives and possess the ability to defy the gods."

"True in many respects, but the gods favor some men above others, and you are one of those men, Javik. When they want you, they will have you."

"By the way, I have 1,000 gold crowns from Allana as repayment of your loan to her. Where should I have it delivered?"

The old witch cackled merrily. "Keep it for yourself. I've replaced the gold I gave her five times over since she left."

Mordah began to growl deeply inside his chest, and rose to his feet concentrating on something behind Javik.

Javik turned to face the expected threat and saw a small deer startled by the presence of the dog. He raised his bow and dropped the deer in its tracks before turning back to Grazhda, but she was gone.

* * * * *

As Javik spent more time with Garen, the boy came to accept him as a member of the family if not his father. He even took Javik's hand from time to time and allowed himself to be picked up on a regular basis by this large, blonde person Dana kept calling father.

Javik stayed at his home village until the first reports of snowfall in the high pass, then began his return trip to Gorgos. He was even gratified when Garen wept at his departure.

Chapter 26

The pirate attacks began on Charlan's warships at the winter solstice. The 5000 crown prize offered by Allana was too much of a temptation for four of the pirate captains. They banded together creating a fleet of six ships. Allana refused their request for cannon.

Javik returned to take charge of the forces manning the beach defenses. His assets included ten cannon in earthen revetments, thirty archers, twenty crossbowmen, 45 men armed with hand cannons, and 200 infantry. He began to drill them on every decent day. With the coming of winter, the island entered its rainy season, and he feared disease. Captain Paolo, the commander of his hand cannon troops, came to Javik one day with a proposal just before drill time. The servant outside Javik's tent on the beachfront announced the Captain's arrival.

"Captain Paolo is here to see you, Lord Javik.'

"Send him in immediately. You know my Captains are always welcome."

Paolo entered the tent.

"Lord Javik, I think I've found a way to make our hand cannoneers more effective."

"Come in, Paolo. Tell me about it." Javik said.

Paolo set a handful of stones on the table and began lining them up in three ranks.

"I've been worried about the time it takes to load our weapons. I've noted that it takes a good man nearly a count of twenty to load and be ready to fire again. In that same time, two men can aim and fire. If we use three ranks, like this, the first rank can fire and begin reloading in a kneeling position. The second rank can fire immediately afterwards and kneel to reload while the third rank fires. By the time the third rank fires, the first rank will be ready to fire again. The process can be repeated as often as needed keeping up a steady fire."

Javik studied the idea for only a moment. "A very clever idea, Paolo. We'll try it today at the drill."

"Thank you, Sir. The men are very excited about it. They're sure it will make us invincible."

"I don't know about that, but it's a definite improvement."

Paolo's tactic proved to be quite feasible, and it was adopted as the usual method of employing the hand cannon troops.

Noka matched this innovation with one of his own. He came to Javik one day with a peculiar looking leather bag.

"What's that?" Javik asked.

"A new load for your cannon. I thought about your situation here on the beach for a long time. You'll be facing an army landing from transports. Though you may sink many before they reach the shore, some of them are bound to get through. Once the men land, they could overrun your cannon and silence them. This round will help stop them.

Javik inspected the bag. It was filled with lead balls the size of small pine cones stacked on top of a circular piece of wood. "How does it work?"

"The cannoneer loads this with the piece of wood going in first. When the powder is touched off, the wood forces the balls forward while the bag burns up. When the balls leave the barrel, it's just like when we use shot in our hand cannon. They spread out to cover a larger area."

"I see," Javik mused as he contemplated the carnage the flying balls would create in advancing infantry or charging cavalry. "What a terrible weapon. Noka, we've taken the glory out of war with our cannon. It's no longer man against man, but man against machines of death."

Noka pondered Javik's remark. "I see what you mean, but why should we give up such a formidable advantage for a bit of glory? Our enemies would not show us any mercy if we didn't use cannon. They'd slaughter us and be thankful for our stupidity."

"That's not it, Noka. I see a time when all men will fight with cannon. The bow and the sword will be relics of the past one day, and a man will be less a man for that."

"Javik, you've grown too philosophical to be a warrior."

"No, Noka, I won't hesitate to use our advantage, but I will always think of the sword as the preferred weapon of any true warrior."

The war fleet continued to grow with three ships launched from the dry docks each month. Gorgos now boasted four ships on patrol, five warships guarding the island with two more in port as reserves. *The Queen of Gorgos* was now being fitted with its stern cannon to match the other vessels. Food and strategic materials were stockpiled in quantities sufficient to last six months. Allana felt she was ready for any contingency. She wasn't, however, prepared for Artun's treachery.

Javik entered her chambers one morning with a long face.

"Why so glum, my darling?" she asked.

"Artun is nowhere to be found, and Avra says we're missing 3,000 crowns from the treasury. Barinosh has taken a fast warship in search of him, but he fears the villain has a good head start and one of the faster fishing boats."

"I can't believe that. Artun was the backbone of our mining operations."

"It seems our 'backbone' was spineless, after all. The money he stole was supposed to be spent on mine improvements."

"There's nothing to be done for it now. Who could we put in charge of the mines?"

"I've had his second in command arrested. He may have been part of the fraud. Barinosh will find out when he interrogates him. Noka recommends Giolo, one of the Gorgon supervisors."

"I'll issue the order immediately. We didn't need this right now, Javik."

"We'll survive. It's just disappointing when we thought he was one of us all these months."

"Perhaps he lost his eagerness for our cause once I rebuffed his advances."

Javik kissed Allana on the cheek. "We're well rid of him, then."

The losses to Charlan's fleet began to build as the pirates collected their bounties. Allana was not surprised to see Bradish, Charlan's chief advisor, land at Thatos with an official entourage. She met him with Barinosh, Sigurd, Bogard and Javik at her side.

The courtier stepped on to the dock dressed in ornate armor. His open-faced helmet shone so brightly it almost blinded anyone viewing him from the wrong angle. The crest was a golden dragon with ostrich plume wings. His heavy leather breastplate carried the crest of Tulla, and the sword hanging at his side would have been of no use in any battle because of the large number of jewels in the grip and guard. He was not so much a menacing warrior as an armored peacock. He strutted toward the waiting group of Gorgos's leaders with an arrogance belying his short stature and extremely bowed legs. He bowed before Allana.

"Welcome, Bradish. Carriages await us. Won't you join us for some food and wine before we take up official business?"

"I'm sorry, Lady, but I have orders to return to Ollon as soon as possible. We must talk here," Bradish said.

"Very well, go on," Allana said.

"My Lady, as you are well aware, our fleet has suffered considerable losses to pirates lately."

Allana didn't like the inflections of Bradish's voice. They seemed to hint she knew too much about the pirate attacks.

"I've heard what you've heard, Bradish," Allana answered.

"Yes, Lady." Bradish bowed to acknowledge the admonition. "These attacks have depleted our sea forces at a critical time. We fear an attack by the Philisians in the spring after the rivers are back within their banks. We can manage the land battle with some help from King Oliga, but if the Philisians land a force behind our lines, we would be lost. Sea power was our guarantee against such a landing, but we can't continue to protect our trade routes and defend our coast in the face of these losses. Count Charlan bids me ask you to deploy your fleet in defense of the Tullan coast should Philisia attack."

"And who will defend Gorgos?" Barinosh asked.

"My Lord proposes sending a large garrison to reinforce

Gorgos and insure victory in the event of any landing on the island."

Allana smiled inwardly. Charlan's plan was exactly as she'd expected.

"Lord Bradish, our island is only capable of housing a small force in addition to our own troops. Without our ships to protect us, the enemy could land a large invasion force from transports. Our defenses would be overwhelmed in short order even with your help. No, we must keep our fleet near at hand. Tell the Count we will keep our fleet here until it is plain no attack on Gorgos is imminent."

"Lady, my Lord now requests, but he could command," Bradish smiled as he said this.

Javik stepped forward. "Tell Count Charlan that commands may be obeyed or disobeyed. They are only as good as the power wielded by the man issuing them. Your spies have seen our fleet in action, and they have mapped our fortifications. I think you'll agree that enforcing such a command would require your entire fleet and a good portion of your army, leaving Ollon an easy target for the Philisians and your trade routes open to the pirates. You might succeed in gaining control of Gorgos, but you'd lose Ollon in the process."

Bradish bristled at Javik's remarks. "This is treason! You refuse to come to the aid of your sovereign?"

"Not at all," Allana said. "I told you, we will attack any fleet menacing your shores when the time comes, but I will not have Charlan's troops stationed on Gorgos. We have ample forces to repel any invasion, if it's directed this way."

"I will report your reply to Count Charlan. He may see fit to appoint a new governor for Gorgos." Bradish's voice was haughty, and he lifted his nose into the air as if he'd smelled horse droppings.

Sigurd spoke, "Charlan may appoint all the governors he wishes, but they will always be subject to the Queen of Gorgos."

"I shall take great pleasure seeing you all hanged as traitors. Good day." Bradish turned and strode back to his ship without even the courtesy of a bow to Allana.

When he was gone, Allana let out a long breath. "Well, the fat's in the fire now."

"The attack from Philisia must be more imminent than we thought," Barinosh said.

"The snow came early to the passes this year, and when I crossed the mountains there was already more snow on them than I've seen in years. The Philisians know the signs. The spring floods will be worse than ever. They will attack while the rivers are still low, before the thaw comes," Javik said.

"When the rivers flood, their forces will be cut off from supply by land," Sigurd said.

"Meaning they'll have to be supplied by sea," Barinosh added.

"Then we will hold the key to the fate of Ollon," Allana said as a smile spread across her face.

"Don't smile too quickly, my darling," Javik cautioned. "With Gorgos as the prime threat to their plans to supply the army by sea, they'll attack here first, and in full force."

"We will be ready for them," Allana said with a grim face.

The pirates continued to sink Ollon ships, but Charlan made no move to invade Gorgos. Several days after Bradish's visit, one of the pirate Captains came to Allana with grim news.

"Lady, I captured an Ollon warship two days ago, but I was

chased away from my prize by a squadron of Philisian ships. I lost them in a fog bank, but when I emerged near the shoreline, I saw a great fleet of warships and transports anchored in the lee of the Nagan peninsula. I sailed here to warn you. They may be headed for Gorgos."

"You've done well," Allana said as she turned to Avra. "See that this man gets a double bounty for his ship and send in Barinosh and Javik."

Avra led the pirate captain out of the audience room. In a short while the other two men appeared.

"What did you need?" Javik asked.

"A pirate captain just informed me the Philisian fleet could be right behind him. Do we have our warning vessels out?" Allana asked.

"Yes, Lady," Barinosh answered. "They should give us several hours warning of any approaching fleet."

"That fellow saw them off the Nagan peninsula two days ago. If they sailed directly here, when would they arrive?" Allana asked.

Barinosh walked over to a large map hanging on one wall and placed his middle finger on the peninsula stretching his thumb to Gorgos. He checked the distance on the map's scale before answering.

"They would be just over the horizon by now. One of our picket boats should have spotted them," Barinosh said.

"I think we'd best put our forces on alert," Allana said. "Send word to the fleet and tell Sigurd to prepare. Javik, take charge of the beach defenses."

Barinosh had the signal fires lit on the watchtowers while Javik readied the beach forces. Sigurd put the garrison of

Thatos on alert for action either on the walls or to reinforce the beach. They didn't have long to wait. Shortly before midnight, one of the picket ships sailed into the harbor with the news the Philisian fleet was only a few hours behind.

The harbor defenders raised the great chain across the harbor entrance, and the men were allowed to eat a hot meal and nap until dawn.

As the sun rose, the attacking fleet came into full view. The Philisians had poor timing, as the sun was in their eyes. Their target was the beach, and they stayed well out of range of the cannon on the harbor defenses. Javik's guns had the only shots, and they began pounding the fleet at maximum range.

Sigurd's troops joined Javik's men in front of the beach guns as they lined up for battle and waited. Several ships fell to the beach guns, but two of the warships managed to get close enough to launch fireballs at the troops. Sigurd ordered a retreat to avoid heavy casualties, and the lines reformed. Cannon fire soon sank the warships, but others were coming behind them slinging fireballs and rocks onto the beach. They stayed out in deeper water as the transports headed for shore to disgorge their troops.

The cannon sank several transports, but several managed to land. Javik ordered the gunners to load with Noka's bag shot and ordered the hand cannon force into the three rank position they'd practiced.

The Philisians formed lines on the beach and archers began to launch volleys of arrows toward the Gorgon lines. Javik responded with his own archers, and the cries of the wounded on both sides soon filled the air between the thunder of the cannons.

The bag shot tore gaping holes in the Philisian lines, and

Javik saw body parts flying through the air. The sight nearly made him sick as he thought of the cannon's effect on war. Transports disabled by the cannon now filled the beach. The ones behind them began unloading in deeper water with their troops wading into shore to meet the fury of the bag shot. Some of the infantry managed to form a charge and ran toward the cannon. Javik ordered the hand cannon troops to aim for those lines and gave the order to fire.

A steady roll of gunfire began, and the charging men fell into great heaps impeding the progress of those behind them. The attackers leaped over the dead and dying to be cut down in their turn until a wall of bodies made further progress impossible. The charge continued around the flanks of the human corpse wall, and the crossbowmen began to make themselves felt.

Javik ordered the guns to concentrate on the ships with round shot now, and the battle was joined in the usual fashion by the infantry. A Philisian warrior staggered toward Javik waving his axe and bleeding from a stub where his shield arm should have been. Javik dispatched him with his sword and picked up his pollaxe. Karl joined Javik on his left side and Bogard on his right. They began the slaughter with Mordah keeping a careful watch in the rear of the trio.

The sound of distant cannon caused Javik to pause a moment. Smoke from burning ships and the haze of cannon fire smoke obscured his vision, but it could only be the Gorgon fleet attacking the invaders from the sea. The Philisians kept coming, though they seemed fewer with each moment.

Javik and his friends fought while retreating, as he had taught all his men to do. Their lines were now even with the cannon revetments, and the gunners reloaded with bag shot and lowered the barrels to point blank range. Javik could hear nothing now, but a steady ringing in his ears. A large warrior charged him. The man was obviously screaming his battle cry, but Javik only saw his mouth move. The charging man wore a shining helmet covering his ears but leaving his face fully exposed. He eyes were red from the irritation of the smoke, but they shone with a madness known only in war. Javik remembered the same look on the Wallan war leader who'd been his first kill. The man wielded a mace of prodigious proportions and carried no shield. His armor was a series of iron plates sewn onto a heavy leather garment reaching to his knees. He held a dagger in his left hand.

Javik waited for the man to telegraph his blow and ducked to the left bringing the pollaxe blade up into his opponent's stomach. The axe hit only iron plates, and the warrior quickly recovered wheeling to strike with his dagger. He caught Javik's right shoulder between his breastplate and his shoulder guard causing Javik to drop his grip on the axe with his right hand. The man sensed the lapse in Javik's attack and brought the mace back sharply toward his head.

Javik ducked the swing and drew his sword with his left hand. The attack was a surprise to the Philisian, and before he could recover with his dagger hand, Javik's blade found a space between the iron plates. He drove it home with all his might and watched as the warrior's eyes took on a blank stare. He seemed to be suspended in time on the blade of Javik's sword. The mace fell from his hand as blood gushed from his mouth. He fell to the ground gasping for air.

A trumpet sounded in the distance and no more men

appeared in front of the Gorgon lines. As the smoke cleared, Javik saw the terrible carnage. The ground was running with red rivulets everywhere he looked. The groans and pleas of the wounded were as loud as the cannons had been. A melee of battle was moving steadily toward the beach as the Gorgons pursued the retreating Philisians. Ships began to make their way back out to sea under the guns of the fleet. Soon all was silence as infantry began dispatching the wounded enemy. Javik walked through the blood and bodies toward the beach, when he noticed a finely armored warrior leaning against a pile of corpses. It was Artun, and he was still alive, though a large hole in his breastplate marked the entrance of a deadly hand cannon shot.

"Hello, Javik," Artun managed between wheezes.

"Well, I was wondering who you worked for."

"The Philisians paid me well for my intelligence on your defenses, but you and Sigurd surprised me. I told them you were two bumpkins from the mountains with little war experience. It just goes to show, you should never trust me." Artun fell into a fit of coughing up blood.

"Will they be back?"

"Oh yes, they'll be back. This attack was little more than a probe to test your firepower. They need Gorgos if they want to take Ollon. They won't give up easily."

"Will they strike here again?"

"Yes, they fear the harbor defenses, and this is the only other possible landing site. Javik, I want you to know…" Artun fell into another coughing fit and rolled over on his side. Great gouts of blood came from his mouth and his eyes rolled back in his head.

Javik felt his once friend's neck, and there was no pulse. "I know, Artun, I know," he whispered as he closed the warrior's eyes.

The water washing up on the beach was red as Javik saw Sigurd approaching.

"They'll probably be back, Javik," Sigurd called. "We only bloodied them a little. Did you see all those ships?"

"I found Artun among their wounded. He told me this attack was only a token force. I don't think they'll be back until they can regroup. Can we move some of the cannon down from the harbor fortifications?'

"Artun? Where is he?' Sigurd's face took on an angry look.

"Over here, but he's dead now." Javik led Sigurd to the fallen traitor.

Sigurd leaned over and pulled a purse from Artun's belt. He counted out the contents.

"Only twenty crowns, but it and his armor will repay some of his debt."

"He's paid with his life, Sigurd."

"Too bad he didn't get to me. I would have enjoyed killing him. What did you ask about cannon?"

"Can we move some down from the harbor? I think if we position them on that cliff over there, we can fire upon the whole fleet without fear of an infantry attack."

"You should have noticed that position before, Javik. It's an excellent place to put cannon."

"It was my next spot, but I felt the beach guns were first priority. Can you do it?"

"I can try. I'll get some men on it right away, but what if they attack the harbor?"

"Artun told me they fear the harbor defenses. We'll have to put something in place to make them think the cannon are still there after we move them."

"I think I know just what to use for that purpose. My men are at your disposal, Javik. I'll see to the cannon personally."

Artun was wrong. The Philisians did not attack again that day, but the picket boats found the fleet still waiting out to sea preparing for the next attack.

Chapter 27

Javik walked back to the hospital area past rows of wounded men in various stages of treatment. The healers were doing all they could, but the gray pallor of death showed on many faces. Fortunately, none of his friends were among that number.

Avra saw Javik approaching and turned his current patient over to an assistant.

"Lord Javik, you're hurt," Avra said.

"Nothing serious, but I felt you should take a look at it."

Avra's white apron was spattered with blood in so many places it looked as if it were some sort of pattern in the material. His formerly white headband was gray with sweat, but his hands and bare arms were spotlessly clean. He helped Javik remove his armor and the cushioning skins beneath it then inspected the wound.

"It will need to be closed. Come over to the brazier."

Avra led Javik to a large brazier of glowing coals. Several bronze instruments protruded from the red glowing mass, and the healer selected one. He held it up to his face to test the heat and nodded. Two burly men suddenly held Javik tightly.

"Would you like some opiate?" Avra asked.

"What is that?"

"Something to dull the pain," Avra answered.

"I've found those potions also dull the mind, and I'll need all of my wit until this battle is over. Are these men really necessary?" Javik asked.

"They will hold you steady so I can make a good seal."

"I thought you preferred being a seamstress."

"Normally, I would, but there's no time for that now. Are you ready?"

Javik nodded, and the two men tightened their grip.

An involuntary scream escaped Javik's lips on the first application. The smell of his own flesh burning nearly made him sick, but he fought it off. He felt consciousness slipping away at the second application, and he never knew if there were others.

Javik awoke to see Allana in a blood stained apron standing over him.

"Avra says you're not hurt badly, darling, but I had to see for myself."

Allana held a cup of wine to Javik's lips as he rose to one elbow. He took a large drink and revived a bit.

"I'm sure there are others here who need your help more than I do."

"There are many, but they've received all we can give them at this time. I fear many will die in spite of our best healer's attentions."

"Have you seen the beach?"

"Yes, it's so terrible. The cannon extract a heavy sacrifice of blood for the war gods."

"Artun was with them."

Allana looked shocked. "Artun? He was with the Philisians?"

"I talked to him just before he died. He was one of their spies. He said they would attack again today, but they didn't come."

"Barinosh is in the harbor. I went to see him, and he said the Philisian fleet has been badly damaged. They've retreated to a captured port down the coast to make repairs. *The Queen of Gorgos* was damaged by fireballs, but they're making repairs now. All the ships are reloading supplies of shot and powder. Our damages were light," Allana said.

"That's good. Any news from Ollon?" Javik asked.

"A courier arrived today from Charlan. The Philisian invading army is stronger than he expected. They appear to have a large force of Karrans with them. He regrets he can send no troops to our aid." Allana smiled, showing her satisfaction with the news.

"Just as well. Sigurd is moving some of the harbor fortress cannons to the cliffs above the beach. With them in place, I think we can turn back any attack in that quarter. How many men have we lost?" Javik asked.

"Sigurd thinks less than 10%. As far as we can count, the Philisians lost over 1,000 men in the attack. They lost ten warships and five transports to our fleet. We don't know how many men that accounts for."

Javik did some mental calculations and sipped more wine. "I'd say that's another 1,000 or more easily."

At that moment Avra called Allana to another patient. Javik put his armor back on over the bandaged shoulder. His right arm wouldn't move as well as he wished, and there was some pain, but he could stand it easily. He made his way back to his tent on the beach and found Sigurd and Bogard there along with Karl.

"Javik, we thought you'd deserted," Sigurd joked.

"I did desert the world of the conscious for a while after Avra closed my wound with one of his instruments of torture," Javik said.

"Aghh, another scar," Sigurd acted as if he'd been slighted. "I haven't earned a single one since the fighting started."

"I'm starving, is there anything to eat?" Javik asked.

"The cooks are bringing around some of that terrible fish stew these people seem to love," Karl said.

"I like the taste," Bogard said, "as long as there's enough good wine to wash it down."

The men ate dinner and made their plans for the next day as they ate. Javik agreed he should stay out of the battle line due to his impaired ability with his sword arm. The night was spent in fitful sleep.

The Philisians did not come at dawn the next day, but a rider from Thatos told of the arrival of six ships of the Ollon fleet to help the Gorgon vessels. They'd sailed that morning to intercept the invasion force when a picket boat brought word they were on the move toward the island.

Javik made sure his men got a hot meal and ran a quick check of all the gun positions. The new battery on the cliff tops commanded an excellent field of fire on the beach approaches, and were sure to wreak havoc there. These men would see the invaders first, and Javik ordered them to use a signal flag to warn the units on the beach as soon as the ships were visible. All he could do now was wait.

The men had a noon meal and a nap before the cliff battery signaled the approaching armada. Distant cannon fire told of the sea battles raging just over the horizon. The black shapes grew into transports and warships, and the cliff batteries opened fire. Cheers went up from the men on the beach as one ship after another fell prey to the barrage. The beach battery joined in the slaughter as soon as the ships came within their range, and it seemed that none of the vessels would ever reach shore, but several transports ground to a stop on the sand disgorging their warriors in large groups.

The archers began a steady hail of arrows on the advancing invaders as fireballs from the attacking warships rolled harmlessly across the sandy meadow behind the beach. Javik made sure to position his men well out of their range today.

An answering barrage of arrows from the beach caused the Gorgon warriors to use their shields as umbrellas against the rain of death. Javik stood under a wooden roof with Noka. Mordah lay beside Javik panting contentedly in the shade. Sigurd was now in command of the hand cannon troops while Karl led a squadron of cavalry he'd hastily assembled from immigrants used to horses. There were no proper warhorses on the island, but the draft animals available looked fierce enough.

This time, the attackers did not charge the guns. They pushed the transports on to the beach, turned them on their sides to form walls and retreated behind them. Javik saw the ploy immediately and ordered fire arrows to burn the ships. At the same time he ordered his guns to raise their aim and lob bag shot over the overturned hulls. In a few moments, a messenger rode up from the cliff batteries.

"Lord Javik, the Philisians are assembling catapults behind the barricades. Shall we continue to fire on the ships or should we fire on the catapults?"

"Fire on the catapults, but watch for more transports. Change your fire to them if it appears they wish to land a larger force."

The messenger rode away as a hail of fire arrows from the attackers began to fall on the gun positions. Javik formed bucket brigades to douse the flames, and was glad he'd stored his powder kegs in earthen bunkers. One lucky arrow found an open keg, however, and the gun was blown off its carriage along with the loss of all gunners.

The cliff guns soon began to take a toll of the beach catapults. The rain of stones and fireballs slowed to a trickle. In spite of valiant efforts to quench the flames, the barricade ships were now burning fiercely. Javik noticed the cliff battery shifting its fire to the sea as other transports headed for shore. The heat from the burning ships prevented close-in landings, but the warriors waded ashore and formed on the other side of the fiery wall.

The heat made the attacking lines form up much closer to the gun positions than the day before. The hand cannon troops were cutting great openings in their ranks, and the guns reloaded with bag shot to further decimate the attacking horde. In spite of the cliff guns, transports continued to disgorge warriors at an alarming rate. The Philisians charged toward the guns.

Javik ordered the guns to cease firing and sent his own infantry to the front as Karl's horsemen charged from the right. The makeshift cavalry was effective in slowing the advance of the attackers, but only a few made it to the safety of the Gorgon lines on the left. Sigurd's hand cannon forces were still taking a heavy toll, but he was forced to withdraw them after only a few rounds of fire.

The battle now came down to Gorgon against Philisian, and Javik ached to be in the thick of the fight. He could hear the war cries of the attackers now that his guns were silent, and the sound triggered an automatic response deep inside him. He started to draw his sword, but Bogard placed his hand on Javik's arm and shook his head. He handed Javik a hand cannon.

Bogard and Javik loaded and fired from their sheltered position picking their targets carefully. The Gorgon crossbowmen were now in action defending the guns, but the action began to swirl around the command position. Sigurd crossed in front of Javik wielding a pollaxe with devastating effect. He was covered with blood, and Javik couldn't tell if any of it was Sigurd's.

The cliff guns continued to roar, and Javik thought he heard other guns joining in. He looked at his own battery, but each cannon was surrounded by the melee of battle. A surge from Javik's rear area told him the final reserves were committed now. This would tell the tale. The Philisians would be defeated or Gorgos would be theirs.

Three Philisians broke through to the command shelter. Bogard drew his sword and took on the first one as Javik drew for the second. He commanded Mordah to attack the third who turned and fled at the sight of the huge beast. Javik fought left handed, but he was losing ground when a pollaxe split the skull of his opponent. A smiling Sigurd wiped the blood from his face with his sleeve.

"Must I always take care of you?" Sigurd said.

"Look out, Sigurd," Javik called as a Philisian pike man ran for his friend.

Mordah acted before Javik and knocked the pike man on his back with a single leap. Javik finished him off.

"I knew that mongrel was good for something," Sigurd joked.

The battle seemed to be ebbing, but Javik couldn't tell in whose favor. Dead bodies littered the ground, and the groans of the wounded were as loud as the cannon fire from the sea, now closer than ever. A spray of dirt hit Javik in the face as a ball landed within a few meters of his shelter. The fire came from the sea. The Gorgon ships were close to the beach and pouring shot into the rear of the Philisian army. A trumpet sounded, and the attackers began to throw down their weapons. Javik called for his men to cease attacking.

Bloodied warriors huddled into groups with their hands in the air. They were all saying the same thing in their language, but Javik had no idea what it was. One of his men shouted the translation.

"They surrender, they surrender. They're asking for quarter," he shouted.

Javik took the man's arm.

"Do you understand them?"

"Yes, Lord Javik. I spent my youth in Philisia. They're surrendering, Sir."

"Call their captain to me," Javik commanded.

The man called out something in Philisian, and a stately warrior approached Javik, sword cradled in his arms. The other attackers bowed low as he passed. He wore fine armor and a helmet with a golden sea bird motif around the edge. He knelt before Javik and held up his sword with both hands.

Javik's man translated.

280 M. L. Hollinger

"He says he surrenders to a powerful magician. He wants to know which god you pray to for the thunder bolts."

Javik took the handsome sword and pulled the man to his feet.

"Tell him it is not magic. Tell him his men will not be tortured or executed as long as they lay down their arms and armor and obey our commands."

A relieved look came over the Philisian war leader as Javik's words were translated. He turned and made a speech to his men who cheered at the news. They immediately began to shed their armor.

Javik commanded his captains to herd the prisoners into an area where they could be watched and guarded easily. They were to be given water and some food and their wounded treated, but only after all of the Gorgon wounded were seen first. The soldier translated for the Philisian's benefit, and the commander echoed Javik's orders to his men. They began to move toward a hollow in the meadow where Gorgon troops were setting up a perimeter guard. The commander started to follow his men when Javik asked him to stay.

Javik turned to the interpreter. "Tell him I would have him stay here. I want to speak with him."

The war leader nodded his understanding to the interpreter and spoke briefly.

"He says his place is with his men, but he will speak with you for a while if you promise to let him rejoin his troops."

Javik thought about the situation for a moment before answering. This man was, obviously, someone important. He might even fetch a large ransom. If he were allowed to join the men, he could change clothes with one of his friends and possibly avoid being held after the common soldiers are released. Javik decided it was too large a risk.

"What is your name, soldier?" Javik asked the translator.

"I am Darrus, Lord."

"Well, Darrus, tell him I can't allow him to rejoin his men, but he will be allowed to inspect them from time to time and speak with them as long as an interpreter is present. Tell him we will expect a ransom for him, and I must insist he stay separate from the others."

The war leader frowned at this news, but he agreed to the terms.

"Ask his name," Javik commanded.

"He says his name is Vallak."

Javik led Vallak and Darrus to his tent and told Farras to bring food and wine as well as water for washing the blood from their hands and faces. When the two warriors were presentable, they sat down to a cold meal accompanied by a good wine. Vallak ate heartily.

"He compliments you on your choice of wine, Lord," Darrus said as Vallak wiped his hands on the cloth Farras offered.

"Ask him why he surrendered."

"He says his men were frightened by the cannon and several ships refused to land. They said the thunder god was on our side, and they wouldn't oppose him. He thought he could manage a landing with the remaining troops, but our resistance was too strong. When our ships began shelling his army from the rear, he knew his own fleet had abandoned them. He saw no reason to continue the slaughter."

At that moment, Sigurd appeared. He too had cleaned up a bit.

"I might know I'd find you eating and drinking, Javik. How's the wine?"

"Excellent, have some," Javik said as he indicated Farras should pour a cup for his friend.

"Who's this?" Sigurd asked as Farras poured.

"This is Vallak. I think he may be a man of some importance," Javik answered.

The Philisian smiled and bowed toward Sigurd at the mention of his name.

"I'm having some of my men who understand Philisian round up the officers now. We'll find a suitable place to confine them and see how much ransom they'll command," Sigurd said.

"What can we do with the troops? There seems to be quite a few of them," Javik asked.

"Over a thousand, at last count. Most of them are healthy, but some are wounded too badly to survive. I counted over ten hulks on the beach, and all but two of them could be used as prisons. We'll put the prisoners aboard and anchor them out to sea. The sharks can be our guards. Do you want me to take this man now?"

"No, I think he's important enough to warrant special treatment. Notice the quality of his armor and the gold design on his helmet. His sword was also quite elegant." Javik produced the sword for Sigurd's inspection.

"Phew! This is a high quality blade," Sigurd spoke admiringly as he hefted the weapon. He took a towel from Farras and cleaned the blade. "It has an inscription. Can you read this?" He handed the sword to Darrus.

The soldier studied the blade for a few moments before replying. "It's in an old version of their language, but I think it says something like, *let all unbelievers die."*

"Unbelievers in what?" Sigurd asked.

"There is a secret sect among the Philisians who worship a god they say is superior to all others. This man must be a member of that sect," Darrus said.

"Hmmm, a religious zealot, yet he surrendered. Those kind usually fight to the death," Javik said.

"Then we must watch him very closely. Your idea of keeping him separate from his men is a good one, Javik. I think there are some old dungeons under the palace that may prove suitable for this one," Sigurd said.

"Take charge of him, Sigurd. I'm sure Allana wants to have a conference at the palace as soon as possible. We'll talk with him more after that. I need to see to the clean-up of the battlefield.

Sigurd detailed a trusted captain and several men to escort Vallak to the palace and find a suitable cell. Javik asked Darrus to remain with Vallak as interpreter, and the business of cleaning up after the carnage began.

Chapter 28

Allana called a council meeting that evening. Barinosh was the first to speak.

"The Philisian fleet has retreated. Our picket boats tell us they've gone far to the North to support their army from that direction. I think we are safe, at least for the moment."

"How many ships did we lose?" Allana asked.

"Only one, My Lady. A Philisian fireball caught it when the captain sailed too close to the attacking ships. We managed to rescue most of the crew, but the ship and its cannon are lost," Barinosh answered.

"How many of their ships are lost?" Sigurd asked. "I counted over twenty hulks on the beach and in the shallow water offshore."

Barinosh counted to himself for a moment. "That would make over thirty five of their ships sunk. Most were transports, but I think at least ten warships."

"Wonderful news," Allana said. "Your fleet did well, Barinosh."

"Thank you, Lady," Barinosh said as he acknowledged the applause of the other council members.

"Their losses on land are just as devastating," Javik said. "We've counted over three thousand dead and hold nearly

1,500 prisoner. Sigurd and I think at least six of them will bring healthy ransoms."

"I understand one of them is a general of some sort," Allana said.

"Yes, I believe he is," Javik replied. "His name is Vallak, and the men quit attacking us on his order. Would you like to see him?"

"Yes, have him brought in," Allana said.

The council waited in quiet conversation, sipping wine. The mood was jubilant. The Philisians were defeated with only moderate casualties, and the fleet would soon be repaired and expanded to insure success against any subsequent attacks.

Four guards accompanied Vallak into the council chamber with Darrus beside him. They stopped before Allana and the chief guard saluted.

"Your Highness, this is the prisoner named Vallak."

"Very well. Stay close by in case you are needed," Allana said.

Darrus translated the situation to Vallak who faced Allana and bowed low.

"He says he's honored to meet such a beautiful queen," Darrus translated.

"He knows how to flatter if nothing else," Sigurd said.

Allana raised a hand toward Sigurd, who fell silent.

"What would you have me do with you and your men?" Allana asked Vallak.

Darrus translated the general's reply.

"He asks you to let them return to their homes. He gives his pledge they would never attack Gorgos again."

"Hah!" Sigurd reacted. "The pledge of an enemy is useless

once he has a sword in his hand again."

"Vallak impresses me as a man of honor, Sigurd. Look at his clothes. He's certainly no ordinary general." Allana turned to Vallak. "Who are you?"

Once more Darrus translated.

"He says he is Prince Vallak of the royal house of Philisia."

"A likely story," Sigurd said with an air of disbelief in his voice.

At that moment a guard entered the room carrying a sealed scroll.

"Your Highness, a ship from Philisia just arrived flying a white flag. The emissary aboard asks an audience and sends this for your eyes only." He knelt before Allana and handed her the scroll.

"Where is the emissary now?" Allana asked.

"Outside, Your Highness."

"Show him in."

The guard saluted and left, returning with a small, fair skinned man in dark blue robes. He wore a curiously shaped hat made of velvet, and a large gold chain with links shaped like dolphins hung around his neck. His hair and beard were blonde, and his eyes were a piercingly bright blue. He strode to Vallak and bowed deeply before repeating the performance for Allana. He spoke with a heavy accent.

"Your Highness, I am Tulliga, chief counselor to His Majesty King Xeno of Philisia."

"You are more welcome than your army, Lord Tulliga," Allana said as she offered her hand to the man.

Tulliga kissed her hand and stood before her. "The scroll you hold contains the terms of our peace treaty with Gorgos.

Will you read it?"

"Gladly," Allana said as she broke the seal and unrolled the scroll. She perused it for a moment before turning to the council.

"The King of Philisia proposes a treaty with Gorgos. He will vow never to attack us again in return for our neutrality in his war with Tulla. He offers two million gold crowns as reparations for his latest attack and pledges his son, Vallak, as hostage until the war is over. He requests the return of all men captured on Gorgos, but will pay 100,000 crowns ransom for each of six officers, if they are still alive. He does not ask to use Thatos as a port until the war is over, and then only for commerce."

Allana set down the scroll and looked at the stunned council members. She turned back to Tulliga.

"I think we'll need time to discuss this in private. My servant, here, will see that you are provided with a comfortable place to wait and anything you may need." Allana nodded to a servant who escorted Tulliga from the room.

"A generous offer," Sigurd said as soon as Tulliga was beyond the door.

"The best part is, he only requests our neutrality," Noka added.

"But what of Charlan? Now that he's seen how effective our cannons are, he'll want us to do a lot of fighting for him," Javik said.

"Perhaps Charlan may make us a better offer?" Avra said as he perused the treaty scroll.

"What more could we ask for? We could easily hold off Charlan's fleet if he should decide to take action," Karl said.

"We could ask for independence," Allana said. "

The other members of the council reacted favorably to the idea.

"What if Philisia wins the war?" Avra inserted a bouquet of thorns amongst their flowery thoughts.

"How could they win if we fight on Charlan's side?" Sigurd said. "We've already destroyed half of their navy, and they don't dare attack us again if they want to defend their supply routes by sea."

"We must send an emissary to Charlan to test his reaction," Avra said.

"I was in Charlan's court just before the war began," Margan inserted. "He still has dreams of conquering Allana, if not Gorgos."

"Still, we must see what he will say about the Philisians' offer. If we remain neutral, he may lose the war," Allana said.

"I will take the message to Charlan, Lady," Avra said. "If any bargaining is to be done, I'm better at it than any of your other counselors."

"Very well, you shall take our offer, Avra. Scribe, take this down. We will accept the Philisian offer unless Charlan relinquishes all claim to tribute from Gorgos, grants the island complete independence and recognizes me as queen. We will remain allied to Tulla and fight on their side in this war, but he must vow never to attack Gorgos in any way and to allow full and free trade between Gorgos and all other nations of the world. Any questions or suggestions?"

The other council members shook their heads in the negative.

"Then make haste, Avra. We will need Charlan's reply before we can answer Tulliga."

* * * * *

The little Argani was not feeling very comfortable as he walked down the long carpet toward Charlan and Brianna. Stopping in at a friend's café for breakfast that morning, he'd learned Charlan was applying a great deal of pressure on the moneylenders to extend payments on his debt. They feared persecution soon, and Avra would be no exception since Charlan owed him money also. He bowed low in front of his nominal sovereign.

"What brings you here with such urgent business, Avra?" Charlan asked.

"My Lord, I bring you good news of the defeat of the Philisian force sent to conquer Gorgos. We sank many of their ships and killed most of their army. We hold several officers and lords for ransom along with over 1,000 other prisoners."

"I know all of that, you didn't need to come here to tell me," Charlan responded with an air of impatience.

"There has been another development, Lord. The Philisians have sued us for peace."

"Their armies still attack our forces in the North. How can they sue for peace with Ollom?"

"Not with Ollom, Lord, with Gorgos."

The assembled court let out a gasp of surprise at this announcement. Charlan rose from his throne and was about to strike Avra when Bradish held him back. He whispered in Charlan's ear.

"Hear him out, Lord. This may work to our advantage."

Charlan shook off Bradish's grasp and resumed his seat.

"A brash thing for them to do. Why would they think Gorgos could speak for me?"

"They do not, Lord. They offer very generous reparations for their attack in return for our neutrality."

"How can Gorgos remain neutral?" Charlan raged. "Gorgos is part of Tulla and Ollon! They will fight beside us or suffer our wrath later."

Avra could feel the moment slipping away. Obviously, Charlan was not in any mood to give up Gorgos now that he'd seen the power of the Gorgon warships. Bradish once more counseled Charlan.

"Lord, without the help of Gorgos, we have no hope of defeating the Philisians. As long as they can resupply their forces by sea, they will continue to advance. Our emissaries to Oliga have produced little in the way of help from the capitol. His armies are not yet recovered from the civil war. We cannot afford to anger Gorgos. If Allana sides with the Philisians, all is lost. Even if she remains neutral the question of our victory is seriously in doubt. I suggest you make her a better offer."

"A better offer!" Charlan whispered through clenched teeth. His face was now bright red, and saliva was beginning to leak from the corner of his mouth. "I'll let her live instead of ripping out her guts for the amusement of the people."

"Be calm, Sire. Allana is your friend, not your enemy. You know she covets the throne of Gorgos as her rightful inheritance. Why not give it to her?"

"Give it to her!" Charlan seemed a long way from calm. "I told you what that whore did to me, didn't I? I'll have my revenge."

"Revenge is for the victors, Sire. If Allana joins Philisia or remains neutral, she will sit where you do now with Gorgos as only a part of her kingdom."

"What should I do?" Charlan seemed to compose himself a bit.

"Ask to see the Philisian terms, then we can develop our offer in council."

Charlan nodded and turned to Avra.

"Have you brought the Philisian proposal?"

"Yes, Lord." Avra handed the scroll to Bradish.

"Good! We will study this before we compose our offer. You may stay in the palace until then. We'll call for you when we're ready."

Two guards escorted Avra from the audience chamber as Charlan moved to private rooms with his council close behind.

* * * * *

In the council chambers, Bradish studied the Philisian scroll then spoke.

"A very generous proposal, Sire - two million crowns in reparations and several hundred thousand crowns in ransoms for simply remaining neutral. I can hardly imagine what King Xeno would offer for an alliance."

"We certainly can't match two million. This is useless. We'll send an invasion force as soon as we can get one ready," Charlan said. He slumped back in his chair with a sour face.

Charlan's Admiral spoke, "I saw what the Gorgon ships did to the Philisian navy, Sire, and our spies tell us that half the Philisian fleet lies as charred hulks on the Gorgon beach. Our navy would fare no better."

"From the number of transports sent to Gorgos, I'd say the Philisians landed over 3,000 troops there. Even if we managed to get some ships past the cannon, we'd face stiff opposition on the beach," Charlan's General offered.

"We have no choice, Lord," Bradish spoke. "We cannot attack Gorgos, and if we don't have them with us, we will lose this war. We must offer Allana independence and the crown."

"Oliga won't stand for it," Charlan said. "Even if we defeat the Philisians, he'll never allow the loss of Gorgos now that it's profitable again."

"Oliga can make no move against Gorgos without your navy, Sire," Bradish said.

Charlan stood up and began to pace the floor rapidly. After a few moments, he stopped with an evil grin on his face.

"We will give the bitch her crown for now, but we'll take it away again when this is all over. Scribe! Draw up a treaty with Gorgos granting it independence with Allana as queen as long as she stays allied with us and attacks Philisia. I also want all prisoners sent here to Ollom. The ones suitable for ransom were captured while Gorgos was still mine. I'd have them also."

The scribe nodded and began to write.

"Any objections?" Charlan asked. His counselors nodded in the negative.

Avra took the offer back to Allana, and was glad to set foot on Gorgos once again in one piece.

* * * * *

Allana perused the scroll then sent it around to the other counselors.

"It's what you wanted, but I don't think we should give up the ransom money," Sigurd said.

"Nor I," Karl added.

"I think Charlan will negotiate on that point," Avra said. "We need to make a counter offer on that part of the treaty."

"We'll keep Prince Vallak and let him have all the others. The Prince will be our guarantee against another attack from Philisia," Allana said.

"There's no need to tell Charlan about him at all," Javik said. "The Count doesn't know how many people we plan to hold for ransom. We simply keep Vallak here as a guarantee against another Philisian attack and they can ransom him after the war is over."

"I agree," Allana said. "Bring in Tulliga," she instructed a servant.

Tulliga entered and bowed to Allana. "What is your answer, Your Highness?"

"We may not accept your King's very generous offer. We were weakened by your attack, and I fear Charlan will not tolerate our neutrality. If I am to save this island from ruin, I must stay allied with Tulla. The Count has ordered me to send all prisoners to him, but I will keep Prince Vallak here for his safety and as a guarantee against any attack by Philisia. Tell King Xeno I regret we are still at war." Allana handed the treaty scroll back to Tulliga.

The ambassador seemed to slump a bit, and his face took on a gaunt look. "Then our war is doomed to failure, Highness. I will advise my King to withdraw his forces from Tulla as quickly as possible."

"Wise counsel. We will be forced to attack your ships if you continue the invasion," Allana answered.

The ambassador bowed low and left the room.

"Send for Prince Vallak," Allana ordered.

In a few moments the Prince appeared accompanied by Darrus. Allana explained the situation to him, and the Prince fell to one knee pleading woefully in his own language. Darrus translated.

"The Prince says his place is with his men. He begs you to let him go with them and promises you half his fortune if he can do so."

"A noble statement," Sigurd said. "I'm almost moved to let him go."

"A war leader's place is with his men," Javik said, "but we should hold him here until this war is settled. The Philisians could return at any time."

"Tell him we sympathize with him, but we must hold him here as a guarantee against further attacks from his country."

Vallak wept openly at the translation, but he allowed Darrus to lead him back to his cell.

Within two weeks the Philisians withdrew completely from Tulla under the guns of the Gorgon fleet. Charlan grudgingly gave the island independence and recognized Allana as Queen. The only thing remaining was a coronation ceremony and a wedding.

Chapter 29

Margan begged for the privilege of planning the glorious events, and Allana couldn't deny him. The minstrel proved to be a fierce taskmaster as he ordered the palace staff about and dealt with dozens of merchants. Invitations went out to over two hundred different special people including Javik's family, many friends in his home village and all those who helped Allana along the way. The new bureaucracy of Gorgos was invited, and Charlan's court was issued a special invitation. The big event was scheduled for six months distant to allow for travel and the time needed to prepare for the double ceremony.

*****

The contingent from Holliga arrived with Browdat seasick from the ferry ride to Gorgos. Javik was at the dock to greet them, and he helped his mother step onto the pier.

"You look as lovely as ever, Mother," Javik said as he embraced her.

Dana held him at arm's length and studied his new form of dress and expensive clothes. The tunic was now velvet instead of leather, and a chain of office made of gold dolphins draped across his shoulders. The crest of the royal house of Gorgos blazed on the left side of the top. Heavy woolen trousers were now silk, and the boots were suede instead of polished leather.

The sword of Aelin the Red hung on one side with Zuban's dagger on the other.

"I'd hardly know you, my son. You seem so much more mature and so rich looking I think I should bow to you."

The rest of the party joined Dana on the pier, and porters rushed to carry their bags to waiting carts.

"You never will bow to me, Mother. It's I who should bow to you." Javik said. "I thought you might bring Garen."

"She thought of it," Goldar said as he embraced his adopted son. "But I told her you and Allana would need some honeymoon time before taking on a child."

"As usual, your third father gives wise council," Dana said.

"You can bring him on your next visit, Mother," Javik said.

Frieda was next to embrace her adopted son. "We're so proud of you, Javik, but I think your second father will need some time to recover before he can tell you himself."

"I never knew water could be so bumpy," Browdat said as he took Javik's hand. He was quite pale, and his black beard showed flecks of that morning's breakfast. "I am proud of you, son. You've brought great credit to our house."

"And to your own," Goldar said. "As your third father, all I can say is that I wish you'd been my own son."

"You care for my mother, and that makes me a true son of yours," Javik said.

"Don't forget me," Berda said as he stepped forward with his wife. She was just beginning to show her pregnancy, but she was every bit as lovely as Javik remembered her from the village.

"And your beautiful wife, Clara," Javik said as he embraced her very cautiously.

"The baby is quite safe from your strength, Javik," Clara said as she pulled Javik closer. "Berda never stops talking about your adventures together. You'll have to tell me how much of what he says is true."

"I'm sure everything he says is true. I've never known Berda to lie," Javik said.

"So there really are fierce sea monsters and men with two heads here," Clara said with mock seriousness.

The group laughed at the obvious joke, but Berda blushed beet red.

Tao Shan was the last person in line. He greeted Javik with a broad smile on his face.

"You have done well, Javik. I don't number many princes among my students."

"I owe much of my success to your training, not to mention the fact that it saved my life many times over," Javik said as he embraced his former mentor.

"How is Allana?" Tao Shan asked.

"She's more beautiful than ever. Wait 'til you see her. I know she'll be happy to see you."

Javik turned to the whole group.

"Allana apologizes for not being here to greet you, but I'm afraid she's tied down with preparations for the coronation and our marriage. Right now Margan is with her in the temple of Godon helping her rehearse for the coronation. She'll join us for dinner."

"I can't wait to see your wild girl in royal robes," Tao Shan said. His remark elicited laughter from the group since all of them were familiar with how she looked when Javik first met her.

Javik changed the subject. "Come, carriages are waiting to take us to the palace. Karl is busy at the farm terraces, but he'll be back for the evening meal, and Margan will give us all a song of the old days afterward. It's good to see all of you again."

The party was soon settled into the palace enjoying the luxuries associated with the royal residence. It was still a month until the big day – plenty of time to catch up on all the events since their last meeting.

* * * * *

Margan, on the other hand, was feeling the press of time. With only a month remaining, he was very worried about the preparations as he inspected the temple of Godon, the sea god. It was an impressive building built half on land and half over water. The entrance was at the top of six steps, one for each of the known seas. Six wide columns supported a frieze depicting various sea creatures with Godon in his usual form of half-man, half-porpoise at the center. It was one of the first buildings restored under Allana's rule.

Most of the structure could be re-created from paintings on the walls of old buildings in Thatos. Former citizens of Gorgos helped fill in the missing pieces from their own memories. Inside the temple, the prospective worshiper saw a large, bronze statue of the half man, half porpoise god on a green marble base surrounded by a wide mosaic floor showing scenes from the sea – a shark devouring a sailor cast overboard from a sinking ship – fantastic sea creatures jumping from breaking waves – ships battling with fireballs and ramming their enemies. Seashells and starfish dotted the remaining space.

Behind the statue, and facing the sea, a large stone altar rested upon huge marble conch shells with immense bronze braziers burning on either side. The part of the temple built over the sea was open, and the water came inside to break on a marble shoreline just in front of the altar. Along each of the sidewalls, smaller columns supported the roof structure rising from wide galleries. Margan looked up to see a circular window in the dome over the altar. The sun cast a beam through the opening illuminating the statue of Godon and scattering golden reflections around the altar room.

Biddish, the high priest of Godon, met Margan as he approached the altar. The priest wore sea-green robes held in place with gold dolphin clasps at each shoulder. He was a tall man with severe features, invoking an air of authority with his appearance alone. His voice was the crowning feature of his personality, however. It was deep and stentorian, befitting the duties of his office.

"Good morning, Lord. Welcome to Godon's temple."

"It looks wonderful, Biddish. Is the ceremonial room ready?"

"Yes, there's still some leakage, but I don't think it will interfere with the ceremony. Come, I'll show it to you. I think you'll be very pleased."

Biddish led Margan to one side of the temple and opened a small wooden door. He led the minstrel down a long, twisting stairway lit by torches.

"This stairway was filled with rubble. It took us a month to clear it, but the result was well worth our efforts, as you will see."

At the bottom of the stairs, Margan calculated they were well below sea level, even at low tide. Workers were still busy cleaning and repairing a large bronze mechanism, green with years of neglect. They stopped their banging and clanging on the arrival of the High Priest and bowed low.

"You may take a break," Biddish said, and all but one man left to breathe some fresh air. The room was heavy with the smell of sweat and bronze corrosion.

"This is Harlan, our chief engineer for these works," Biddish introduced the burly man who bowed to Margan.

"What is this?" Margan asked.

Biddish nodded to Harlan as an indication he should explain.

"Sir, this is the chamber our Queen will use for the coronation ceremony. She will enter here," he indicated a hatch in the cylindrical main chamber. We will then fill the chamber with seawater and open a hatch on top. Four men will pull on these ropes to lift her to the surface."

"Isn't this dangerous?" Margan asked.

"It's all part of the coronation ceremony. Our Queen must rise from the sea if the people are to recognize her as the true queen. It only involves holding her breath for a short while. We'll help her practice until we're sure she can do it," Biddish said.

"What if something goes wrong?" Margan asked.

"Once the upper hatch is open, she can easily swim out of the chamber. As long as that hatch is closed, we can dump the seawater from the chamber into that pool." Biddish indicated a large, empty marble pool. "The upper hatch cannot be opened unless the chamber is full of water. If the chamber is only partially full, there's plenty of air for her to breathe until we can dump the water."

"Speaking of air," Margan said. "Why is it that the torches down here don't burn up all the air?"

"There is a ventilation system powered by the action of the waves. It doesn't keep the air completely fresh, as you've probably noticed, but it does prevent suffocation in this confined space."

"Truly a marvel, the effect must be spectacular," Margan said.

"No one here has ever seen it before. The last coronation was Princess Allana's mother, and that was many years ago," Biddish said.

"Will the mechanism be ready in time?" Margan asked.

"Aye, Sir," Harlan answered. "We only need a few more days to finish and test the mechanism."

"Test it well, Harlan. Your device will hold a precious cargo," Margan said.

"Never fear, Sir. We love Queen Allana," Harlan assured him.

"Come, let me show you the dolphin pens," Biddish said as he led Margan back up to the temple. He led the minstrel down the left gallery from the altar to the sea and stopped at a bronze grating in the floor. The unmistakable squawking and clicking of a dolphin rose from the pen.

"These are my addition to the coronation ceremony," Biddish said as he proudly pointed into the pen. "There's another pen like this on the other side."

Margan looked over the edge of the floor to see a dolphin circling inside a small pool.

"What will they do?" Margan asked.

"They are being trained now, but we hope they will escort our Queen from where she rises from the sea to the front of the altar."

"Very fine, but don't risk anything. If you're not completely sure of them, don't use them," Margan said.

"I'm confident they'll be ready. Come to the other side of

the temple, though. The best part of this is yet for you to see."
Biddish smiled broadly, as he led the minstrel to the other side
of the temple and a heavy steel door with formidable padlocks.
The priest opened the locks and swung the door open. Pulling a
torch from one of the sconces along the wall, he led Margan into
a short hallway opening up into a large chamber filled with
wooden chests.

"What is this?" Margan asked.

"When we opened the ceremonial chamber below the
temple, we found these chests. I think you'll like what's in
them." Biddish waved a hand at the closest chest indicating
Margan should open it.

The minstrel lifted the heavy lid revealing gems, pearls, gold
coins and jewelry. He gasped at the sight. "There's a fortune
here," Margan said.

"And, there are ten chests just like this one. This is the
hidden treasure of Gorgos. Allana's father must have put it in
the chamber when the Voldunee attacked. He filled the
stairway with rubble to discourage entry. This all belongs to the
Queen now."

"We must tell her of this miraculous find," Margan said.

"In good time. This will be the sea god's gift to her on her
wedding night," Biddish said.

"How fitting," was all Margan could manage.

* * * * *

At last the day came. The honored guests assembled in the
Temple of Godon to witness the coronation ceremony. Javik sat
with his parents and the other guests from his village on one
side of the altar while dignitaries from Tulla and Ollon sat on
the other side. The council of Gorgos and other officials of the

island sat in the gallery on one side of the artificial inlet, while the other gallery was reserved for heroes of the recent battle. The throng grew silent at the sound of a large gong.

A chant arose outside the temple, and a procession of priests and acolytes made its way to the altar. First came four young boys dressed in short skirts and swinging incense censures. Behind them came a dozen women in white gowns with golden trim, playing musical instruments. The song was a mysterious blend of sea sounds and hymns to Godon. Next came the priests chanting in a dirge-like monotone. They were dressed in sea green robes with white trim and wore a wreath of plaited seaweed around their heads. Bringing up the rear, another party of women in white dresses beat tambourines in time to the priest's chant while four men in short skirts carried two chests slung on poles.

The women musicians took up a position behind the great statue of Godon while the incense boys stood on either side of the altar. The priests surrounded the altar with the High Priest standing on a raised platform behind it. The tambourine women and the chest bearers moved to the edge of the water in the artificial inlet. When all were in place the music and chanting stopped.

Only the sound of waves lapping on the marble beach and the cries of gulls broke the heavy silence. The smell of the incense mingled with the natural salt fragrance of the ocean in a pleasant blend of aromas invoking dreams of distant lands. The light beam from the hole in the dome shone on the High Priest alone. He raised his arms and began.

"Great Godon, we gather here a people without a monarch. Too long you have withheld your blessings from our island.

Grant us your favor that we may prosper again. Grant us a queen blessed by your almighty hand."

Once more the temple was silent, then water in the inlet began to boil and foam near the center of the waterway, and the crowd sucked in a collective breath. The great gong sounded once more, and expressions of awe and wonder greeted a head arising from the water. It was Allana with her hair tied behind her head in a pearl encrusted clasp. She didn't blink or shake her head to clear the saltwater from her eyes but stood still as her body down to her waist came into view. Her breasts were bare, and Javik gave a startled gasp at the sight.

He had little time to wonder at the sight as the cries of two dolphins split the quiet of the temple and echoed off the marble walls. They swam to Allana's side and circled her screaming their staccato calls as they did so. As the new Queen began to walk toward the altar, the dolphins continued to escort her. Once she reached shallower water, it became obvious she was completely naked. The crowd gasped in astonishment, and Javik stood up automatically. The rest of the group thought it was a cue and stood with him.

The dolphins beached themselves on the marble shoreline, and Allana walked to the altar where the tambourine women surrounded her. The High Priest spoke again. "Oh great Godon, we are thankful for your blessings. This woman is truly a gift from your benevolence." He dropped his arms and spoke to the tambourine women.

"Does this woman bear the mark of Godon?" the High Priest intoned.

"Yea, she does bear the mark," the women replied in unison.

"Then let her be clothed and brought to the altar," the High

Priest said.

The dolphins returned to the water while the women toweled off the seawater clinging to Allana's body before slipping a pure white gown with gold trim over her head. Golden sandals completed the outfit, and Allana walked proudly to the altar opposite the high priest.

"What sacrifice do you bring to Godon?" the High Priest asked.

Allana raised her hands and bowed low to the statue of Godon. The light from the hole in the ceiling now shone directly on the altar.

"I bring treasure from the land and sea." She motioned for one chest to be brought forward and opened. Gold coins and bags of pearls spilled out on the altar as the burly men dumped the chest's contents.

"Godon is pleased," the High Priest intoned.

"I bring the heads of Godon's enemies to show my loyalty."

The other chest contained four skulls, and the men placed one skull on each corner of the altar.

"Godon is pleased," the High Priest repeated. "Bring forth the crown of Gorgos."

A gong sounded, and two priests appeared from a bronze door carrying a golden crown on a purple velvet pillow. It was two snakes consuming each other with a silver conch shell on top. The eyes of the snakes were precious gems and their bodies gleamed with smaller stones. The priests stopped in front of Allana, and one moved behind her holding the crown over her head.

"Godon has consented to give us a true queen. All praise to Godon."

"All praise to Godon," the crowd responded.

"If you accept this crown, you assume the responsibility for Godon's people and their welfare. Should you fail in your duties, the wrath of Godon will fall upon you and all the people of Gorgos. Do you accept Godon's burden?"

"Gladly, for myself and my people," Allana responded.

A large gong sounded as the priest lowered the crown on Allana's head. When it was in place, the women began a song of celebration and the priests led the new Queen in a procession six times around the altar stopping where they began. The light from the rooftop hole now shone directly on Allana.

"Let all here now swear allegiance to Queen Allana," the High Priest shouted.

"Hail Queen Allana. We salute you and pledge our loyalty," the crowd responded in unison.

Javik noted that Charlan remained silent.

The crowd filed past Allana paying their respects to the new queen. Javik was the last in line. He dropped to one knee before her.

"Rise my love. Today we will be wed, and though I be a queen, you will never bow to me again," Allana said as she lifted Javik to his feet.

"I never thought this day would come," Javik said. "May I kiss you now?"

He moved to embrace her, but Allana pushed him back.

"That's considered bad luck here on Gorgos. There's plenty of time for that later.

The dignitaries left the temple of Godon and entered carriages for the ride back to the palace. Allan's carriage was in the middle of the line. Every flower in bloom at this time of year on Gorgos adorned the conveyance, and that meant a profusion of color. Javik joined her inside the carriage.

Behind Allana's carriage, the carriages of Gorgos's nobility followed. Sigurd's carriage featured gold leaf trim, and the horses were coal black with huge white plumes. The rest of the group opted for less opulent arrangements.

Happy subjects lined the procession's route through the city and up to the palace. In each square they passed, people were feasting from great tables laden with food of all kinds. Music filled the air and people danced anywhere there was room. The palace was decorated with banners and pennants, and the guards were dressed in their best armor. The wedding quests waited in the great audience chamber where the tables already groaned under the weight of the many dishes waiting to be consumed.

Allana's carriage stopped at the main entrance, but she did not move to get out.

"Javik, I will put on more suitable clothes for our wedding," she said. "You get out here and join our guests. I'll be in shortly."

Javik looked at her. Even with the residue of the salt water clinging to her skin, she was beautiful, but he understood her wish to look her best.

"I will count every second until I see you again," he said as he kissed her hand before stepping down from the carriage.

The great hall was alive with merriment. The orchestra played lively melodies while the guests stepped through the intricate patterns of the various dances. Javik knew one or two, but he made a note to learn several more now that times would be less frantic. He made his way to a table Browdat set up to display Berglauni food, but his chief interest was the large keg of qush resting on heavy supports. Most of the Gorgons and Tullans were bypassing it for the more familiar wine amphora at another table, but Javik's mouth watered as he smelled the aroma of the strong brew.

Sigurd, Karl and Noka joined Goldar in sampling the quality of Browdat's gift to the bride and groom. Javik joined them, and immediately found a huge mug in his hand, courtesy of Browdat.

"To the new groom!" Browdat shouted loudly enough to be heard in Harrish.

The other guests stopped what they were doing and turned to the thunderous noise. They raised their wine goblets in answer to the toast, and Browdat began the bawdy ballad customary at Berglauni wedding celebrations. Fortunately, most of the guests didn't understand the words. Frieda cast a black look at her husband, and he stopped after one verse.

Javik was on his third mug by the time the trumpets sounded to announce Allana's arrival. He'd vowed to pace himself, but between Browdat, Goldar and his friends, he was hardly allowed to finish one drink before another appeared in a mug seemingly larger than the last.

All heads turned to the staircase leading from the royal apartments to the great hall. At the top of the marble stairs, Allana stood like a goddess.

Strands of pearls twined through the ebony hair piled high on top of her head, adding highlights to its already elegant sheen. Large, silver and sapphire earrings reflected the light from the dozens of candles around her. A silver necklace with diamonds and sapphires adorned her throat. Her dress was a delicate shade of blue and so flimsy it could have been made of spider webs. It draped across one shoulder and hung to the floor leaving her other shoulder bare and exposing the tops of her bosoms only slightly. A silver armlet wrapped three times around her bare arm while silver bracelets hung on her wrists. As she stepped forward, silver sandals graced her feet.

Barinosh appeared by her side and tamped his staff on the floor three times. The crowd fell silent.

"Her Majesty, Queen Allana of Gorgos," he intoned in an official voice.

The orchestra took up a regal tune as the guests bowed before her. Allana walked down the stairs very slowly, not stopping to acknowledge anyone until she reached Charlan and Brianna. She stood before them for a moment relishing the situation.

"Rise Count Charlan, Countess Brianna," Allana said in her most condescending manner. "You are the most honored of my guests because you have made all of this possible."

She lifted the Count to his feet and turned to the guests, raising one arm for silence. The orchestra stopped playing as she turned, and Allana spoke loudly enough for all to hear.

"The bond between Gorgos and Ollon will always be strong. I pledge here in the presence of all to always hold Ollon as a special ally. May our two realms always enjoy the happiness and prosperity they do now."

The guests applauded wildly as Allana took Charlan's hand and held it high for all to see.

"A very fine speech, *Your Majesty*," Charlan choked out the last two words.

"I mean it, Charlan. Now all of these people know about

our 'special' relationship, and they would be most distressed to see any enmity between us. Please enjoy the party." Allana whispered through clenched teeth.

Javik took this occasion to join Allana, but she was still waving to the happy crowd. Charlan spoke to him.

"I trust you enjoy being spanked like a child?" Charlan said in a low voice.

Javik smiled broadly. "Why Count, my ass is thickly calloused from my lover's attentions." He left Charlan there with his chin hanging.

Allana led Javik to the table where King Oliga sat with his Queen. She bowed before him as the King rose to greet her.

"Cousin Allana," Oliga smiled as he took her hand and lifted her to her feet. "We are forever in your debt for helping destroy the Philisian fleet. You've been instrumental in preserving our province of Ollon, though it cost me the island of Gorgos."

"Gorgos is still yours, Cousin. I will always respect your throne and honor your name," Allana replied.

"Introduce me to your consort," Oliga said indicating Javik.

"This is Lord Javik of Berglaundia. I owe him my very life," Allana said as Javik bowed before Oliga.

"I heard about your actions in freeing your Queen from the Turrek. You are a brave warrior indeed, Javik," Oliga said.

"Thank you, Majesty, but there are other warriors here from my homeland whose deeds make mine pale into insignificance," Javik said.

"I will meet them later, Javik. I think your Queen is anxious to start the wedding ceremony." Oliga indicated the center of the great hall where Barinosh and Biddish, the priest of Godon, were waiting.

"It's time, my love," Allana said as she led Javik to the waiting officials.

Javik and Allana walked to the center of the room. They knelt before Barinosh on purple velvet cushions, and the crowd grew silent.

"Javik, Lord of Gorgos, do you wish our Queen as your bride?"

"I do, with all my heart," Javik responded.

"Queen Allana, do you accept Lord Javik as your consort?"

"I do, gladly," Allana said.

"Then by the power vested in me as Chief Admiral of the Gorgon fleet, I declare this union valid."

The priest stepped forward now.

"Queen Allana, do you accept this man, Lord Javik as both a subject and a mate in the eyes of Godon?"

"I do," Allana said as she looked lovingly into Javik's eyes.

The priest turned to Javik.

"Lord Javik, do you promise to honor your Queen and obey her in all things?"

"I do," Javik answered.

The priest turned to an acolyte who handed him a silver crown. He turned back and placed the crown on Javik's head.

"I now crown you Prince Javik of Gorgos and pronounce Godon's blessing on your union with our Queen."

The priest lifted the pair to their feet and turned them to face the guests. Javik took Allana in his arms and kissed her to the applause of the crowd as the orchestra took up a joyful tune.

The party went on until well into the morning before the quests began to leave. Dana and Goldar came up to the new couple to say their goodnights.

"My son, I'm so proud of you," Dana said as she embraced Javik.

"Mother, you've made all of this possible," Javik said as he held her at arm's length and admired her beauty even though she was his mother.

Goldar took Javik's hand. "No father could ask for a better son," he said.

Allana embraced Dana. "You are mother to me also, Lady Dana. You will always have royal status on Gorgos."

"I have you and Javik in my heart, and that's all I need," Dana said.

Next was Browdat and Frieda. Browdat was not too steady on his feet from the effects of the qush. Frieda helped him approach the couple, and the war leader smothered his adopted son in a bear-like embrace.

"Who would think there'd be a royal in my household?" he said then whispered in Javik's ear. "I didn't think much of that ceremony – all that stuff about obeying a woman."

Javik whispered back. "The priest only says what we all know to be true, Father."

Browdat's eyes took on a merry twinkle as he pushed his son to arm's length.

"Aye, but we can't let them know that."

At last, those of the court still capable of walking that far escorted Allana and Javik to the royal apartments. The huge wooden doors closed behind them, and they were alone. Javik took Allana in his arms and kissed her tenderly.

"I've waited for this night for a long time," Javik said.

Allana laughed lightly. "Javik, you sound like we're making love for the first time."

"Well, it is our first time as man and wife. That's something special."

"We must never let this night end," Allana said as she led Javik to the huge, silken bed.

The End

Title: *The Adventures of Regen the Bremen*
• Author: M. L. Hollinger
Publisher: TotalRecall Publications, Inc.
• Hardcover, ISBN: 978-1-59095-110-1
• Paper Back, ISBN: 978-1-59095-111-8
• eBook, ISBN: 978-1-59095-112-5
•: Audiobook, ISBN:

Regen is a Bremen. By nature he loves only his pet skeen, sensual women, money, and adventure in that order.

REGEN is an earthy, pragmatic, drug smuggler who cares little for anything but money, beautiful women, and his own highly unusual pet. The animal is a skeen, and they are usually shot on sight for the pests they are. Most people marvel that Regen managed to tame such a nasty creature. On top of everything else, he named the skeen HITLER after a 20th Century Earth dictator with a personality as evil as any skeen's. Regen is a Bremen. Bremen are known for their tough exterior, sexual prowess, and their tendency to leap before they look. I hope you enjoy following this arrogant, self-confident, egotistical and narcissistic bastard through a series of adventures in disparate sectors of the galaxy.

Title: *Josh and the Cargan*
• Author: M. L. Hollinger
• Publisher: TotalRecall Publications, Inc.
•: Hardcover, ISBN: 978-1-59095-124-8
•: Paperback, ISBN: 978-1-59095-125-5
•: eBook, ISBN: 978-1-59095-126-2
•: Audiobook, ISBN: 978-1-59095-254-2

Science tells us the speed of light is absolute, but is it? If physical objects can't go faster than 186,000 miles per second, maybe something else can.

Josh Smith is your average teenage boy. His hormones are raging and he can't wait to have sex with a girl. He also wants to be a rock star, and has an amateur band of his own. One evening after band practice he learns his rich, eccentric great grandfather, Charles Evans Bastin, is dead.

When the will is read, Josh inherits one of Charley's ugly sculptures while his father inherits the rest of the fortune. Back home, Josh accidentally discovers his sculpture is a CARGAN, a device used for interplanetary travel as a ghostly presence called an ENTITY. He travels to the planet destination of his cargan and finds it's a very exotic place indeed.

- Title: *Snow*
- Author: M. L. Hollinger
- Publisher: TotalRecall Publications, Inc.
- : Hard Cover: 978-1-59095-303-7
- :Paperback, ISBN: 978-1-59095-304-4
- : eBook, ISBN: 978-1-59095-305-1
- : Audiobook, ISBN: 978-1-59095-258-0

When her husband is reported as dead, she escapes to the United States and takes up a new life. Unfortunately, she runs into Jeff again, and he wants to take up where they left off. Naturally, Snow resists him until he traps her into resuming their relationship.

Title: *Josh Martin – Space Commander*
- Author: M. L. Hollinger
- Publisher: TotalRecall Publications, Inc.
- : Paperback, ISBN: 978-1-59095-282-5
- : eBook, ISBN: 978-1-59095-283-2
- : Audiobook, ISBN: 978-1-59095-284-9

A bored teen-aged boy escorting his little brother at Disney World finds love and adventure on Space Mountain.

While waiting in line at Space Mountain, Buzz Lightyear presents Josh with a pin and suggests he'll enjoy the ride a lot more now. Josh and George board the sled, but Josh doesn't notice the cast member pushing a button on the sled. As they start the ride, Josh is suddenly propelled into another dimension where he's the Commander of a space ship. The ship is a battle cruiser, and receives an order to rescue a princess who has been kidnapped by pirates. With the help of the ships Executive officer and his staff Josh develop the perfect plan to accomplish the rescue. What could go wrong?

Title: *Mauhad*
- Author: M. L. Hollinger
- Publisher: TotalRecall Publications, Inc.
- : Hardcover, ISBN: 978-1-59095-104-8
- : Paperback, ISBN: 978-1-59095-105-5
- : eBook, ISBN: 978-1-59095-106-
- : Audiobook, ISBN: 978-1-59095-272-6

A boy struggles to pass Mauhad, the manhood test of his people, and falls in love in the process.

Javik lives in a country surrounded by mountains and covered in old growth forest. His ambition is to become a warrior like his father, Tolda, but he must pass Mauhad before he can realize that ambition. When is father is killed saving the others in his raiding party, Javik despairs of ever reaching that goal without his father's training. Goldar, who led the raid when Tolda was killed, convinces the King to allow Javik to train with Tao Shan, the finest mentor in the kingdom. Javik finds himself among the sons of the wealthy and must adjust to the situation quickly. While in training he encounters a girl in the forest. She is Allana an escaped slave, but Javik falls in love with her. He convinces her to come out of hiding, and she teaches the sling to Tao Shan's students.

The First book in the Javik series.

Title: *Love and War*
- Author: M. L. Hollinger
- Publisher: TotalRecall Publications, Inc.
- : Hardcover, ISBN: 978-1-59095-285-6
- : Paperback, ISBN: 978-1-59095-286-3
- : eBook, ISBN: 978-1-59095-287-0
- : Audiobook, ISBN: 978-1-59095-288-7

Allana goes in pursuit of a crown, and Javik is trapped into an unwanted marriage before the fates conspire to free him from all obligations except finding the woman he loves.

Javik goes off the war. He gains glory and gold in the war but returns home to find Allana gone. He's dismayed when Dana tells him she doesn't want him to follow her. He's also promised Tao Shan another year of training. He begins the training, and Tao Shan gives him a bonus by letting him in on the secret of a magic powder (gunpowder) and the weapon called a hand cannon.

The second book in the Javik series.

www.ingramcontent.com/pod-product-compliance
Lightning Source LLC
Chambersburg PA
CBHW020330120726
47904CB00002B/351